PENGUIN BOOKS
VIRTUAL REALITIES

The author of three previous works of fiction, Neelum Saran Gour has also been a book critic, a humour columnist, and writer-in-residence at the University of Kent. She lives with her husband and two sons in Allahabad, where she teaches at Allahabad University.

BY THE SAME AUTHOR

Grey Pigeon and Other Stories
Speaking of '62
Winter Companions

Virtual Realities

Neelum Saran Gour

PENGUIN BOOKS
An imprint of Penguin Random House

PENGUIN BOOKS

USA | Canada | UK | Ireland | Australia
New Zealand | India | South Africa | China | Singapore

Penguin Books is part of the Penguin Random House group of companies whose addresses can be found at global.penguinrandomhouse.com

Published by Penguin Random House India Pvt. Ltd
4th Floor, Capital Tower 1, MG Road,
Gurugram 122 002, Haryana, India

First published by Penguin Books India in 2002

10 9 8 7 6 5 4 3 2

ISBN 9780143028062

Typeset in Galliard by Mantra Virtual Services Pvt Ltd, New Delhi

Printed at Repro India Limited

www.penguin.co.in

This is a legitimate digitally printed version of the book and therefore might not have certain extra finishing on the cover.

Dedicated to the great storytellers in my family
who never wrote a line

1

Ponds like panes of glass set in the paddy fields. Polished pools of a laminated jade. In the mist of the mornings, under the musty palms, they turn into bowls of smoke. In the afternoons their dark liquor brews brackish light.

The road, where it is metalled, curves like the blade of a sickle, steel-sharp with sun. At noon the State Transport bus from Narendrapur brays down it, crunching pebbles under its wheels. Vendors walk, baskets on their heads, to the weekly market at Vishvakarmagram. Sometimes a lone rickshaw utters a sharp honk as it careers round the mildewed wooden bridge. But by sundown all is quiet and the surface of the pond brims over with slick sky-gloss. This is the hour when the house seems a-sail.

It is a landscape carved with a sharp scalpel, washed in a slurp of wet, glowing green. Powdered in early mist and then suddenly, an hour later, bristling with chill sun.

Amalendu sits upon his string cot, brooding. Watching the ducks paddle across the pond, cleaving a furrow across its dense treacle. Cutting through the thin scum of shade that has settled on its face.

He stopped, read over the paragraph he'd completed. Those lines needed to be combed out. Thinned. He didn't like those tiny knots between the sentences. Needed a bit of lubrication to make the lines flow. Maybe if he broke up each line . . . And Amalendu still had to be visualized clearly. A wizened man, sour before his time.

Footsteps on the landing. Then a soft thud in his mailbox. Three letters arrived together, one an innocuous-looking inland, one a large brown official envelope, the third a dog-eared postcard.

He tore open the inland first. He was used to hate mail, so it made no dent on his composure. But this man's handwriting rattled him. Had done so for years. He remembered entire days laid waste by the sight of this spidery hand. There was no attempt at anonymity, even if the letter was always unsigned. Obviously written in a state of advanced intoxication. Seething with an old and confirmed rage, thought Sravan as he tore it into small pieces. Banishing the disturbance from his head by an effort of will, he opened the second letter, the official one, and scanned the contents with satisfaction. He decided not to break the news to anyone yet.

The postcard was from Buddhoo. Undated, postmark smudged, handwriting cranky. As though the words had been shaken out of a salt shaker and had landed, skittering, on the card. 'Arriving Thursday, 5th, Kalka, seeyouthen!' Dot, dot, dash. Buddhoo's brisk wireless. Sravan cursed the bastard. He hadn't mentioned *which* Kalka! There were two, one from Delhi and the other from Howrah.

The latter, as it turned out. Running two hours late, it disgorged Buddhoo's dishevelled, grinning face and faded shoulder bag on to Platform One. Buddhoo's raucous greeting floated across to Sravan: 'Arré, saala, what you done to yourself? You're thin as a sugarcane stick. Your face has sat down, man!' He'd always loved shocking Sravan with his most outrageous Indianisms.

When people remarked upon Sravan's attractive trimness, he'd usually shrug and answer: 'It's because my life's got just the right blend of satisfaction and dissatisfaction.' But he didn't dare throw that line at Buddhoo.

Now Buddhoo lolled on the divan in Sravan's sitting room, rolled rum round his mouth like mouthwash and observed airily: 'Bilingual author, wah! Mutlub, sort of a hermaphrodite, na?' He followed it up with a double-decker axiom: 'Fools build houses and wise men live in them. And fools write books and wise men sit back and read them!'

'I thought you were into writing, too.'

'Ah, that was when I was a fool. Wiser now. I'd much rather read a first-rate book by you than write a third-rate book myself.' He paused, smiling engagingly.

Buddhoo all over. He could tease and please in the same breath. No trace of ridicule in his banter, no formal flattery in his compliments. None of that undertow of delicate jibing that characterized Sravan's current companionships. Good to see the blighter again.

'Besides,' went on Buddhoo, 'I can't speak this furr-furr English like you.' He made a fluttering sound like the flurry of wings in a staircase. 'My stomach won't fill, bhai, with these saltless English words. I won't let myself turn into the bania in the old saying, the guy who went up to Kabul and learnt so much Persian that he began saying *aab* for plain homely water and forgot the word *paani*. Know what happened? Fellow died crying out for "aab" and no one knew what the fuck he wanted and he couldn't for the life of him reach out to the pitcher of water at his bedside!'

'Oh, I know all about you, Buddhoo,' was Pragya's breezy welcome. 'Sravan's told me fabulous tales of your escapades.'

'Actually, I almost met you at your wedding,' said Buddhoo.

'Almost?' Pragya was mystified.

'Buddhoo organized a gents' sangeet a day before the wedding,' Sravan said. 'Complete with harmoniums and drums. Lewd songs and booze—a riot it was. Buddhoo spent the wedding itself horizontal on the carpet in the hotel room.'

'Really?' Pragya smiled at Buddhoo. 'Sravan didn't tell me. I'd have gone to the hotel for your autograph! You're such a celebrity prankster.'

The guest cocked a rakish eyebrow. 'Sravan? You mean this bloke? I quite forgot his name's Sravan. To me he's always been Ravan.' Buddhoo settled himself snugly against a silk bolster. 'Personally, I'm always a bit staggered seeing his name on books. Sravan Nishit, wah, bhai, wah! To me he's always been Ravan

Shit. Or don't you know this one? He hasn't told you? Let me tell you how the name stuck. In the old days, when we shared a room at the Jai Ma Kali Students' Lodge in Morrisgunj, Ravan here was writing his first book. Up to his teeth in it he was. Had it coming out of his ears. He'd worried himself sick. Wanted a poetic pen name and a suitable title. We had lots of damn serious discussions. Like, he'd say to me: "Something refreshing. New-minted. The pundit says it's got to begin with the letter *f*." I'd say: "Yaar, don't make me laugh." He'd persist. I'd search my head and suggest: *Fractions and Frictions*. Or *Factions and Fictions*. Or something like *An Infictious Disease*. He'd demand: "What's infictious?" I'd answer discursively: "Infictious means to infect with fiction. Infuction means to infect fiction with fuction. Fuction means the action of . . ." He'd shout, "Oh, fuck it, saala! I've though of something else. What d'you say to *Briefs and Blueprints*?" I'd crack my sides with laughing. Say, "Yaar, don't give me ideas. I'm getting visions of pretty blue-flowered underwear!" '

Pragya laughed politely, a little out of her depth.

'The search for a pen name was funnier still,' continued Buddhoo. 'The *urf*. Sort of a capsule to hold the essential quality of the guy. We ran through *tanha* and *parishan* and *saaz* and *alfaz* and I suggested *pyaaz*—he used to stink of onions then—and a few more profane ones, but nothing clicked. So he stuck to his own name.'

'And you abbreviated it to Ravan Shit?'

'In still crazier circumstances.' Buddhoo took a long, sussurating sip. 'There was this sleazy bar we were fond of. What was it called?'

'The Somnath.'

'Right. The Somnath. I scratched his name into the wooden panels of the loo. Wrote up the college phone number. And underneath it:

OMNISEX CHAMP SRAVAN NISHIT

PASSIVE / ACTIVE / MEN / LADIES

ALL AGES AND PREFERENCES WELCOME

SPECIAL 20% DIWALI DISCOUNT

—that sort of thing. Sravan went in to piss and was aghast. Spluttering with fury he was! Tried frantically to scratch it out, but could only scratch out three letters. And there you have it—Ravan Shit.'

'Were there any phone calls?' Pragya wanted to know.

'If there were, we weren't informed.'

'You'd hardly expect the college office to taken down and deliver the message. But it proved a historic inscription.'

'Yes, and Buddhoo's called me Ravan Shit ever since. As for me, I keep forgetting he's called Prabuddha. To me he's always been Buddhoo.'

'Buddhoo!' exclaimed Pragya. 'What a name to carry all your life.'

'Actually,' confessed Buddhoo, 'I rather like it. Think of it. Prabuddha means "wise" and Buddhoo means "fool". It isn't everyone who has the privilege of enjoying wisdom and folly at the same time—eh? Mutlub, a transcendental name, na?'

Pragya's laugh this time was one of genuine delight, and Sravan was relieved. He'd been a little apprehensive about Buddhoo's reception in his home; now he knew he needn't have worried. Trust the rogue to charm his way into any sort of company.

'How did you come to acquire such an interesting nickname?' Pragya asked.

'Long story,' sighed Buddhoo, pouring himself another drink. 'That was just after I went into the design biz.'

'Design biz?'

'I was in shirts.'

'Aren't we all?'

'No, I was designing shirts. You know—the famous Pissitoire Collection. Harlem Shirts. I almost had an ad campaign—macho model with hatchet raised—a strong sexual message. Alas, it fizzled out. I was also the author of Buddy's Signature Exclusive Animal-wear. That was just before my portable-automobile venture and my Jug-Mug Animal Restaurant.'

'Animal restaurant?'

'Tell you later about that one. Plenty of time. In between creative ventures I had a dose of social-upliftment fever. Thought of opening a school back in my native Etawah. It wasn't exactly what you'd call a progressive city, and I had noble plans of community welfare. Get the idea? Research and development, the works!'

Pragya nodded, amused.

'It had to be a convent and it had to be named after a saint. The Pauls and Peters and Josephs and Xaviers held no attraction for me: I wanted something original. I finally hit upon calling it Saint Buddha's Convent. Nice, what? Considering that my name's Prabuddha. And a good, guaranteed, respectable, international Indian saint, too. Alas, the public went one better. They disfigured it to Saint Buddhoo's Convent! Hardly the sort of name to encourage right-thinking parents to send their kids. There were also some speculations about my saintliness . . .'

'Once,' interrupted Sravan, 'in a small English village, I came across a school with an abbreviated name of the same sort. Saint Dunce, for Dunstan.'

'Ofo! Did you find out how many kids it had, that school? No, after one small foray into the education racket, it was a stint at law college for me.'

'Which came to a similar entertaining end. But what then? What were you up to after you disappeared some years back? Someone told me you'd been in jail.'

'I was.'

'Politics?'

'Crime,' said Buddhoo sedately. 'An interesting case of imposture.'

'Let's hear it.'

'Ah, well,' sighed Buddhoo. 'It was like this: hectic night on the Jhansi Road. Drunken driver, red Maruti van and drunken self. Sab daru ka khel, if you know what I mean. It all began as a daredevil proposal from the driver. "Sir," he drawled, "I know the VIP signal well. Bet you I can stop all the lorries on this road." In the beginning I took no notice. But then, you know how these ideas grow on you. "Bet you, sahib," whispered that voice of Shaitan, "that I can even pass you off as the regional transport officer." "Listen, you fucker," I swore, "when does the RTO ever travel in a Maruti van? It's always a jeep, or maybe one of these obese white official Ambassadors, for the likes of him." "I bet you, sir, they won't know the difference," he drawled, grinning from ear to ear. So the fellow braked and parked the Maruti slantwise across the highway and got down to doing his stuff. So what happens? The VIP signal—get the idea? Eh, shabash! The lorries began stopping! One, two, three, five, a long row. I sat, face hidden behind a newspaper, cursing. Then I saw what the son-of-a-bitch was up to, the double-crossing cur! Saala! He was actually extracting money from the drivers on behalf of *me*, the fake RTO! God knows how many hundreds he raked in from those poor suckers! Coolly examining their papers, hectoring them in police-station bluster. And he wasn't even sporting a constable's moustache or uniform, the haramzada! At last, along came this UP State Transport bus. The fellow smelt a rat. Grew as meek as you please and drove off. And reported me at the next police chowki!'

'I heard some such thing,' remarked Sravan when the laughter in the room was under control. 'Actually, in another version of your adventure, the real RTO was riding in the bus . . .'

'Ha! Damn lies! Trust the rascally lot to make up the tale! Well, one thing led to another. By now the situation was out of my control, and what does a man say when that happens? Goli maro, yaar, what must be must be. High words passing between cops and self. What with this and that, I'd become convinced that my rights as a citizen were being buggered by the Indian police and I was wrathful and self-righteous. Rhetorical, too. Arguing points of protocol between the transport department and the police department. Ready to fight anyone who challenged my word.'

'So what followed was inevitable.'

Buddhoo nodded sadly. 'Naturally. Was handcuffed, hauled off and clapped in jail. And this is where the real fun begins.'

'Oh, dear, there's more?' giggled Pragya.

'If you knew Buddhoo, you wouldn't ask that.'

'Now, after all this I was in no mood to compromise my dignity. Fortunately something happened to make a deep impression on the bastards. They went through my pockets, whacked my wallet and found my pocket diary. Now, my diary is full of the addresses and phone numbers of VIPs—DMs, commissioners of income tax, ministers past, present and aspiring, notorious student leaders of five state universities . . . Those cops paled at my collection.' He took a slurp from his brimming glass and smacked his lips.

'Returned your wallet?' kidded Sravan.

Buddhoo threw him a reproachful grimace. 'With each flick of the page they grew more respectful, until halfway through my diary they were positively fawning. I was carrying my angina papers and was pronounced medically unfit and consigned to the jail's hospital ward. Best holiday of my life. The jailor turned out to be from Etawah, too, and a Thakur like me. That was it! Sahib! Hot puris and spicy vegetables from his house. I tell you, it was rigorous hospitality! Transistor radio, portable TV, *India Today*, *Filmfare*, *Sportsweek*, novels by Ranu and Mastram and Shobha Dé for timepass. I lay back and had a fantastic time. The other fellows in detention were mostly from my part of the world, too, and took a kindly interest in my well-being. Etawah ke ho lala? they enquired courteously. And when they learnt that I came from the same district and belonged to the same caste, they threw themselves on to the reception committee with great gusto. No son-in-law was ever more spoilt! They washed my clothes, they pressed my feet, they massaged my scalp with scented oil and even filled my chillum, which came courtesy of the warder, fags being unavailable.'

'And then?'

'All good things in life must end,' said Buddhoo with a sigh. 'My father came and bailed me out and hauled me home by the scruff of my neck.'

Sravan took a sip and smirked significantly, allowing the dramatic pressure of his impending verdict to build. 'Badly composed, but good plot, passable narrative pitch and convincing episodic succession. Marred by two fatal flaws.'

'Eh?' Buddhoo leaned across the table.

'That bit about the fags being unavailable when so much else was,' declared Sravan triumphantly. 'I don't know if village thanas have hospitals. Also, sitting there in your Maruti van, exactly what were you doing with your face hidden behind a newspaper? It was night, I thought you said. Were you reading in the dark?'

Buddhoo leapt to his feet, lunged across and fetched Sravan a resounding clap on the shoulder blade. The glass of army rum teetered on its perch and crashed to the ground, splattering its contents on Pragya's Kashmiri carpet.

'Arré! Sorry, yaar!' exclaimed Buddhoo.

'I'll get it cleaned,' said Pragya in a strained voice. She rose to call the maid.

'You've just tested my wife's patience to its limits,' chortled Sravan. 'She's a stickler for good housekeeping. I warn you, if you want to stay on her right side you'd better watch your step. None of your chillums and bidis and Bohemian mess here.'

'Okay, boss.'

'As for this adventure of yours, I don't believe a word of it. What you've just narrated is the finest yarn of your life.'

Buddhoo's face broke into a slow, conspiratorial beam. 'Not the finest,' he protested. 'There've been some finer ones.'

Lolling against the bolster, his grimy feet stretched in front of him, Buddhoo began to laugh, swallowing big gulps of laughter like draughts of a delightful fizzy drink. Soda laughter, thought Sravan. He looked at Buddhoo's uncut toenails, so out of place among Pragya's elegant raw-silk cushions.

'Still living by yarns—your old game,' he remarked.

'Living by my wits—that and the credulity of the world,' said Buddhoo. 'Didn't work with you—you know me too well. And are in a same-to-same dhandha yourself.' He guffawed.

'You're as mad as you always were.'

'Who was it?—one of your writer johnnies—who said something like, "When we remember that we are all mad, the mysteries disappear and life stands explained?" '

After dinner Sravan put the question uppermost in his mind as delicately as possible: 'So I understand, Buddhoo, that you're presently a gentleman of leisure?'

'Unemployed, if that's what you mean, and very nicely put,' Buddhoo replied cheerfully. 'And I've come looking for a way to relieve my leisure as profitably as possible: enjoy your hospitality and exploit your patronage.'

Sravan digested this in silence.

'Let's get this clear. Other than spin yarns, exactly what's your area?'

'Area?'

'I mean, what can you do? Accounts, proofreading, typing?'

Buddhoo uttered a hoot of laughter, totally unsettling Pragya, whose first easy acceptance was now quite complicated.

'Typing! Is it possible that you've forgotten that fiasco of mine back in '70?'

Sravan flushed suddenly as an uncomfortable and ridiculous memory came flooding back into his mind.

'Hell, no! Not that one, please!'

'What's this now?' asked Pragya, her curiosity aroused.

'I'll tell you all about it,' said Buddhoo, sweetly malicious. When Ravan and I were lodge-mates, we tried all manner of things to earn a bit of cash. Once Ravan said to me: "Buddhoo, you good-for-nothing oaf, we all know you can talk at the speed of light, but why don't you learn to type? You can type out my scripts and I'll pay you enough for your bidis." Ever a tight-fisted skinflint, this. Well, I'd do anything for him, so sure enough, I learnt to type double-quick. Now there was once a bad-tempered English district collector who rather plumed himself on his literary gifts. Somewhat like our Ravan here. This gentleman wrote poetry in the time sandwiched between dispatches and reports, and he had a native Hindustani babu to type them all. One day the poor babu was terrified to behold the sahib emerge from his chamber, raging like a furnace, frothing at the mouth and tearing his auburn hair. "Babu!" he fumed. "You have ruined my poem! The poem I wrote for little Richard-baba." "By your leave, Sahib, the undersigned has typed the same with painstaking punctiliousness . . ." quavered the babu. "Oh, damn you and damn your nigger English!" shouted the sahib. "See the mess you have made. I began my poem with the noble apostrophe, "My son, my pigmy counterpart!" Now look what you have done to it. You've inserted a space right in the middle of the word *pigmy* and a goddamned comma where it's got no business to be and the wretched thing now reads: 'My son, my pig, my counterpart!' And it's already been posted to the

Statesman!" '

Buddhoo waited for the commotion to subside.

'So what happened to me during my tragic experiments with the typewriter was similar. Next door to our lodge lived a young lady who Sravan was rather sweet on. Once he composed a lengthy ode dedicated to her which began with the solemn address, "My pen is mightier than the sword." '

'I'll tell you what happened, Pragya,' interrupted Sravan. 'This treacherous bastard offered to type it out and post it! I might have known . . .'

'Absolutely inadvertent, my dear Ravan.'

'Nonsense. You intentionally joined the words "pen" and "is" together so that the opening line . . .'

'My penis mightier than the sword!' Pragya shrieked with laughter.

'I was only learning to type. A raw hand.'

'Rubbish!'

'But how did she take it?' asked Pragya.

'Oh, that was the woeful end of a tender romance which had all along stuck to chivalrous lyrics and gifts of jasmine gajras for her chignon and courtly salaams in the direction of her balcony. She wasn't amused. And her brother, who was a numbskulled tough, took it as an insult to the family izzat and his chaste sister's maidenly modesty. We were almost constrained to change house.'

'Your typing days ended?' Pragya chuckled.

'Unfortunately, yes,' admitted Buddhoo, mock-rueful.

'That was about twenty-five years back. I trust you've learnt to practise greater responsibility in your scripts,' retorted Sravan severely. 'But seriously, what're you planning to do now?'

'I think its hardly fair to push Buddhoo around so soon,' intervened Pragya. 'Let him settle down and give us the pleasure of his company and liven us up a bit. We need it. An overdose of seriousness in this house, Buddhoo-bhai.'

She threw one of her arch, sidelong looks in Sravan's direction, irritating him enormously. Then she took charge in her prompt, decisive way. 'We're rather cramped for space, as you can see, but you're most welcome. Only you'll have to share Babuji's room, make do with a foam mattress on the floor. D'you mind?' She looked at him anxiously.

'No problem,' assured Buddhoo.

'Babuji's unwell. Recovering from a stroke. The physiotherapist visits every day.'

Buddhoo clucked in an appropriately sympathetic manner. 'I'll be fine. Babuji and I shall get along like a house on fire.'

'I'm not so sure,' Sravan speculated. 'He's very peevish. A problem parent. Likes no one but himself.'

'I promise to be charming,' grinned Buddhoo, unfazed.

'You'll have to work overtime. Exert all your magical appeal.'

'That's settled then,' said Pragya. 'That's where we'll put you. It's just next door.'

2

'There's this potential fortune I've amassed, yaar. All packed away in two aluminium trunks. You'll never guess what it is.'

'I won't even try.'

'Fifty nameplates. Politicians, writers, lawyers, even a bit star in the films. All collector's items. Taken me half a decade's devoted labour. Braving risks to life and livelihood, to say nothing of my immaculate reputation. Night after night of planning, military scouting, escapades. You could say it's my love of adventure, pinching the nameplates of bigwigs.'

'Never got nabbed?'

'Just once. My advice to the artist-pincher is: never diversify. The fruit of that shattering chapter. See—I was on the point of pinching two nameplates in one night. Two high-class, keenly competitive lawyers of the high court. The night was fair, the moon hid behind a cloud. Away in the bagh a jackal bayed—you get the scene. Okay, now just as I was about to pinch the second one, a reckless thought surfaced in my mind. Why not exchange the two? I mean, why not? Let's wait and see what happens. Wait and see I did, and there was lots to see. And hear. In short, Mathur's clients headed for Misra and Misra's clients headed for Mathur and their munshis went stark mad trying to restore order and the two learned counsels nearly came to blows in the Coffee House, each accusing the other of using touts to grab the other's clients! Uf! Some spectacle, with the manager of the India Coffee House bleating, "Order, order" and of course there's no such thing as contempt of coffee house, so there were the two learned counsels, having a field day. Should've seen their ugly mugs. The law of contorts and distorts, ha! Okay, the case was duly investigated, the swapped nameplates discovered and they got their chowkidars to lie in wait for me. I will now skip over the next few sequences as irrelevant to the central argument of my theme . . .'

'You let them rough you up?

Buddhoo sighed. 'What to do, yaar? It was a case of IPC Sections 379, 380. Who can stop a lawyer from taking the law in his own hands? A man's got to—what's the damn word?—ah, adjust, adjust at all costs, so I thought it best to adjust my hide to the lathi and practise some active passive resistance. Not the Gandhian brand, because I'm vicious and vindictive, let me tell you. I had my vengeance by pissing into the learned counsels' mailboxes for weeks afterwards . . . But coming back to my fortune, pretty soon it'll be time for me to e-mail Sotheby's. Stolen nameplates—Amitabh Bachchan's dad's, Shahnaz Hussain's dad's, Firaq Gorakhpuri's, Nirala's, Mahadevi Verma's, Munshi Premchand's, Sushmita Sen's maternal granddad's! This collection's got a great future—I just know it. Just waiting for the price to escalate a bit more and *buss*!'

They sat up late, remembering old times.

'Remember that All India Poetry Festival in Aligarh? And how you and I represented the All Allahabad Federation of Creative Artists?' asked Sravan.

Buddhoo shuddered. 'Do I? It haunts my sleep.'

'Me president, you secretary.'

Pragya was interested. 'Great! Who were the other members?'

Sravan answered with a straight face. 'There were no other members. The All Allahabad Federation of Creative Artists comprised just two members, Buddhoo and I.'

'And no one can dispute the fact that we were the two most creative artists in the city.'

'Well, Pragya's had an overdose of my creativity for fifteen years now,' laughed Sravan. 'To your creative talents she hasn't had complete exposure, but you've already given her a mild demonstration.'

'You certainly have,' agreed Pragya. 'And I'm looking forward to more.'

'You little know what you're in for,' said Sravan. 'Anyway, to come back to the All India Poetry Festival in Aligarh, Buddhoo and I sent out handbills and collected about three hundred bucks. We went to the festival and were received with great ceremony.'

'Ravan read out his famous "negative poem".'

'What was that?' Pragya asked.

'This humbug here, your husband, used to have a lot of literary gimmicks up his sleeve. For the festival he composed an eight-line poem and crossed out each odd line. The special thing was that the cancelled lines weren't excluded from the text. They were part of the original poem and expected to stay right there.'

'Sort of an inverse text,' explained Sravan.

'So there were two poems dovetailed into one. Eight lines adding up to one sense, and the four cancelled lines adding up to something quite different.'

'The even lines moved forward in meaning. The odd ones moved backward in meaning. Ingenious it was. Poem, anti-poem, sense, counter-sense, experience and its alter, get me?'

'How exciting!' exclaimed Pragya. 'What became of that poem, Sravan? I never saw it.'

'Oh, a squib,' dismissed Sravan. 'It wasn't meant to be taken seriously. The funny thing was that it was.'

'But really, it was a marvel. We raved over it at the Jai Ma Kali Students' Lodge. Some of us swore it was one of those rare ideas unthought-of in the whole history of literature. Ah, you humbug. You shrugged and put on your self-effacing face.'

'At the festival the poem proved a problem,' recollected Sravan. 'How on earth was I to read the blasted thing? Those cancelled lines. It was the pre-audiovisual-aid age, remember? Luckily they brought a blackboard and I wrote up the cancelled lines.'

'Yes, I remember. You alternately read out the forward lines and pointed at the silent lines written on the board. The audience got the hang of it. An unconventional sort of reading.'

'But it was a hit. And that play we did for All India Radio, remember that? I did the protagonist's voice and you did all the rest.'

'Including the heroine's,' laughed Buddhoo. 'Ha, some play. Classic tearjerker. *Usne Kaha Tha*.'

'We needed cash to buy text books—we'd spent our money from home. We thought of roping in a few other fellows but the fuckers were unwilling, so we said to hell with it, we'll go it ourselves. And it had a biggish cast!'

'Did you manage?' asked Pragya.

'You bet. We got the books we wanted—though as usual I plugged that year.'

'Buddhoo had sound reasons for plugging every year,' chuckled Sravan.

'It was my love of learning, Pragya. I believed in devoting two or three concentrated years to each year's syllabus. Nothing slipshod or hasty. Solid education for me, see? It's because I repeated each year that you'll find me one of the most educated guys in your circle.'

'That play turned out so well that we actually went up to Delhi with it, this time as president and secretary of the All Allahabad Federation of Dramatic Artists.'

'My God!'

'At Delhi we didn't make it to the competition.'

'Got sozzled,' informed Sravan. 'And trapped in a subway.'

'A subway?'

'Yes. We kept going down the steps, crossing the street underground, climbing the steps at the other end, and staggering across the same street and so back down the first flight of steps . . .'

'Very confusing,' injected Buddhoo. 'I didn't know where the fuck we were going. Finally we accosted an auto-wallah who'd been watching our antics with keen relish. We said, Oye, Srdaarji, Sasriakaal, Waheguru da Khalsa, Waheguru di Fateh, all the rest.' To which he said, "Oye, hullo-ji, puttar. Sasriakaal. And what you are trying to do, ji?" Cross this road, we told him. Which road is it, can you tell us? He said, exploding into laughter, "Kissturba Gandhi Marg, ji." Kiss *who*? we asked. He repeated the name. 'You've been on it for the last hour, puttar.' I remembered thinking what a long road it was—and built on several levels. India was getting impossibly advanced for me. I said so. "Very advanced, ji," agreed the sard. "And going round and round." He made a rotatory movement with his hirsute hand. "Up like this, yo! Down like this, yo! Exactly like the two of you." What? we slurred. "Hanji." He grinned. "That's what the two of you have been busy doing for the last hour. Into the subway, out at the other end, across the street, into the subway, out at the other end, across the same street! Heh, heh, heh!" '

'But did you finally reach wherever you were trying to get to?'

'The sardar took us into his auto and stormed down half of Delhi, beeping like mad round the buses like a giddy mosquito, but we were too late. Our turn had come and gone. But drama in real life, we'd had more than our fair share.'

'What fun,' breathed Pragya.

'It wasn't fun all the time,' said Sravan. 'Not in those years when there wasn't money enough and nobody wanted our scripts.'

'All of us used to write in those days. It was the fashion.'

'And all of us wrote the same way.'

'I have a name for that grand manner. I call it the Socially Progressive Post-Victorian Rhetorical Cadence.'

'We had great theories on social change.'

'I wasn't ever part of that set,' said Buddhoo. 'Some of you were such phonies. So many little writers talking unstoppably of writing. Wearing their little vanities on their sleeve. Failed writers who'd lost faith in literature, or turned critic. Everyone dreaming of making it big. A regular rogues' gallery. Each one affected some individual perversity, and most of them had a contrived image. But there was one thing I noticed. Most of them were paisa-smart. I once asked Ravan about it: why are the lot of you such low rats? And Ravan crushed me with that bombastic line of his: "Arré chup! Genius lies outside your conventional judgements." '

'Did I really say that? Well, as I told you, we were small-time writers. Most of us had never seen print. When we could scrape together the money, we brought out a few crudely printed pages of poetry or fiction. We wrote serious articles on one another's work and read them out at our meetings. Nobody outside our circle had heard of us. And we always read out our rejected scripts and set off a loud clamour of abuse against the stupidity of publishers and editors. And frequently in a mood of reckless abandon, especially round Holi, we made a collage of our collection of rejection slips. Ten of us managed to cover an entire wall! Every publisher and editor in the country appeared to have rejected our work. Quite a distinction, isn't it? Hell hath no fury like an author spurned. The fellows with the most rejection slips were given an award and there was such celebration, such wining and dining and reciting and applauding—even if we had to go hungry for a day afterward. As for jealousy, none. Man hasn't lived in such collective harmony as we did then. There's no fraternity like the fellowship of shared failure. Then, abruptly, I found myself banished.'

'How?'

'Suddenly, out of the blue, I received an acceptance! My novel, *Dhumil Akash*, was enthusiastically taken on by the publishers Mayur-Vriksha.' Sravan's voice preserved some of the injury.

'The day I broke the news to my friends, I became a leper. They thumped me on the back, they clapped me on the shoulder, they shook hands with me, they smiled and congratulated me and wished me luck. They even held a celebration for me and put up their usual wallpaper of rejection slips! Only my slips weren't there. I no longer belonged. There was a chill, a constraint. I'd become an outsider. My presence made them uncomfortable, and I could see that I would never be forgiven. That's when I first tasted the loneliness of success . . .'

'Oh, come on now,' protested Buddhoo. 'You don't regret being lucky.'

'But I've never experienced that kind of comradeship, before or since—nor known such absolute exclusion.'

'You can't have everything,' mused Pragya softly.

'But the loneliness of success is strange—because so few can relate,' reflected Sravan. 'There was just one fellow who was truly overjoyed, who didn't desert me: Hari Mohan Misra. And I didn't want *him* flitting round me.'

'Ah, that's the guy we joked about. Freaked out on you . . .'

'Oh, shut up. I tried explaining to him that mine was a very mainstream sort of promiscuity, that I appreciated his regard . . .'

'Nicely put.'

'Naturally. We were very euphemistic in those days. But the fellow published a slender novel at his own cost—and dedicated it to me! I was laughed at for weeks. It was a shitty novel, and just went under—deserved to.'

'I think he gave you the very best thing he could offer. Or maybe the second-best.' Buddhoo winked. Then added, more seriously, 'Even if it was trash in your eyes.'

Sravan made no comment. They refilled their glasses. Then Sravan spoke: 'You know, Buddhoo, we didn't know it then, as we gnashed our teeth and mutinied and slogged and cursed our lot, but we were just the right mix of intensity and irreverence.'

'Every generation carries that impression,' said Buddhoo. 'Mid-life nostalgia. Pure chemistry. Most of you guys were only writing love poems. Some of your pals pronounced it "law". I remember one solemn discussion on "law"—such tales of passion and heartbreak. It's best to law twenty-five at a time, said one. That's treacherous, said another. Lawing one is a full-time job, frequently overtime. But Lord Krishna managed pretty well, mused the first. Come to think of it, Lord Krishna was a slight, dark sort of a guy. Not particularly smart. Didn't even wear a tie. How come the girls were all over him?'

'Maybe he held a diploma from a personality-development institute,' quipped Pragya.

Buddhoo threw back his head and laughed. 'Your literary success began painfully, I must say. Even if it wasn't the way you saw it.'

Sravan's train of thought led him to ask, 'Do you remember Amrit? Hell of a chap, Pragya. Also dead now, poor bloke.'

'Good chap,' said Buddhoo soberly. 'I think of him quite often.'

'He was one maskhara. You know, once in the lodge he put up a big poster on the wall beside his bed. Ava Gardner in *Mocambo* or some such thing. He pointed at it and told me very solemnly in his rackety English, "Yaar, I have fallen into love with this female." "Like falling into a ditch, what?" I mocked. "My love is pure and holy," declared Amrit piously. "I see all her fillums. But tell me one thing, Sravan-bhai. I've developed a great liking for these Hollywood fillums, only I never manage to understand exactly what's going on. Even rickshaw-pullers seem to understand this language, but not I. I don't know when to laugh or clap or wolf-whistle, when to toss coins at the screen as others do." I tried to sort it out. "Why don't you just watch how laughter in the movie hall starts at one end and sweeps down the rows until everyone is convulsed? I bet no one else there knows when to laugh, either." '

'D'you remember how Amrit used to try to explain you to me and me to you? When we had one of our flaming rows, he always intervened.'

'Doubtless with noble pacific intent.'

'Yes, he tried to clarify us to one another, saying: "One minute, please. What Ravan means is . . ." And he always managed to convey exactly the opposite of what I meant, until I was tearing my hair and yelling, "That *isn't* what I mean, you fucker! You've got it all wrong!" But he'd hold up a patient hand and say: "One more minute, please. I'm just coming to what you had in mind." '

'He managed to bungle and blunder and bosh up the whole issue until he had us totally confounded about what we were originally clamouring about.'

'Instead, our energies went in telling the bugger to shut his trap and lay off trying to restore peace.'

'He wasn't as daft as he pretended, though.'

'And that time the three of us dressed as beggars and sat outside the Sarojgarh temple to raise funds for beer.'

'You financed yourselves in all sorts of adventurous ways,' said Pragya.

'We had to.'

'And how much did you raise?'

'Not the two of us; we weren't authentic enough. It was Amrit who stole the show.'

'Blind singing leper boy. Paws bandaged in grimy rags, eyes rolled back. The fellow had such an ache in his voice, it'd break your heart.'

'Don't forget he'd trained as a classical singer.'

'He certainly put it to good use. The fellow amassed heaps of coins while the two of us got a niggardly ten paise or so. Guys hurrying across the yard took one look at us and their faces hardened.

You could see them thinking—Lazy bastards. Able-bodied parasites! Why don't they work for a living? But Amrit's whining trills twisted the hearts of the toughest.'

'He earned enough to foot our beer bills.'

When they'd finished laughing over that one, they fell silent and looked past one another in shared disquiet. Sravan said, 'How come none of us *knew* he had a heart condition?'

'He didn't know it himself.'

'How did he die?' asked Pragya quietly.

'In his usual cranky way. He used to oversleep every morning, and we had to splash him with cold water to get him to wake up. It used to make us late. When we cribbed about it he'd say, '*Abe*, you benighted sons of the owl, I'll tell you a sure-fire way of waking me up. If I'm lying here stoned or sleeping, just whisper in my ear: "News! You've become the Chief Justice of India!"'

'That's how it happened, believe it or not. We shook him and shook him but he didn't respond. We put our lips to his ear and shouted, 'Wake up, abe haramzade, there's great news! You've become the Chief Justice of India!'

'We shook him and shook him . . .'

Sravan's voice trailed away in perplexity. They sat, faces closed, and did not speak. Years after his death, Amrit had reaped his two minutes' worth of silence as his posthumous revenue of regard from his friends.

'Some people seriously believed it was the avenging manes. His death, I mean.'

'How?'

'On the day Pitrapaksha ended, all the busti-wallahs used to cook piles of goodies: puris, kachoris, karhi, dahi baras. Mutton and sweets, too. They'd leave it all for the spirits of ancestors at the river ghat.'

'Booze, too. And bidis, if the departed had been fond of his drink and smoke.'

'Grub for the deceased seniors, see? Well, that Pitrapaksha, Amrit went and made a sumptuous feast of it all, along with some friendly pariah dogs.'

'He was like that. Bohemian.'

'The busti-wallahs were outraged. It just wasn't done—poaching on the spirits' annual treat! When Amrit suddenly conked off, some folks said, "Ah, there it is. What did we tell you?" '

'Spooky.'

'Yes.'

'That old crone cursed him. What was her name?'

'Malti.'

'Ah, yes. Aunt Malti to you, if I remember right.'

'Who was she?' Pragya asked.

'A servant. She washed our clothes.'

'Remember how she drooled over the memories of her dead husband?'

'He used to be an alcoholic. They were famous for their squabbles; you could hear them down the lane. He beat her up black and blue, yet after his death she was full of him. On the last day of Pitrapaksha she cooked all his favourite food and fondly arranged it on a platter and put it on the riverbank.'

'That was some of the stuff Amrit polished off.'

'D'you know, Buddhoo, she made it into one of my books.'

'That old crone in *The Temple of Sarojgarh*?'

'That's the one.'

'Is she alive?'

'I really don't know. I don't think so. I last met her in '85 or so. I was visiting the city and thought of taking a walk through the old area, since I'd used it extensively in my book. And there she was, pottering about. Her house had shrunk to a hovel. She was very old, almost blind, and she had trouble remembering me. She was ill-fed and sort of bitter and spiteful. Now, *The Temple of Sarojgarh* was a commercial success. Netted a tidy sum for the publishers and a nice bit of royalty for me, and was made into an award-winning film in the mid-'80s with Mrigank Sengupta directing and celebrities like Shalini Swaroop and Pritam Puri in the cast.'

'Yes, I missed seeing it.'

'I have the video; show it to you one of these days. The grandmother's role was done by Manorama Mankad. You probably haven't heard of her but she was a big-time art-film personality. I was more than satisfied with the adaptation: Manorama made old Malti come alive. Every quaver and scowl and toothy smile. She really studied the part. So seeing poor Malti in the flesh after many years was a shock. Even I had somehow come to associate the video image with her, until Manorama was more like the Malti I remembered than Malti herself. Now she was bent, ragged, senile, shockingly ill. I looked at her, and I was ashamed—you know what I mean? I thought of all that the movie buffs had said and the tabloids, the film festivals and the best-actress awards, the parties, the reviews of the Mankad retrospective, the money that had flowed. I felt like a thief. I'd used the content of an old woman's self, over which she could assert no copyright, for which she couldn't claim a percentage. And now she had belied the book, as it were, gone beyond the range of camera focus towards her own separate doom—which was different from the fate my book or the film had assigned her. Like a tragic revolt . . .'

Sravan stared at the ceiling, leaning back in his chair. His voice pursued a tortuous point of conscience. Soul-surfing.

'For a writer it's something of a blow to realize how life constantly defies the expectations of literature. It is always less merciful and more inventive, carrying on with unexpected patterns long after the imaginative function stops.'

'All this sounds great, but what did you do for her?' asked Buddhoo with a crooked grin.

'I wondered what to give her. Like an idiot I gave her a copy of my book. I had dedicated it to all my anonymous sources of inspiration, and I told her she was in it. She looked at it in confusion. It didn't make sense. What I told her was entirely outside her range of understanding, and of course she couldn't read anyway. She threw my book a look of complete contempt. It was utterly useless to her. Quite deflating—to measure your work against a different scale. I came back and sent her a thick cotton sari. Good for the cold weather, Pragya said. But again, too small. I searched my memory for something, some wish she might have expressed in the old days, and after strenuous recollection I recovered a stray remark that gave me a clue: she had desperately wanted to go on pilgrimage to Badrinath and Kedarnath. So I made all the arrangements, sent the cash and sent my secretary at the academy, Srivastava, to accompany her.'

Sravan changed the subject. 'Ever hear from Nandita?'

'Got a letter from her after a year of her marriage. I guess that's the only favourable written testimonial I've ever been given. Kind of a review of my agreeable self.'

'You fucked up your law exam because of that miserable business.'

'Maybe.'

Pragya ventured hesitantly, 'Who was Nandita? Your girlfriend?'

Buddhoo smiled a twisted smile. 'Yes. Shall I tell her the whole disgusting history?'

Sravan grimaced. 'Go ahead. Makes no difference now. It's all too far in the past.'

'Started as a psychological experiment. Two sisters. Sravan and I were trying to write a book each. Back in the Morrisgunj days.'

'Along with the two sisters?'

'No. This was about "law" again: romance, passion, sex. We needed concrete experiences, real characters, authentic material.'

'The girls suspected nothing.'

'Ravan got all the material he wanted. And more than the experience he strictly needed.'

'More than I'd bargained for or was capable of handling. Hell, she was a furnace!' He'd always enjoyed parading his past affairs for Pragya's benefit.

'You led her on, yaar.'

'She stuck to me like a leech. For months.'

'She had a breakdown afterwards, don't forget.' There was a murk of resentment in Buddhoo's voice. 'We despised you. Your book was fantastically written, though.'

'I wonder what became of her?'

Buddhoo shrugged. 'Don't know. Mine was the other one. Nandita.'

'Did you get a book out of her, too?' asked Pragya in a strange voice.

Buddhoo sparked up. 'Me? I forgot the fucking book. Forgot

everything. Filled out a thick pad with letters. All the while Ravan was scientifically studying each mood and desire, getting a great book out of it, carving out his sentences, there was I, scribbling letters to her. She gave them back afterwards. She was scared to keep them. Oh, we were a mess. It ended, of course.'

'How?'

'She got engaged. The old story. I was going to burn all that trash I scribbled, but Ravan here said, 'Here, let's take a look, Devdas.' I passed them on and they passed into literature.'

'What?'

'Yes, Sravan, wrote them in—his second draft was much more concentrated than the first.'

'That book got great reviews.'

'Must have. As for me, she wrote me that one letter a year later, saying something like, "All my life I'll care for this man I've married but I'll be measuring him against you and finding him less"—that sort of thing. The only review my letters got.'

There was silence. Sravan heaved a sigh and said, 'Oh, that first book. Every unpractised sentence a discovery, every insight dearly bought.'

'Only the price wasn't yours to pay,' said Buddhoo softly.

'Still sore? Anyway, yaar, to each his own. At least I got a book out of it; you didn't even manage a girl. Jo jeeta woh Sikandar.'

'Yes. And jo haara woh mast kalandar.'

Buddhoo's eyes had a fluid shine, and his nose was oddly full. He cleared his throat and Sravan said reflectively, 'That's why I often feel that all this art stuff has been just artifice. Counterfeit. Others might swallow it. I can't.'

'Nice speech,' said Buddhoo. 'Especially on a fattened ego.' He turned to Pragya with a knavish smile. 'Is this what you called Ravan's overdose of high seriousness?'

'D'you know the time?' said Pragya. 'It's past two.'

3

'Each time I realize how close I've come to making my million and how dumbly I've let the chance go, I could beat my breast and howl like a banshee,' said Buddhoo. 'Now this news item in the *Statesman*—three enterprising young college boys kidnapped their pal and got the guy's pa to cough up a fortune. Why couldn't Amrit and I have thought of that?'

'Who would you have kidnapped?'

'You, why not?'

'No go—my father wouldn't have coughed up. Besides, you'd have had to maintain me, and I have finicky tastes in food and drink. I never repeat a shirt. I smoke expensive fags . . .'

'Why wouldn't your father have coughed up?'

'He's never thought me a worthwhile proposition. At the best of times my credit with him's low. Right now it's touching rock bottom.'

While Buddhoo digested this, Sravan plucked up the courage to propose an employment-hunting expedition.

'Time for business. There's a guy—Arora, chartered accountant—in the colony. Needs an office assistant for his private set-up . . .'

Buddhoo waved a dismissive hand. 'Sorry, I've other plans,' he said loftily.

'Arora'll train you in accounts and computers.'

'My tastes incline to the rustic arts.'

'There's a small room with attached bath on his terrace. He'll let you have it on a nominal rent.'

'What I'm looking for is the moon with attached bath. Leased or freehold.'

'You've got to plan right.'

'I've joined a correspondence course in homeopathy and alternative healing.'

'Are you serious?'

'As serious as damnit. I want to set up as an alternative-healing vet. I tried it once but things went wrong. I mean, how does one manage acupressure with a dog? There was this cur with a limp. I tried a spot of acupressure, but the cur proved a greater master of the art: buried his fangs in my calf. I stand forever cured of an old toothache, I grant, but I'm reluctant to pursue my mission, knowing animals as I do and fully sharing their mistrust of human motives . . . So let me complete the course and take the exams and frame my diploma. In the meantime I might turn critic. I propose to write monographs on your future works, and you can accordingly tailor your books to fit my criticism. The next step in post–post-modern criticism. Let the criticism precede the work.'

'Stop kidding around.'

'No, think what a breakthrough it will be. Standing the cause-and-effect formula on its head. Temporal concurrence . . .'

'Quite a conference intellectual, Buddhoo,' observed Pragya. 'I'm disappointed. Where did you pick all this up?'

'Oh, Buddhoo's full of surprises. Don't be taken in by his act,' said Sravan.

'Or else,' continued Buddhoo, 'I've thought of applying for a place in a home for the aged. A permanent residency. Full board, lodging, medical facilities, leave-travel subsidy, cultural and recreational benefits, income-tax exemption, free rail and air travel as a senior citizen. If my friends would only subsidize and sponsor me.'

'Perish the thought. You won't be a senior citizen for three decades at least.'

'I can entertain the senior citizens.'

'That you can, seeing what a hit you are with Babuji,' remarked Sravan wryly. 'What was he telling you last night? I heard the two of you getting pretty riotous.'

'That? Oh, that was all about his contribution to Britain's War Effort. 1942.'

'What did he ever have to do with it?'

'Didn't you know? He was a respected member of a dedicated group called Ha Ha Hi.'

'What?'

'Ha Ha Hi, my dear Ravan, wasn't any laughing matter, as its name tempts you to think. It used to be a committed cell of the Hindustan Scout Association to assist wounded victims during the blitz. Dramatic, what? The Germans on the rampage, the Japs baring their fangs on our eastern front, the French fallen . . .'

'There was no blitz here. No blitz could ever hope to submerge Babuji. He's always been the prince of all blitzes. Besides, the only place where a blitz was expected—and that only by rabid pessimists—was Calcutta, and to the best of my knowledge, information and belief, Babuji's never set foot there.'

'Ah, but fellows in the United Provinces weren't going to miss the fun. What d'you think? Most were on the side of the Germans. All except the toadies, who seized their chance to demonstrate solidarity. And your father actually enlisted as a scout in this Ha Ha Hi.'

'What the fuck does that *mean*?' cried Sravan, exasperated.

'Hawai hamle se hifazat,' said Buddhoo in high glee. 'Fantastic, what? Babuji was a First Aid scout.'

'Funny,' mused Sravan. 'All these years, he's never once mentioned this little detail to me. I just can't see him rendering first aid to anyone. It's out of character. If there ever was a determined candidate for first aid, it was Babuji himself. And he saw to it that he got it—from the entire world.'

Buddhoo looked intently at Sravan, not missing the bitterness in his voice. Self-conscious, Sravan pulled himself together and changed the subject.

'What I want us to do—right away—is drop in and speak to Arora.'

'Who?'

'The chartered accountant.'

Buddhoo regarded him in stubborn silence.

'We must negotiate with him about rent and salary. Why don't you change your clothes?'

'I'm okay as I am.'

'No, you're not. You're totally unkempt. Put on something presentable. If you haven't got it, I'll lend you something.'

'Fuck-all,' scoffed Buddhoo. 'How respectable we've become! What're the lot of you ashamed of?'

'You,' retorted Sravan, not to be outdone, 'are an elderly flower child. Still practising an extinct hippiehood. Stuck in the sixties. Are you coming?'

The snap in Sravan's voice made Buddhoo rise in immediate compliance, murmuring, 'Okay, boss.'

In a few minutes Sravan was ringing Arora's doorbell, and in a few minutes more they were back in the tree-lined lane, Sravan in deep gloom and Buddhoo in high spirits.

'Sorry,' said Sravan. 'He's found someone already.'

'Sorry yourself,' crowed Buddhoo.

They were dangerously close to a quarrel. Sravan shuddered to remember their old altercations, and struggled to master his face. 'I thought you wanted me to help you find a job.'

'It happens, Ravan, that you're far more anxious than I am. What's it? Want me to pack up and leave? I'll do it right away.'

'Shut up!' shouted Sravan. 'That's not what I meant and you know it.'

'I'm not sure.'

'The day I want you out I'll throw you out on your backside. I've never stood on ceremony with you.'

'Then what?'

'You can't go on like this.'

'Like what?'

'Like a saala junkie. Swadeshi brand. Doing nothing.'

'Nothing? I do much more than most guys. The things I've done in my life would fill a volume.'

'Look, I'm sure you'll give us the story of your life in large doses over the next few days but you're making a bloody mess of your life.'

'It's a good sight better than most people's lives. I see what you're driving at, and I'm leaving first thing tomorrow!'

Sravan stopped. He cursed in a low voice. 'Ulloo ke patthe! Do you think I'll let you? I spent months in your village home when I was dead broke, and you have the nerve to imagine . . .'

Buddhoo studied Sravan's flushed face a long moment before his own broke into a sheepish grin. 'So you're prepared to wait—till I find the right thing? Or don't find it?'

'Have it your own way.'

'No typing, accounts or computers?'

'No.'

'The moon with attached bath for me, right?'

'Designer junkie,' jibed Sravan. 'You can slum it in your own way. I'll explain it to Pragya. Our very own domestic philosopher. For some reason best known to you, you've got a job phobia. You're a full-time addabaaz. Yarn-spinner, tea-stall raconteur, professional sponger.'

'Just for a few months, Ravan, yaar,' said Buddhoo in a small voice. 'I'll pay for my keep.'

Sravan stopped and considered Buddhoo seriously. An idea had just offered itself, promising and entire. One of those swift instants of inspiration had come, fully finished and perfect.

'You just spoke of paying me, right?'

'Uh-huh.'

'You can do it in kind, not cash. You can take my father off my back.'

'I don't get it.'

'Take his mind off his peevish pranks. Entertain him, don't you see? It's perfectly clear. The man's bored stiff and naturally mischievous. I can't devote any time to him, and anyway I don't seem to have anything to say to him. There's all my editorial work at *Swadeshi* and my classes at the Centre for Literary Arts, plus my own writing. And Pragya's tied up with her design company and the kids. Neither of us can open up with him. We've tried—she's better at it than I am—but he used to be such a supremo that all of us go mute, and it's too late to change the pattern now. But come to think of it, yaar, you're made for the job. A natural entertainer, and you seem to click with him, too. Just the other day Pragya was talking of finding a full-time nurse . . .'

'Are you trying to be funny?'

'Not in the least. There won't be much nursing to do. All you have to do is be a companion.'

'Durbar jester.'

'You'll be doing me a great favour. D'you know how much nurses charge?'

'Babysit him round the clock, huh? Running a crèche for the senile.'

'All you have to do is keep him occupied, give him his medicines, help him to the bathroom, help with his exercises and his massages and chat him up.'

'On-site geriatric psychologist,' mused Buddhoo, letting the idea sink in.

'Something like that. And tell him your cock-and-bull tales. I guess he's lonely in his way. Stories, gossip, anything. Let him snarl at you. It has a tonic effect on him. You've got to keep your stories simple, preferably rural and stupid. Won't be difficult.'

'You're very persuasive,' snorted Buddhoo.

'Oh, come on, yaar. This is the first time you're actually going to be paid for telling cranky stories. The right job for you. Full board and lodging.'

Buddhoo threw back his head and laughed loudly. 'Okay,' he agreed. 'I might have done worse. It might suit me for a while. But if I get restless, I'll tender my resignation and walk out on you.'

'Good, that's done,' said Sravan. They walked on. He'd have to do some careful explaining to Pragya. She'd have to understand their old history of reciprocal support. A great idea, he exulted. He badly needed to talk to someone at times, and this was a guy who understood.

As they turned the corner of Block P, Sravan's eyes followed an irresistible upward path along the vertical glass-and-concrete building and came to lodge in their usual place: the window on the extreme left on the sixth floor. The curtains were drawn, but he could visualize behind them the bowl of light that burned at the tip of the slender brass column behind the blue velvet armchair. He tried to pluck his gaze away, sort out his walk. With a voice well practised in guile, he stopped and nudged Buddhoo.

'Listen, I've an important message to send through someone who lives in this building. D'you mind coming up with me—just for a few minutes?'

'Fine,' assented Buddhoo.

Sravan strode briskly into the lobby and made for the lift. He always marvelled at the way his feet devoured the distance across this lobby. He was restless in the lift, fumbling with the buttons. With a bump the lift stopped, the door slid open and Sravan sped on to the landing. They stood before the polished door, number 614, and all Sravan's misery and tension gathered as he pressed the bell and heard it ring within, a pale tinkle of coin against the large ringing walls of the flat.

Malini herself opened the door. Her face lit up in a welcome so rehearsed in its exuberance that all his suspicions returned.

'What luck!' she cried. 'I was just thinking of you. Come on in—there's something fantastic I've managed to acquire today, after two weeks of haggling.'

She led the way, speaking fast. 'Cost me a fortune but I'd set my heart on it. Love at first sight. Luckily, Mridul's out on tour—I'll have to break the bad news to him gently. The poor fellow's going to have a heart attack when he learns how much I've spent. Wait till you see it.'

She was wearing a cunningly designed outfit, an artful affair made up of tiny oblique pleats round a simple yoke that enhanced a provocative fullness, contained at the waist by a stern affectation of sash. Looking at her, his nerves all on edge, he felt sure she had not been alone, and the old rage rose in his heart. He crushed it with difficulty, putting on his cynical act.

'Sit,' she commanded. Then she looked at Buddhoo curiously.

'This is Prabuddha. Old friend. He's staying with us for a while. Buddhoo, this is Malini, Pragya's friend.'

'Oh, hullo,' piped Malini, turning on Buddhoo the torchlight of a brilliant smile. 'What do you do?'

Buddhoo had a problem answering that one. Sravan came to his rescue.

'Prabuddha is a pop philosopher,' he said facetiously. 'He used to be in the sixties, anyway.'

'Oh, I'm impressed,' breathed Malini, mock-serious, eyes very wide. 'D'you write songs on I'm Blue and Make Love, Not War and Say No to Nukes and things like that?'

Buddhoo snorted in amusement and Sravan answered for him. 'He doesn't write. He's a wandering preacher. Come and hear him at it someday.'

They were sitting in an opulent, marble-floored room where the brass gleamed and the china sparkled. Onyx sat on the cabinets like blobs of veined butter. Thick carpets cradled the feet, and ivory lights seeped gently out of silken lampshades and flowed softly along the creamy pallor of the walls and floor. In the green light of an aquarium, brilliant fish wove around tiny rockeries. Mughal queens with liquid eyes and jewelled coronets reclined in rich frames, delicate blossoms poised in their tapering fingers. There were painted screens, filigreed bowls, small rugs, velvet cushions, palm fronds and an outsized portrait of Malini herself on the extreme wall. Somehow this house repelled him—everything in it was expensive and true to type. A house of pretension, clutter and kitsch, with a vague, self-conscious vaingloriousness.

Malini rose to her feet. 'Let me show you what I bought today. I'm terribly excited about it.'

She fetched a small stone head from the marble ledge on which it stood, shells clustered around it.

'Look,' she said. 'Isn't it gorgeous? Such a sublime expression. It looks like the Buddha but it isn't the Buddha. It's a warrior. The headgear is different—see? But there's this little trace of Greek influence. Notice the eyes and the bridge of the nose. The dealer told me it's a Gandhara piece. If it hadn't been a secret deal, I'd have got it dated at the museum.'

Sravan took the stone head and held it appraisingly in his hands. 'Where did your dealer get this thing?'

'It's a piece of the famous Viratgaon frieze. After that earthquake a lot of these bits fell off and . . .'

'How much did you pay for it?' he asked, non-committal.

Her eyebrows leapt up her smooth forehead. The glinting earrings did a little pirouette against the dark curls.

'Don't even ask!' she breathed, mock-threatening.

One of the ways in which his infatuation uttered itself was the savagery with which he loved to disappoint her. In some strange way he earned her respect by proving her wrong, and thereby matched his power against hers.

'This is a Bulunda piece, make no mistake,' said Sravan decisively.

'A what?'

Sravan put the head down on a small table beside his chair. 'It's useless telling you that you've been taken for a ride. You won't believe me.'

'What d'you mean?' she cried, agitated.

Sravan warmed to his act. 'There's a place called Bulunda in Rajasthan where the Aravalli Hills start. Great stonemasons there. And great fakers.'

'Isn't it genuine, then?' she cried anxiously.

He shook his head, saying nothing, enjoying her suspense.

She was aggressive, stubborn. Her savvy discernment was being questioned, and she bristled. 'But Chaudhury said it's authentic, and he ought to know. He even showed me some papers.'

'If it was real, as he claims, it wouldn't be in Chaudhury's showroom. He'd hide it in the basement. Viratgaon!' he murmured in scorn. 'D'you imagine it's that easy making off with national-heritage bric-a-brac? My dear girl, you shop for antiques as though you were choosing a pedigreed pup, complete with papers from the Kennel Club of India! When was this Gandhara influence, by the way?'

'The . . . fourth century, I think.' She faltered, embarrassed.

'AD or BC?' he asked ironically, and loved the way she winced. Having administered that affront, he was now ready to soothe, indulge, and apply the emollient of his fervour again.

'By the way,' he changed the subject quickly. 'I have some great news for you.'

His words were cut short by the shrill ringing of the telephone.

Annoyed, he reached out and picked it up, hulloed, and met complete silence. A charged, waiting sort of silence, like the vacancy of a room in which an unknown assailant lurks. He hulloed again. The line clicked dead. Instant suspicion flooded his mind. He felt sure that if she, Malini, had received the call, the person would have spoken.

Then he remembered what he had come to tell her. 'You're the only one to know so far,' he said in a shabby appeal. The honour he bestowed on her did not go unnoticed. Her face flushed with pleasure and she turned eagerly to him, the affront forgotten. From his chair Buddhoo watched the little tableau with interest.

Sravan lowered his voice. 'I finally heard from Srinivasan last week.'

She gave a tiny gasp. 'The Golden Lotus!'

'Yes,' he confirmed.

'This is wonderful!' she cried. 'Oh, we're proud of you!'

'It's not what you'd call a mega-success.' He brushed aside her outpourings with a fine show of modesty. 'But you could call it a moderate achievement in its way.'

'We must celebrate this. Now. A big bash!' she cried. 'I'll phone Shahani's. What would you like for lunch?'

'No, not right away,' he said, guarded. 'Let's leave it for later.' The look that he shied across at her and that she deftly caught and held was intercepted by Buddhoo, on whom no significance was ever lost. Sravan turned to find Buddhoo surveying him with an expression of cool assessment. A small downcurl of mouth or a minor trick of eyebrow was enough to establish the certainty that Buddhoo had grasped all.

'But what a record!' Malini was gushing. 'Three awards in ten years! And you're the youngest ever to win the Kala Vihar Patra, too! And all your reading tours. Sessions with translators. Interviews! Ph.D.s on your work! It's breathtaking!'

He regarded her smooth, ecstatic face with some misgiving. Her words were gently tinted with laughter. With Malini he could never be sure when she was ridiculing him.

'I'll never be able to take you seriously,' he remarked lightly.

'No? You should know better, then. I'm really most enormously impressed,' she protested.

'As an author I'm not out to impress; I'm out to improve,' he pronounced sententiously.

'Great! That's one of your most quotable ones. I must jot it down. And now how about a tiny drink? I'll have it fixed in a jiffy.'

'No, coffee'd suit us fine.'

'Okay. Give me two minutes.'

And while she chatted up Buddhoo over the coffee, Sravan sat and looked at her. Basically, he liked her because she confirmed his admiration for himself. Or did she? He'd chosen her for reasons he had only partially explained to himself. She belonged to a different class. He was comfortable with her.

He liked that confectionery mouth over that sensitive cleft chin. And her eyes, with their heavy-lidded, thick-lashed lassitude. Malini had a trick of seeming to switch them on and off, dimming them to the right degree of translucence, achieving the right temperature for each moment. Sravan was often aware that he felt a bristling contempt for her pretensions, her compulsive glitter, but this did not diminish the power she had over him. His mind was never so fluent as when it busily transferred the fantastications of his desire into images—the squeeze-beckoning resilience of her shapely arms, the liquid suction of her mouth, the sumptuous resistance of her breasts. And she was articulate. Headstrong. She even had Buddhoo quelled. It was hard to dissent, for Malini had a cultivated voice, a plentiful vocabulary, great presence of mind and inexhaustible malice and was fortified by a streak of native arrogance. Even he, Sravan, who had seen arrogance in many forms—artistic sneers, bureaucratic hauteur, corporate condescension, yuppie patronizing—had to allow Malini her due. Give her time, say ten or fifteen years, and she'd turn into a staccato, overbearing, omnicompetent authority on everything. In the meantime there was no denying her appeal. And to think it had all begun as a calculated move to punish Pragya for what she had done a dozen years back.

There was the telephone again. He reached out before she could and was sucked into an immense conduit of space, a dark tunnel of silence. He clicked in impatience, hulloed again. The line went dead.

'Must be Mridul,' she remarked. 'These long-distance calls . . .'

'Or one of your other admirers,' he said wryly.

She twinkled into laughter. 'Thanks for that word "other". It assumes your eminent self in the first place, then?'

'On principle I never disturb a beautiful woman's illusions,' he retorted. 'So how's the book coming along?' Since she had gotten to know him, Malini had begun fancying herself a potential author, and he knew that any talk of her book would smooth her ruffled feathers.

'I've written a bit more. Shall I read it to you?'

'Do.'

She fetched it, moved a chair close to his, cleared her throat in a pre-recitation cough and began: 'Now, in this stretch Shipra's musing: "By some peculiar chance time seems to have slid off its groove. All mornings are the same. My brainful of the sky's blue with a froth of sun spinning in wisps in its centre. I dislodge the sleep from my mind as I come down the stairs from the terrace. The day awaits me, like a stagnant pool creeping up my ankles as I step into it. The street looks like a long unreeled grey ribbon. But I am ill at ease. A disease infecting my own self chronically. The same words, thoughts, feeling drone in my head, and they are always uttered by the same unaccented inner voice, pausing at the same pauses, rushing in the same spurts. Each morning the disc begins rotating under the clock's needle. Like an obsolete, wound-up antique gramophone. My words on paper cast a shadow, a crawling shadow across a pool of wintry lamplight. My words come like milestones marking my lamplit path. Black rocks of compressed sound . . ." '

Sravan was at once amused and irritated. What a bad imitation of his own style. Wannabe women writers who attached themselves to him inevitably began producing poor copies of his manner. Affected, amateurish. But to her he said, 'Seems to be coming along fine.'

'Shall I read more? Are you interested?'

He lowered his voice significantly. 'I'm always interested.'

She flushed. Read some more in the same strain. Suddenly she stopped and said, 'This is the penultimate chapter. I wonder if you're serious about getting it through to a suitable publisher.'

'Dead serious.'

She was anxious, unsure. 'So can I send the manuscript across to you next week?'

'Better if you bring it personally,' he said.

She persisted. 'I mean, it'll be a surer thing if *you* discuss the deal.'

He was cautious. 'What's the hurry? Let it stand a while. Settle down. A novel's got to resolve itself through a bit of necessary separation from its author, you know. Like a growing child. You might want to write a second draft. Polish it up . . .'

She studied him closely, suspicious. 'I'm desperate that Papa should see my name in print soon. He's terribly excited about it. I used to get full marks in English composition in school. He says he always knew I had it in me. And he's eighty now.'

'Ah, I wish my father felt that way about me,' Sravan said, laughing, and he stood up to leave. 'Bye for now. One of these days I'll see what can be done about it.'

She looked far from reassured, but nodded. He rose to go.

'Bye, then,' she called at the door. 'Tell Pragya I'll stop by tomorrow.'

Out in the lane, Buddhoo cleared his throat. 'And the message, dear Ravan?' he taunted.

'What message?' barked Sravan.

'The urgent message you had to send—through that china memsahib? The message you came to deliver, ha?'

Too late Sravan realized his error. Buddhoo chafed on: 'You won the Golden Lotus, eh? Congratulations, yaar. When I die, a happy business maharaja, I shall bequeath my fortune to a trust that shall annually award a prize, too. I shall call it the Golden Phallus! Not that you aren't a worthy candidate for it; I promise to take your merits into account. By the way, does she wear falsies, or are they real?'

Sravan smarted.

'The point is, yaar,' went on Buddhoo, 'whether you still own that something that's mightier than sword *or* pen?'

Sravan preserved a dignified silence. Buddhoo wouldn't let him alone.

'Quite a lady-killer, wah!' applauded Buddhoo, as they walked back. Then an idea seemed to strike him. 'Is she the only one, yaar?'

Sravan began to enjoy himself. Buddhoo's question had suddenly ignited a range of inventive possibilities. A brave new image of himself began inflating tantalizingly in his brain.

'No,' he answered soberly. 'Not counting my lady wife there are—let me see—I sometimes forget names—yes, six. Malini, Menaka, Atreya, Devyani, Purabi and Mondira.' He struck off each name on his palm, his forehead crumpling with the exertion of recollecting. 'This year, that is.'

Buddhoo grunted in disbelief. 'This year!' he exclaimed. 'One for each day of the week! And what d'you do on the seventh day, may one know?'

Sravan guffawed. 'Like the Lord, I rest.'

'All your women have uniformly beautiful names. As though you named them yourself. Like the names of apsaras round a lecherous sage.'

'Yes. A mere accident. Maybe I go for women with lyrical names. But some of them came to a lousy end.'

'How?'

'Most unfortunate. One died a natural death—but unfortunate all the same. Another killed herself.'

'You must be joking.'

'I'm perfectly serious. She jumped into a well. One was an online relationship and one a classroom affair. Both ended badly. That's what my love life is—messy. I'm now alarmed when a woman starts taking an interest in me. I warn her to keep away for her own good, but nothing helps.'

He had Buddhoo agog, he noted with sly satisfaction. 'Which one shall I start with?' he asked sadly.

Buddhoo considered. 'Menaka.'

Sravan groaned. 'You've selected the most disastrous one, yaar. Okay, let's take another turn round the park. This was the online one.'

'An affair over the Internet?' gasped Buddhoo in awe.

'Right you are.'

'I've only *heard* of Internet affairs,' said Buddhoo. 'Did you get to know what she looked like?'

'Now you must understand one thing. I'm extremely intolerant of crappy moral judgements,' he declared sternly. 'Also understand that in the recent past I've been a serious and dedicated womanizer. I've needed it to fuel my creativity. This woman, Menaka, liked older men. All her men had been twice her age, she informed me the first time we met at the chat site. She was twenty-something, five-three, on the slender side, long black hair and wheatish skin.'

'All that's left is the "convented" tag and the "decent marriage" assurance,' muttered Buddhoo.

Sravan ignored him. 'Over the first few days, I learnt to use words that brought out electric leaps in a million ganglia. I let my fantasies loose. Those words were like magic mantras. Of course, I realized soon enough that they gave the whole thing a tremendous build-up and finally let you down. But imagine playing footsie on a woman's boobs, yaar? All through words. Imagine plugging your engorged nozzle into her, snuggling there, guzzling on her virtual body. All through words. For a while I was convinced that the virtual was a great improvement on the actual. There are things you can do better with your mind than you ever can with your clumsy, lumbering beast of a body. The subtle physicality of words—get it?'

Buddhoo nodded.

'I told her I liked wine, women and words, not necessarily in that order. She said she liked wine and words, too, but naturally, no women. Older men for her, but of late she'd been having problems. Her boyfriend had left her. She was dejected, ill. I tried cheering her up with one of my favourite fantasies. "Welcome," I typed. "You've come calling. I'm opening the door for you." She typed, "Thanks." I continued: "You're dressed in a Gujarati choli. Red, encrusted with mirrors and lots of embroidery." She typed, "Oh, great!" So I developed the picture further. "You're wearing a chunky silver choker. Long dangling earrings. Full makeup. Red lipstick, mascara . . ." She typed, "Lovely. You're making me feel glamorous." Then I sprang my well-timed surprise: "And you're nude beneath the waist." She typed six exclamation marks. I could see she was loving it.'

Buddhoo stared, open-mouthed.

'"You have a silver chain round your waist. A pendant suspended on your crotch." Et cetera, et cetera.'

He cut short Buddhoo's awe with a brusque wave of the hand, laughing secretly to himself.

'Did you manage to cheer her up?' asked Buddhoo eagerly.

'Bless you, no. You'll hardly believe it, yaar, but I learnt soon enough that my images left the lady cold. She was turned on by—of all the bally things—philosophy! Ever heard of philosophy as an aphrodisiac? Well, hear this one, and never fuck a philosopher, my friend, virtually or actually. It can't be done. Our exchanges grew pretty bizarre in course of time. A most arduous and unrewarding exercise. I'd express a particularly juicy thought like: "How about the corridor of a speeding train in the dead of night? You're a total stranger and we run into one another outside the loo?" but she'd come out with something like: "I've only just gotten round to defining peace. Peace is what's consistent with our complexes and doesn't provoke them." I'd be gruff: "Too abstract." She'd persist: "Nobody wants the active disturbance of misery. But I've just discovered I don't much care for the stress of active happiness." Or she'd turn critical and say, "Do you know what's wrong with you? You have no real interest in people. Armchair empathy, practical apathy. You're supposed to be a writer, but why can't you connect?" Anyone could see that connecting was what I was trying to do all the time. But if I said that, it'd be: "There's this kernel of self in you which can't dissolve." '

There were times when she didn't give me the chance to begin. She'd toss the first question: "You worked out this God thing?" Startled, I'd answer, "A bit." She'd type, "I'm bothered about this. I've got a vital stake in the matter." Then, very fast, the words would pour across the screen like a palpitating soliloquy: "I often drop that vowel 'o' in 'God'. Turn it into GD. Suitably abstract. A blueprint encoding the universe in a micro-thought. At other times I feel the need to humanize the abstract, and I replace that 'o'. You ever looked for God, S.?" I'd quip, "Not God but his initial draft certainly." I'd been about to propose a "Me Maratha chief, you Portuguese hostage" brand of fantasy, but she went right ahead and swung at me her next: "I haven't got this good–evil thing sorted out properly. It's become a personal question." I felt like roaring: "Goddamn it, what's this, a nonstop seminar?" But I just said, "Haven't worked that one out, sorry." To which she urged, "Well, work it out now and tell me." A bloody great meeting of minds, this tamasha, but on the screen I offered the random thought: "I guess you can't supplant evil by good, only supplement it." She replied, "Fantastic. I absolutely agree. The hurting motive is so strong in nature, the best that we can do is increase the healing motive—to counter it. Keep the balance." '

I wrote lamely, "You're wise for twenty-five, I must say. What are you? A Holy Master? Koot Homi?" She retorted, "Holy Mistress is more like it." '

Finally, one day she typed, "Suppose I tell you something today, S. I won't be logging on again." I typed an exclamation mark and three question marks. The words strung themselves together on the screen in uncanny finality. "Going into hospital. Desperately ill." I admit I was dashed. I asked the devious: "What's up with you?" She said it was broncho-pneumonia. She'd been running high fever for days and now going into hospital was the only thing. "So, you'll be back soon?" I urged. Then screen stayed empty a longish moment. Then the words crept across it, as though blown in by an unearthly draught: "I don't think I will." For some peculiar emotional reason I was indignant, and thumped down in outrage, "Nobody conks off with broncho-pneumonia." The draught blew more words across my screen: "People like me do." All of a sudden ribbons of words began appearing, reaching across to me: "There isn't anything like virtual pain or virtual death. I mean, you just can't switch it all off, yourself, your pain, your death. I've been turning over the idea of suicide in my mind but I can't really believe that it's a switching off. And medical science in a case like mine is like a bit of extra power from your UPS—a little more time, that's all. So, I get out of this web now, S. In more senses than one! Interesting. I often think of it as the Indra jaal, the net of

Indra, the mesh of maya, call it whatever you like. I must tell you—I'm 61. Male. Gay. Have AIDS, desperately ill. Ex-professor of philosophy. Wanted to get out of this miserable body, become someone else, interact with a stranger. Didn't work out too well, did it? Sorry for being such a clumsy actor. In my state and at my time of life I couldn't rid myself of the things that dog me. Thanks for everything."

'It didn't register for a while. Dying of AIDS. Gay and sixty-one years old! This was a real being out there somewhere. Not a trick of the machine, not a figment of my imagination. And hell! All the time I thought we were interlocked in a common story, the storylines were so far apart. To each his own fiction. It might be fun till it wears off . . .'

Sravan heaved a deep sigh and said in a world-weary voice, 'So there you have it. That was Menaka for you.' He watched Buddhoo out of the corner of his eye.

Buddhoo finished chewing his areca nut in slow deliberation. Then he offered his comment: 'Okay story. Middling. Except for one or two little things. A sick man—I mean—that sick—probably isn't up to all these discussions. And at sixty-one, you can't like men twice your age. It's like those wisecracks they put up in grocery shops: "Credit will be given to all customers eighty-five years of age or older, if accompanied by both parents!" '

4

'I'm working on this new book. A tentative first draft so far. It's all in a state of subconscious gestation. Posing quite a management problem for me—these six characters I'm obsessing over. I'm doing what I call creative waiting. A book's got to stand a while before it starts flowing. There is an estranged married couple, Mondira and Amalendu. Two other characters, Mihir and Devyani. A child, and a senile and malicious old woman.

'What I'm uncertain about is this pentagon of context–personality–event–consequence–law that I've sketched. I've never been convinced that life can be made to fall into facile plots and counterplots and subplots and a whole ladder of atomized minor plots on a reducing scale. Still, there's an apparent order but it isn't easily detected. And everything's got its built-in symmetries and anarchies. My brain and its fantastications do seem to be extensions of the concrete physical universe and therefore real and continuous with it. There's no parallel reality but the same reality with a different consistency . . .'

Buddhoo's flat voice broke into Sravan's monologue: 'So in this novel of yours, who sleeps with whom and who kills whom?'

Sravan frowned, aggravated. He spelt out his idea in a voice of strained patience. 'What's important is who learns what and reaches where. There's an old fantasy of mine that I'm trying to realize. Suppose a dead man, someone I've never known, were to leave his incomplete storyline as . . . a subtle presence in the air. A sort of psychic code. And I were to pick it up without knowing.

Suppose I were to carry on, adding my own private story to it. Like . . . recording my voice on a pre-recorded tape. And suppose, when I die, this double-decker plot were left as a sort of vibration in the air and a third person were to pick it up and add to it his own story, without erasing all of mine . . .'

'Does it have an end?' asked Buddhoo.

'How can it? The circle is beginningless and endless.'

'The reader's patience isn't.'

Sravan clicked in exasperation. 'Go to hell—it's all lost on a joker like you. But if you just hear me out, you'll see what I'm driving at. It isn't critical theory I'm obsessing about—it's a vital life issue. Is there a pattern or not? What was that thing Wittgenstein said, about philosophy being a battle against the bewitchment of our intelligence by means of language? It's roughly like Sankara's maya. Language does both the things Sankara stated—*avarana*, camouflage, and *viksepa*, distortion. But the opposite is equally true. If you study bio-genesis or particle physics, there's no denying the existence of fundamental patterns. Plots. Purposes. So Indian philosophy talks of the word with a capital W—calls it *aksara lakshmi* and *vakya devi*. Talks of the mantra calling truth out of the void . . . where are you off to?'

'Sorry. This is nature calling truth out of the void.' Buddhoo made for the loo.

'Funny that nature should call truth each time I start discoursing, no?'

'Funny,' agreed Buddhoo with a grin.

The right tone wouldn't come just yet. The first draft was often like a lump of clay, laboured over and left, into which God breathed life in the second draft. And he was not ashamed to bring in God, so long as God stayed off the record and didn't embarrass or compromise his own public poise. He went back to his immediate problem: Purabi. He'd only just begun to apprehend her visually. Short, slightly bent, a puckered parchment face intricately lined. The shaded eyes of a cow, large and drowsing beneath deeply folded eyelids. And a big-toothed, too-broad sudden smile. Big, crumpled knuckles on puffy paws. What he still couldn't invoke was her voice. Probably rusty. Something of an off-key strum. When she spoke at length it was like a tuneless harangue and a lament in one. He wondered if he'd seen Purabi somewhere. The characters of the present might well be like much of adult life—an unconscious working-out of the encoded cryptograms of childhood. He sat and breathed in her presence. Slowly his head filled with uncooked images, the shredded parings of future sentences.

> The little boy dogged Mondira's footsteps. Straggling across the paved courtyard and into the kitchen, then up the rough stone stairs to the threshold of the cavernous prayer room. To the terrace, where the jars of pickles were stacked and the dal nuggets sunned on faded sheets.
>
> He persists: 'Then why did she jump into the well?'
>
> 'Who?'
>
> 'She.' The boy's eyes are hot little rapids of baleful black. He draws nearer. 'Did you push her in?' he asks.
>
> Mondira feels a prickle of panic. Shrill, she swings round and snaps: 'I'll smack your face and skin your buttocks for you, you little burnt-face, you! Someone's been telling you a pack of lies.'
>
> The kid backs away against the wall. She realizes her mistake, flushes, quickly dabs her perspiring face with her sari and steps forward. 'Believe me, son, don't doubt my word.'
>
> The shabby note of wheedlesome appeal empowers the child with impetuous confidence. 'You are not my mother!' the child shouts, pale with loathing. 'You stole me!'
>
> 'I am your mother, child, as God's my witness. I am your mother.' She begins to tremble. Her brittle voice cracks with pain.
>
> The child turns to Mihir. 'Are you my baba?' he asks, grave as an inquisitor at a crucial trial. Mihir looks away, saying nothing.
>
> 'Tell me, Baba. Are you my baba?' The child's voice

has risen to a delirious shriek.

Mihir turns to look at the child, at the inky puddles of his eyes. An impenetrable cloud gathers on Mihir's face. 'No,' he answers, expressionless.

The child is seven and his reasoning is seven years old. If Mondira says she is his mother, how can Mihir not be his father? But Mihir clearly denies being his baba, so Mondira must *not* be his mother.

That night Mondira quarrels with Mihir. 'Why did you tell him?' she demands. 'Do you realize what you've done to all of us?'

'I couldn't lie to that child.'

'So much for your virtue, my truthful Harishchandra! And where was your truthfulness when you lied to her?'

He answers in an even voice, his fastidious face frowning. 'I never lied to her.'

'Oh, no. You didn't have to. She never thought of asking, so you didn't have to answer! But if she'd asked, would you have lied?'

He looks at her, heart-sore. 'I don't know,' he says.

'Tell me the truth, my mother,' implores the boy. 'Did you do it? Did you push my mother into the well?'

Mondira freezes over the fish she is cleaning at the running tap.

'No,' she answers firmly. 'I did not push her. She killed herself. She jumped into that well. The times were bad.'

'Was she my real mother?'

'No. She was your aunt. She was my sister. I am your mother. Look at me, child. I am your mother!'

'But Baba says he's not my baba. How can you be my mother then?'

She is at a loss, pitted against this child's merciless logic.

'Who's been telling you these lies?'

The child turns sullen, then spits out the defiant words: 'That old woman. The Didimoni who died in hospital.'

Purabi!

'Devyani was your mother's name,' the old woman had told him, her fawning eyes slurping at his face. 'The lovely, lonely Devyani. I remember her going to the mutth for kirtan. Oh, she was noble, she was! Veiled, like all high-born ladies of the village. Two saris were held betwixt doorstep and buggy—yards and yards, child, two walls of cotton, and the veiled lady passed between them. So sad, the poor little Devyani, your mother . . .'

The boy twists out of Mondira's grip. She pursues him down the courtyard and out into the banana clump. 'That old crone was a liar!' she shouts.

'No! You're lying! You're the liar! You pushed her down a well!'

Mondira is in tears. Mihir rises from his veranda cot and says: 'Listen, boy. Listen to me. Your father's name was Amalendu. He was killed. During the bad times. The troubles. And Devyani was your aunt and my wife.'

The child is baffled: 'How can she be your wife? She was my ma and you say you are not my baba . . .' he whimpers, defeated.

Mondira's voice is clenched. 'You see now what you have done?' she hisses. 'Try answering. With your accursed truth, try answering him!'

'Only the truth can work now,' he says lamely. 'Nothing but that.'

The last chapter would need careful doing. Sravan had the episodic sequence plotted out in his notes. The child disappears. A search is organized. A weeping Mondira charges Mihir with having upset and estranged the child. The search party returns without a clue. A scene in Lalbazar Police Station. A visit to the morgue. Then a nocturnal visit from the reporter of a local daily. The whispers of malicious neighbours. Photographs of the child in the daily Missing Persons column. Mondira stops speaking to Mihir, threatens to leave him. Finally, a phone call to the ashram where they live and work, from an acquaintance in Siliguri. News of the kid. He has been sighted at the bus stop. Reported to have wangled a ride up the Sikkim route. Mondira and Mihir rush to Siliguri. Comb several cities—Gangtok, Pelling. Pick up stray bits of information. They trace the kid to a small Tibetan monastery some distance from Rumtek. The scene with the abbot needed reflection: the abbot refuses to let the kid return. The kid is too disturbed, denies his parents, will not go back. Let him stay here for a bit, persuades the abbot. The turning of prayer wheels shall calm his rage to a rhythm, the chanting of serene prayers shall bring peace to the disordered little soul. We say in our discipline that the desire to assert, 'I am the parent, the author' shows a mind not yet spiritually adult . . . Let the boy go—do not cling to him. Return when he is twelve and we shall then ask him whether he is prepared to go back with you or whether he desires to take the robe as a novitiate.' But Mondira can't bear to return. She takes up a housekeeping job in a small tourist lodge so as to be close to the monastery. Mihir returns to Calcutta.

There were a few scenes Sravan was having real difficulty visualizing: the abbot sequence and the journalist and police sub-inspector bits. There was a problem with the kid's 'Did she jump or was she pushed?' question, too. Mondira's agony over the child had to be more intensely realized. He had to feel these things in his nerves. He left it to time. All he had to do was invoke the images patiently, sitting at his desk every morning for an hour.

Sometimes it was best to do no active work, to exert no compulsion upon the mind to throw forth potential personalities. It's quite possible, reflected Sravan, that these characters I think up are people long dead, their essence preserved in the air that I, like a medium, allow to manifest in my imagination. My mind may be a fluid screen on which old sequences are projected! It's best to let them form and fulfil themselves, rise to the surface of my consciousness, bringing their own histories. I must not command them into existence, I must not compel, I must only accept their materialization. There seems an infinite reserve of potential beings. Tune in to any one and he or she shall gather into form, an entity emerging out of the soil of my receptivity. God doodling on the sheet of my vacant sensibility.

Suddenly he saw a complete sentence just ahead of him, fully finished and waiting.

> She rattled the phlegm in her throat, brought it up with a rusty snort. She expelled it in a jet into the spittoon that Mondira held.

Somehow a symbol of ejected guilt? Ugh! What an image. But the picture was a sharp one. Why did Mondira tend the old woman with such devotion? Sravan wondered. First, to overwhelm her with shame. An avenging compassion. Second, to sublimate her own revulsion of stench and decay. Third, to act on an abrupt insight into the old woman's real state—a demented, pitiable creature, a suffering animal. But these diverse complexities would have to find expression by suggestion, the grades of motive smoothly fused, seamless.

And meanwhile the old woman, the one who wrought such havoc in Mondira's life, lies in the old people's ashram where Mondira and Mihir work. Her bedsores stink. She will not die. (No, didn't the kid refer to her as the Didimoni who died? That bit would have to be rewritten.) She waits for her sons and daughters to come, but they despise her for her habitual home-wrecking ways and her history of destructive malice. So the days pass. When at last, tired of fighting the tow of nature, the old woman's foggy mind releases its stubborn clench upon her will, she goes off one dank, misty morning, her glassy eyes wide open, still frozen upon the door.

Exhausted with visualizing the old woman's death labours, Sravan stopped to wonder where it all came from. Not out of my head, I'm sure. I've never witnessed this death or anything like it as far as I can remember. Perhaps back in the misplaced past there was something my mind couldn't handle. What I'm trying to connect here is the old woman going crazy, confusing Mondira's small son in his mother's absence. Then the bashfulness of the girl bride, Devyani, on her wedding night. And how her mother-in-law, that wise matriarch, had the four-poster double bed artfully removed and a single bed put in. Devyani, his favourite character.

The door to Sravan's study blew open ever so slightly, and along the blade of sunlight floated Buddhoo's animated voice.

'That was my pal Vikas. Lived to be a millionaire stockbroker and a proper old seth in Bombay. Son of a district judge with pots of the stuff and but three loves in life—booze, wenches and his old man's official car. One hell of an awesome car, that, a blaze of lights glimmering on its bald head, and his old man didn't put up any objection to his piece-of-the-moon using it as often he pleased. Well, one day, bloke oils up to our man and fawns: "Kahiye Vikas-bhai, we've grown up together and all the rest. Been chums of the loincloth, as they say. And now I have the pleasure of bidding you welcome to my cousin's wedding. The best booze that a feudal baron's money can buy. And," he winked, "the comeliest of village wenches, ah, such dancing fillies, chilli-hot lasses, wickeder than you can fancy! As luscious on their feet as on their backs! All on the house, mind. We zamindars know how to look after our guests. The pick of the bunch shall be yours, believe me. So what d'you say?"

"Okay, if you insist, I'll come," grunted Vikas-bhai.

"A thousand thanks, brother mine!" gushed the wily fellow. "I knew you would not fail us. We shall meet on Thursday, the fifth, then. I shall come to your house and we shall proceed to my village together—no?"

"How do we get there? Train?" asked Vikas-bhai.

"Oh, no, no!" squealed the fellow. "My mistake entirely. A little detail of the programme that I forgot to include. We drive down in your most splendid car of the many lights."

"Hold it!" barked Vikas-bhai. "What's this now? What's my old man going to say?"

"Never mind that, big brother," assured the other. "The sons of district judges may with pride grace the weddings of village barons. As the lights on your car, so be the gems on our turbans in our ancestral portraits."

"Oh, all right," agreed Vikas-bhai, deciding not to let his old man in on the project.

'Vikas-bhai drove through dust and pothole, stoically steering the awesome Ambassador with his jabbersome host beside him. His thoughts, no doubt, drew ample comfort from the delicious prospects of the evening ahead. He drove and drove until they reached a remote village, innocent of road or rail. To discover, ah, too late that the feudal mansion was a tumble-down shack and his fellow guests-of-the-groom's-party a miserable gaggle of garlicky rustics, all agog over his car!

"A thousand welcomes!" gushed Vikas-bhai's host. "The wedding party leaves for the bride's village in an hour. I am sure, O Venerable Uncle," he addressed the hoary old patriarch, "that my friend shall generously consent to drive the groom yonder in his glorious car of the many lights, and shall also happily drive the wedded couple back tomorrow after the nuptials have been tied and the feast is over."

'Well, Vikas-bhai seethed in fury. His car, not his presence, was the object of the sly invitation. He swore he'd give the rascal who had brought him to this godforsaken hole the finest hiding of his life, but decided to bear the outrage with fortitude—in view of the delights promised him ahead.

'Soon enough Vikas-bhai found himself driving a yellow-robed rustic bridegroom and a horde of betel-munching, hawking, belching, bad-mouthing drunken brethren down to the village-but-one-along-the-river where, he hoped, better conditions for repose and jollity existed. Aha, none of it! At the wedding all he got was cheap, gut-flaming hooch, a string cot under a tree and for bedfellows, lo, no country songstress lasses but only swarms of mosquitoes making music in his ear! And worse—no loo! The wide-open fields for his royal lavatory, whither he betook his suit-clad, tie-knotted self on the morrow, head spinning with bilious hooch waves and bowels churning with a red-hot mess.

'The bride's family was speechless with awe to behold the groom arrive a twinkle-lighted car, chauffeured by a suit-and-tied attendant! But Vikas-bhai, it may be unnecessary to remark, was in a bitter frame of mind. It was also unfortunate that one innocent serving-guy committed the unforgivable blunder of addressing Vikas-bhai as "Driver Sahib"! Hate burned in his bosom. He lay awake all night scheming revenge, and hit upon a choice method of wreaking it.

'The next morning Vikas-bhai sat patiently on his string cot, biding his time. The wedding party, complete with bride and dower, was to return to his host's village at noon. Vikas-bhai showed great readiness to accommodate as many village brethren as his car could hold. So when the sun vaulted up the pole and stood roaring in the middle of the sky that blinding-hot April day, the groom, the bride, the host, the groom's father and two uncles piled on and Vikas-bhai drove majestically out of the village with showers of rice and benedictions following him. He had not gone far when the car began to show signs of reluctance. Vikas-bhai braked and got out, a worried frown darkening his brow. He opened the bonnet and tinkered about. He shut it with a resounding bang that made his passengers jump and hastened back to the driver's seat, apologizing unctuously all round for the delay. "This car," he explained, "is an old one. Often gives trouble." He started the engine and drove cautiously on. A couple miles further down the dust road, the car began chugging in strangled convulsions. Vikas-bhai swore and braked, got out, opened the bonnet again and peered into the innards. He emerged clucking like a hen, a look of embarrassment on his face.

"I regret to say that my car has developed serious engine problems," he disclosed. "I'm ashamed to put you to this trouble, but I must request that you get off and assist this old hulk by lending its old battery the cooperation of your muscles. In short, heave it a mighty push, and carry on pushing till its stubborn sinews begin to pulse again."

'His passengers were sympathetic. "We quite understand," they assured him. "When our bullocks evince similar dullness, we've got to fetch them a hefty one on their arses to get them to move. No problem, sir."

'So out they clambered, all except the little bride, and, arraying themselves in ordered formation behind the car, they dealt the Ambassador a most mighty shove. And Vikas-bhai, at the same instant, stepped on the accelerator and was off, flying like a falcon down the dusty expanse without a look behind! Oh, yes, he left them stranded on the dirt track there—not a nice thing to do at all and I don't for a moment exonerate him—but he wasn't so hot on being nice that day and that was that, ha!'

And as Buddhoo's raucous narrative came to an end, Sravan heard an unfamiliar sound. A strange, sputtering squeak, like a door creaking on a rusty hinge. It took him a minute to realize that it was his father laughing!

Manfully he forced his mind back to Devyani, but somehow Buddhoo's silly narrative had put him off his own. He suddenly remembered that he needed to call Malini to fix up the evening at Amirbagh.

5

For some weeks Sravan had been giving Malini a steady dose of soul in a tactical effort to conquer her sensibilities. The gathering of shabby-genteel writers in Ranjana Devi's Amirbagh bungalow wasn't a bad location for an effective exercise.

Malini was dressed just right for the sort of role she saw herself playing—the unspoilt lady of sensitivity and subtlety, subdued of voice and dainty of step. She wore a pale-lemon outfit in Dhaka cotton, a simple, elegant cut that flattered her form and allowed the fine muslin dupatta to swing in a languid hammock from shoulder to shoulder, cradling the teasing weight of her breasts. Her eyes were finely kohled and her lips a mellow peach, and on her small, well-tended feet she wore a cunning pair of sandals of an ingenious basket weave.

The gathering assembled in the sprawling drawing room, with the furniture moved back against the discoloured walls, the floor covered with spotless white sheets and a large number of cushions and bolsters strewn about. There was an elaborate alpana at one end and an arrangement of Ranjana Devi's favourite crotons in decorative earthen pots painted with intricate patterns, each crowned with a circlet of mango leaves and a deepak. Marigold garlands were festooned in scallops round the white-sheeted divan reserved for readings and speeches. In its customary corner stood a small table holding an outsized oil portrait, Maheshwar Dayal Saxena gazing morosely into space.

Sravan knew everyone in this crowd of literati, regulars of

long standing at the Amirbagh house. His nose twitched as he abandoned his sandals and stepped into the room. There was always an air of the prayer meeting about these posthumous birthday celebrations. Was this some sickeningly strong rose attar or a cheap joss stick? The room was already full when they arrived. Ranjana Devi, grown frail and stooped with her arthritis, signalled her inability to rise to her feet, inviting them in graciously from where she sat between the portrait and the divan. They stepped through the throng of seated guests, carrying on a spirited mime of greeting, namaskaring, nodding, smiling, waving until they found a place to sit near the veranda.

He could tell Malini was impressed. This wasn't her usual crowd. Surely she found the faces of these bearded relics inspired and these khadi-draped frumps intellectual, he thought with a stab of malice. It was her first exposure to a circle where the same affectations operated, though in less obvious ways, as in her own. Personally, he'd sized them all up long ago, every one of them. Humbugs. Rancorous in their rivalries, poisonous in their jests and as covetous of each paisa as any petty grocer but without the grocer's frankness. He'd observed this lot and many more like them for over twenty years now, and there was nothing more to know about them.

A sitar trailed the thin thread of a raga in the humid air. Ranjana Devi always favoured *Mian ki todi*, the sort of lugubrious stuff played by All India Radio to announce a state funeral. The sitar shook out a final tassel of notes into the incense-heavy air and subsided. The last invitees had arrived and Ranjana Devi's rigmarole commenced. The portrait was garlanded. Maheshwar Dayal Saxena regarded the proceedings in resignation. The deepak was lit by old Abhishek Agnihotri. Then came Ranjana Devi's speech, cast in the form of a poem. Sravan groaned. He knew each pause and impassioned quaver by now; she'd only added a couple of extra sentences. Soft perfumed words with a sweetish, unaired sort of mustiness. Last season's stale scent trapped in the folded lines, as though they'd just been unpacked for their annual appearance out of a trunk in the boxroom. Ugh, that speech! But then, lots of senile people went on writing senile stuff. Like those two old jokers

Srinivas Avasthi and Javed Farooqui, sitting there like a pair of dusty dodos.

Farooqui's sallow face had shrunk with the years, but nothing could change that downturned mouth, those lips purpled with nicotine or that enquiring grimace. His smiles, his salutations were all dour self-deprecations, and when he spoke—in careful, mincing Urdu—he swirled the words artfully round his mouth in a slow, vindictive chomp. Avasthi was large and as diffuse as his bluster, a man tipsy on his own wit. When he uttered a sentence he usually found himself so surprised and delighted that he repeated it half a dozen times, swaying and staggering like a drunk.

Sravan's musings were interrupted by Malini's hushed voice close beside him. 'How lovely! It's just too much, isn't it?'

He turned to stare at her. She had a curious shine in her eyes, as though she were on the verge of tears. He realized she was talking of Ranjana Devi's poem, and nodded agreement with exaggerated respectfulness.

'I'd love to have a copy of that,' whispered Malini. 'I just can't get over some of the lines.'

'I'm sure she'd be delighted,' he said drily. 'I'll ask her.' He regarded Malini's subdued ecstasy with contempt.

'Please do,' she begged. 'And who is that lady there?'

He followed her gaze. 'That's Asha Neogy,' he told her. 'Another veteran poet. I've known her for years.'

'And those two very old men?'

'They're a couple of vintage novelists. Srinivas Avasthi and Javed Farooqui. One wrote in Hindi, the other in Urdu. Great friends and terrible enemies for a large chunk of their lives. But friends again apparently—for the present.'

She studied them with keen interest. 'D'you think if I invited them to read at one of my lunches, they'd come?'

He almost shouted with laughter. 'Would they?' he snorted. 'Just give them a chance. And send the car round or pay them a handsome TA.' Malini seemed nonplussed by his scorn. 'They'd like to dictate the menu, though. And see your wine list first. They'll probably send your driver down to the hooch bar. Maybe they'll approach your husband to help them get their hovels allotted in their names.'

Malini's perplexity deepened. Sravan, she noticed, had a look of dark venom on his face. Such savagery. She'd never seen that expression before. He seemed to hate this crowd. She didn't ask any further questions. Tedious encomiums about Maheshwar Dayal Saxena's genius, his generosity, his breadth of vision, his depth of inspiration, and little vignettes of his life that the guests had shared—Sravan had beard it all before and longed to make a nice, perverse, hard-hitting speech of his own. Ranjana Devi had never asked him to speak, so it came as a surprise when today she did. And Sravan, enjoying himself enormously, warmed to his role as iconoclast. His parting para was good and stinging.

'For a decade and a half we've spoken of Maheshwar Dayalji as the provider of our ideas, an institution unto himself, an ineradicable legend, never mind his verse, about which opinion shall always be divided. I'm what I am today considerably due to Maheshwar Dayalji's literary example. Personally, I learnt from him inversely, which, too, is a valuable form of tutelage. I made up my mind what poetry should never be. Yes, I began persistently pursuing an antithetical ideal. I learnt to recognize words that had been chewed tasteless until only their husks remained.'

A disturbed silence had fallen. No one dared to applaud. Sravan came down from the podium, congratulating himself for having at last given voice to what a great many writers felt about Maheshwar Dayal's work. He looked around for signs of approval, but no one met his eye. Only Malini looked straight at him with a stricken face, and then she looked away.

It was with unnatural haste that Vinod Rastogi began his rendition of ghazals written by Maheshwar Dayalji in the late fifties. A smug, dishonest voice, thought Sravan. A voice greased with sickly-lavish unguents of drama. Then it was Pandit Sheel Kumar Thakur singing Maheshwar Dayalji's devotional verse, followed by a sentimental reading of those miserable Saraswati poems that had won Maheshwar Dayal that wretched award. He's growing old, jeered Sravan, he's acquired a nasty, wheezy rasp, and there's an ugly flutter of phlegm in his throat that he can't quite overcome. And then, oh hell, it was Maheshwar Dayal's blank verse recited by Asha Neogy. The same speculations about Maheshwar Dayal's unfinished magnum opus, *Antim Aadesh*. The same pieces as last year and the year before. This was the problem with a writer long dead. Everything could only be rehashed! The same old tired stuff, recycled. No oxygen left. And the dreariest part of the evening was still to come: having run through the entire scale of Maheshwar Dayal's work, the guests were now invited to give select readings of their own work. Two women poets cried out for the blood of man in embittered quatrains. Like a pair of vampires, Sravan thought.

As the next reader climbed to the podium, Sravan caught his breath—there was something familiar about that spare figure, the way the fingers of his left hand dithered about the collar. Sravan found himself staring at Veerendra Vyas. He wore his hair long, and his pale face looked unclothed in any practised expression. As he read the opening lines of an extract from an old novel, his squeamish tongue tested each syllable cautiously, resulting in a peculiar halting manner that was both submissive and somewhat affected.

The passage he read unnerved Sravan, as he recognized each stilted phrase of it. He could still, after all these years, anticipate the next line. An unbearable oppression weighed down upon him.

'Enough,' he whispered to Malini. 'Let's get out of here.'

She looked at him, wondering.

'They're going to drag on for hours, these interminable readings by little pen-pushers. Let's go have dinner somewhere before we . . .'

She accepted without protest and followed him out.

'At least one can have a decent meal in this restaurant,' Sravan sighed, unfolding his napkin.

Malini stirred her soup. She was silent.

'Well?' he asked. 'What did you make of this evening?'

'I enjoyed it very much, thank you,' she answered in a formal voice.

'They're a pretty exclusive lot,' he said. 'The best in the arts in every field.'

She looked at him with a strange smile in her eyes. 'Which

explains your own presence there, I suppose.'

He looked at her, surprised.

'Tell me about that lady—the one who read that poem about Assam—Asha Neogy, I think you said.'

'She's been on the lit. scene for almost thirty years now. Lost her husband in a plane crash years ago. Built a beautiful house—I'll take you to see it someday—I mean, it's really unusual—got real character. She keeps dogs and writes middling verse, mostly yearning trash about her past. Oh, yes, she spent some time in a mental home after the death of her husband. Now she's rebuilt a life of convincing sanity for herself.'

'Interesting,' murmured Malini, sipping her soup. Then she added slowly, staring meditatively into her bowl. 'I find it rather grand. I mean, her verse may be middling to you but her survival's grand to me. Isn't it wonderful to think that maybe that middling verse has helped her pull through—that human beings do manage to survive on the strength of those so-called middling writings?' She looked up suddenly with piercing intensity. 'So what if her poetry isn't up to your standard? It's pulled her out of her particular crisis—which even the world's best poetry may not have done for others . . . And anyway, I thought she had lovely hair. I kept wondering how to describe it to myself. Kind of metallic ash. Or silver flax.'

There was a peculiar note in her voice.

'That's one way of looking at it, I suppose,' he said guardedly.

'I liked the look of her,' Malini went on. 'She was so free from this . . . this poet thing. The way she took her knitting out of her frumpy bead bag and then fished out a diary of poems. You wouldn't think of a poet knitting at a reading, would you? It's contrary to the current literary stereotype—seems kind of funny . . . but so human.'

'What d'you imagine? That writers aren't human?'

'Are you?' she threw him a piercing look. 'I liked the way she opened the diary and some torn pages fell out—and she rifled through them real fast—like a cashier rifles through a wad of banknotes. Maybe they're her only wealth, who knows?'

Sravan laughed outright. 'She's filthy rich.' He guffawed. 'What an old romantic you're getting to be. Who'd have believed it of you! One evening in that dump and you're hooked. I must say that atmosphere's catching.'

'Don't be nasty,' she said. There was an uncomfortable pause. The waiter brought a second course.

'So what about those two old men, the vintage writers?'

'Ah, those two.' He grinned. 'Interesting pair. Old Srinivas Avasthi used to write novels in Hindi in the late fifties and sixties, and Javed Farooqui wrote novels in Urdu around the same time.'

'Which ones?' Malini wanted to know.

'Unfortunately, they're the only ones who remember the names of their books—their own and the other's. A minor splash, a small coterie of fans, a few good reviews and then—phut! That's what happens to most small-town writers.'

'To which category you obviously don't belong,' was her flat remark. Sravan marvelled at the undercurrent of animosity in her voice. What had got into her? he wondered vaguely, then chose to ignore it.

'Well, those two were great enemies, horribly jealous of one another. Always bickering—it was fun watching them at it. Then, sometime in the late sixties, they came to an agreement. Mind you, in spite of their constant wrangling they had a curious respect for one another—anyone could see that. One day at a boozing binge Farooqui swore that a writer must know when to lay down his pen, but few writers ever know when the time has come. So Avasthi sprang to his feet and declared with a flourish that he, Avasthi, would undertake to inform Farooqui when his writing days were over. And Farooqui, no doubt made emotional by booze and verse, rose to the occasion and thumped Avasthi on his back, shouting, "Done! As you to me, so I to you!" '

'Quite a story.'

'Oh, a great one. One of the most interesting literary feuds I've known. Of course, I wasn't around then, but the story's been handed down by word of mouth. Well, soon afterwards Farooqui's magnum opus was released and it made quite a splash. Farooqui was cock-a-hoop over it. Then, one day, at the height of his success, Avasthi appeared, congratulated his rival and complimented him on having produced a masterpiece. He also announced that he had come to fulfil his promise—to caution Farooqui that his writing days were over. “This is when you must stop, bhai-jaan,” he said. “You’ll never write anything better than this. Lay down your pen before you start producing trash.” Farooqui was furious. “Nonsense!” he scoffed. “You’re resenting my success, that’s all. You wish you’d written it yourself, don’t you? You’re afraid I’ll write better and better, so you come here with your petty advice, hah!” That was the most violent quarrel they had. Avasthi left in a froth and they did not see one another for some years.’

‘But how did they come to be friends again?’

‘Well, slowly they began to understand that no one remembered them any more. They were both outdated. They hadn’t been all that important as writers go, and now times and tastes had changed. There were fresh faces and names. I suppose there came a time when they realized that the only person who knew their work intimately was the other one. They’d disliked one another so bitterly that they’d read all the other’s work to poke holes in it and could practically recite it from memory. Quite gratifying to the other at this point. That’s when they began appearing together. Sometimes they’d get drunk and sit in their corner, reciting passages from one another’s work and applauding one another hysterically, lost to the rest of the world. Sometimes I actually envy them. I wish I had at least a single reader who knew every sentence I’ve ever written.’

‘For that you’d need a serious enemy first,’ Malini said, smiling.

‘Oh, I have plenty of those,’ he replied. ‘I’d feel neglected by my friends if I didn’t have a handful of people actively hating me.’

‘D’you think you’ll know when to stop?’ she asked unexpectedly. ‘I mean, d’you think you’ve done your best work yet?’

‘I don’t know,’ he answered gravely. ‘I do think at times that the book I’m currently on may be substantial. It’s hard to know. I rather dread reaching that peak of performance, though, I don’t mind telling you. You know that story about Rodin?’

‘No.’

‘When friends complimented Rodin on a particularly splendid piece of sculpture and told him it was the best thing he’d ever done, Rodin began to weep. He said he knew it well, that he'd never be able to repeat that excellence and that this was the biggest tragedy that could befall an artist.'

He could see that Malini was moved. She looked away pondering the matter. Then she remembered something.

'Who was that person, that crushed-looking man who read that piece right at the end?'

The one question Sravan didn't want to be asked. He cursed her sharpness.

'You didn't seem to want to stay after he came on. He put you off, no?'

'That guy? He's a tiresome fellow I knew once. We run into each other at readings and writers' meets.'

'What is he? A novelist?'

'Sort of. A poor one. He did a novel called *Maut ka Muhurat*. The critics tore it to shreds, and he's never recovered from the blow.'

Malini concentrated on her bowl of ice cream, then reiterated her admiration for Ranjana Devi's poem. 'You really liked it? That third-rate poem?'

She arched her eyebrows. 'Third-rate?' Her eyes were icy.

'Absolutely. That's not poetry, yaar. That trumpet blast of tragedy. A dripping, syrupy spongeful of sentimentality. Couldn't you see the funny side of it?'

'No,' she retorted, anger quickening in her voice. 'Unlike you, who can only see the funny side of everything.'

'What's this now?'

'She probably loved her husband the one-in-a-thousand-marriages way and she declares it without embarrassment, that's all.'

'Not a savvy thing to do at all,' he rejoined suavely.

'No. You're too savvy for simple things. They've been—how did it go?—"chewed tasteless until only their husks remain", right?'

He was irritated. 'What *are* we talking about exactly?'

'We're talking about love, exactly,' she mimicked him.

'That's something I like making, not discussing.' He made a thin attempt at flippancy.

'Naturally.'

He stared at her. This was a tone of voice he'd never heard before.

'Coming to this one-in-a-thousand-marriages thing, you seem to know what that is.'

'No. And I'm sorry I don't. If I did, I wouldn't be here with you.'

'What's wrong?' he questioned, with solemn and injured dignity.

She scrutinized him uncertainly for a long moment. Then she put down her spoon and, placing her elbows on the table, clasped her knuckles in a tight clench.

'Okay, I'll tell you. I thought you were rotten this evening.'

Surprised, he could only frown at her in stressed silence, not trusting himself to speak.

'You were very unkind,' she went on, speaking with deliberate precision. 'I wish you hadn't said all those things.'

'I haven't the foggiest idea what you're talking about.' He felt obliged to put on a token act of confusion. Buy time to collect his wits before he squashed her audacity with a suitably withering snub.

'All those cutting things about a dead man.'

He guffawed, a harsh stage laugh. 'You're beginning to sound as pious as Pragya,' he jeered.

Her eyes engaged his in a swift interlock. 'I wonder if you're aware that the tone you use with Pragya is far, far worse than Mridul's worst voice?'

He looked at her, incensed. 'What's this? A women's issue?'

She sat in hostile silence. She was going fast, he realized abruptly. Passing rapidly out of his spell and there was nothing he could do. He had only his unpleasantness to armour him, give a counterfeit power against her.

'I have yet to see a feminist who deliberately and willingly makes herself unattractive to spare a fellow feminist the pain of losing her husband to her. No,' he sneered. 'Feminine vanity is seldom sacrificed at the altar of feminist solidarity. But then, I'm a poisonous old cynic.' Suddenly he recalled what they were wrangling over. 'And Maheshwar Dayal! All this tamasha over him! If he was alive and fucking I'd be suspicious, my dear girl.'

'Witty,' she muttered. 'And in such wonderful taste.'

That was the last straw. A tart like her preaching taste! He controlled himself, with effort.

'More and more like Pragya,' he said again. 'The problem,' he reflected, 'is that a girlfriend of long standing starts acting more and more like a nagging wife. I'm flattered that you should feel such personal responsibility for my misconduct.'

She ignored the jibe. 'Did you have to spoil it for everyone? I mean, look here, the evening meant a lot to that old lady. Everyone knew it—or did you actually think they were out for art's sake, poor Sravan? Nobody cared two hoots for the old man—he's dead and gone, but everyone was there to humour the old lady. It stuck out a mile.'

'You're very perceptive,' he snarled.

'Pity you aren't,' she said. 'To tell you the truth, I was very touched. It isn't often you see love on that scale.'

'The love beyond the grave, eh? Author, please rephrase.'

She flushed, ready to scream. 'Let it go,' she said. 'Forget it.'

They looked at one another in strained silence. The waiter brought the bill, a welcome distraction. Sravan prolonged the process of taking out his wallet and counting out the cash to allow his head to quieten. They left the restaurant, the strain between them mounting.

He normally left her later, around midnight. When Mridul was out on tour and the kids asleep in their room, there would be time to slake the uneasiness disturbing his limbs. In the lift there would be time for a brush of the lips and a quick, snatched fumble or squeeze, which would give him a sharp and sordid thrill. He had come to associate the lift with the quickening drumbeat of desire by which he waited impatiently to taste the peppermint flavour of her skin and submerge himself in her moist warmth.

But today she slammed the car door and strode up the stairs to her building without a word.

6

'Atreya was a student at the Centre for Creative Arts, where I teach a creative-writing course,' Sravan told Buddhoo on one of their evening walks. 'Around twenty-eight or twenty-nine, slightly older than the rest of the class. She'd done well in the entrance exam. At the interview I discovered she'd opted for the evening batch because she worked in a bank. I asked her why she had joined. Wasn't she fagged out at the end of the day? Didn't she want to rush home?'

"I want to write just one book," she said.

"Many of us do," I pointed out. "Maybe all we full-time writers do is write one book, cunningly chopped up into a dozen."

"No, but this is different," she said. "I don't want to write for the sake of art or creative expression or recognition or anything like that. It's to save my mind. My marriage . . ."

'That intrigued me. "What?"

"I want to write a book to put everything right."

"Ah, a confessional work," I observed, wondering what horrific thing haunted this attractive young woman's consciousness.

"No." She jerked impatiently, lifted her arms in a restless gesture and slapped the loose bun at the nape of her neck. Even on that first day she struck me as vaguely familiar. I was sure I'd met her somewhere, seen that quick movement of the brown arms slapping her bun in place. But I couldn't place where. "Not that way," she asserted.

"Then?"

"It sounds a personal thing, but it's bound up with my joining this course," she confessed awkwardly.

"You can absolutely depend upon my professional discretion, madam," I recited in Sherlock Holmesian mimicry, and she laughed. That broke the ice.

"For some time, Mr Holmes," she recounted, "I have had the eerie feeling that everything is wrong in my life. Has been wrong from the start. But it just might have gone right—missed being right by a hair's breadth. See, I was born a fourth daughter. I had the wrong sort of home. The wrong sort of parents. I went to the wrong school. Had the wrong teachers. Read the wrong subjects in college, and naturally all my choices went wrong. Finally, I thought I married the right man, but things just went wrong between us. It's a spell I've got to break."

"This course doesn't undertake to provide the frog prince," I said seriously.

"No, I wouldn't risk calling you that," she said demurely, and it was my turn to laugh. I tell you, yaar, we got along like a house on fire. I really enjoyed that girl's company.

"Carry on," I prompted.

"It's a grim story," she said.

"In that case you and I'll be the Brothers Grim," I retorted.

'She flashed me a quick smile. "I've been telling myself—maybe I'm seeing things wrong. But I've been seeing them this way a long, long while. So I hit upon this: If I were to rewrite my life, making every wrong thing right, changing every situation and every character, then maybe it'll all cancel out in my head. Work out right." Her voice trailed away. There was an eccentric urgency about this girl. I took an instant liking to her. And damnit, that's the strangest and most striking reason for wanting to write a book that anyone's ever given me.

"I get it," I said. "It's creative correction, is it? But you don't necessarily have to enroll for a course to be able to do that. Much of the time I drill my students in routine stuff."

'But she was firm. "I want to learn. Just one book, no more."

'Of course I selected her. After a few lectures I made an astounding discovery: I placed her. You'll never believe me, but she was exactly like my character Mondira. And I'd framed Mondira long, long before I'd even set eyes on this woman. I've heard a Swiss painter say that he'd chance upon exact copies in nature of landscapes he'd painted years ago. She even had a tall, lanky husband called Amresh! In my book I'd named him Amalendu. Such an uncanny coincidence. I almost smelt disaster, wondering if she'd take the hatchet to him as Mondira does in my book. Now I'm going to tell you something very strange. I had the whimsical idea that if I hurried up and let my fictional Mondira expend her rage on her fictional husband, then some resource of psychic fury in the universe might be used up and this real girl and her husband spared. Or, better, if I changed the plot of my novel and let Amalendu be killed by someone else, I might help avert tragedy in this girl's life. So I did that—changed my book. Call it writerly superstition. And all these problems I'm having with my novel spring from that change. I haven't solved half of them, but at least I have the satisfaction of feeling I've helped avert some catastrophe . . . It's ridiculous! No one will ever understand why I did it.'

'I do,' said Buddhoo. 'It's the most gallant thing you ever did in your mean little life, Ravan. Maybe it's the only kind of chivalry you're capable of. Did she appreciate it?'

'She never knew. Will you be surprised if I tell you that the only time we spoke to one another was that first interview? We didn't exchange a word after that. The communication was different.'

'ESP?'

'Better still. As her first assignment she wrote a one-act play called *As You Loathe It, or What You Won't*. A perverse little spoof, all wisecracks and black humour. I gave her a B for it. Later, to my amusement, she vented her protest in pithy retorts in her notebooks, which I enjoyed reading as much as I enjoyed going through the assignments themselves.

'The second week she submitted a poem written entirely in the jargon of business management. My comment was: "Excellent. I'm impressed. But to be impressed by dazzling virtuosity is not to be humanly moved. Therefore another B. Don't strike poses on the page." Her handwriting dashed its spitfire script across the margin: "*I'm not striking a pose. This thing I'm trying to say bloody well matters to me*!" Mondira to the core!

'Then she applied herself to the challenge of leaving me humanly moved. Her story was a heart-twisting narrative set in First World War Alsace. A German soldier wanders into an abandoned cottage and is met by a starving old dog who fiercely guards a broken door. The soldier manages to enter the cottage and finds himself menaced by the dog, who has obviously hidden something in the coal scuttle. He is bitten in the calf and shoots the dog dead. Then he explores the coal scuttle and finds broken toys, left by a child when the city was evacuated. It was crisply written, quite overwhelming in patches, and for once I had to concede her an A+. The grade spoke for itself. I made no observations and neither did she.

'But the next piece was a disappointment. I gave her a C and wrote in the margin: "A whole tedious menstruation theme! What's this? A shout? A statement? A gyno-visceral banner? Too bloody uterine."

'She scrawled back, "Bloody is about right! Such a thing as Discriminatory Downgrading by Supercilious Male Examiner!"

'What was funny was that we communicated exclusively through these marginal exchanges. I was half beginning to think of it as a marginal romance.

'I've noticed while working with students that creative growth is a cyclical thing. There's an ascent of the graph, then after a few excellent entries there comes a slump. Like Atreya's next exercise. The idea was original enough. A man caught between two realities, the psychic world "behind the veil" and the cyber world behind the screen. Trapped, he ricochets from one to the other and can't find a foothold in physical reality. I was struck by the theme. But as an idea it was too advanced for the technical capacity of this unusual girl. The execution was shoddy. Reluctantly, I gave her a B and asked if anything was wrong.

'Next day she handed the notebook back without looking at me. After she'd left, I flipped it open and read: "I can't seem to get it right. I don't like my way of writing. Sick of it now. I've tried to change it, but I've nothing to replace it with. Any good waiting???"

'When students reach this psychic point I usually make each

one write a personal story containing at least one actual character in their life. List the characters that are promising and write a story including all of them. Literature isn't your story or mine, but our common story, etc. I assigned her a narrative essay: How It Feels to Write. She turned in a twenty-page manuscript starting with the axiom: "Self-consciousness involves a tale in time but a writer's plots are artificial symmetries." Then she wrote: "It began as a sort of self-indulgence. I was trying to use words to study existence, to render its sense or lack of sense."

'I read on and on. Made an asterisk against one phrase: "ideas like plants, thrusting themselves from the dry soil, obeying a natural law, ready to boil over, overflow." I told her not to mix metaphors.

'She ended, "I love the magic moment when a work begins managing itself, wakes up to itself, and before my eyes, a finished piece lifts out of the pages." I had the distinct vision of a gull, rising in a curve out of an indigo sea.

'Now, I still can't explain why I took this risk. I was seduced by what I'd just read, I guess. In the margin of the essay I wrote not a grade but something foolish, halfway between a proposal and a proposition. I wish I hadn't done it. Under the circumstances it wasn't in the game.'

'So what did she say?' asked Buddhoo, curious.

Sravan just sighed. 'Tell me, yaar. Why are all my relationships such a disaster? Every one of them?'

'Write a book setting the wrong things right,' quipped Buddhoo. 'You haven't answered my question. What did she say?'

'Nothing. She handed in her notebook as usual. I received it with, well, staged apathy. When she left, I grabbed it and flung it open and see what I found: she'd graded my proposal a C–. Worse, she stopped coming to class. So that was it. One false step and I lost her. I have her notebook still.'

'Meanwhile, the novel stays changed to suit her future?' asked Buddhoo.

'A kind of gift, you understand. Or do you?' said Sravan. 'I tried to reassess that brief relationship in another book based on that experience. It was called *Such As I Am*. I believe it would have been something substantial . . .'

'But . . .?' Buddhoo was alert to the hint.

'I couldn't finish it. I was on the last chapter when Pragya destroyed it.' His voice was expressionless, but Buddhoo looked up swiftly and searched his face. 'You've heard of romantic murders? Sounds like the headline of a tenth-rate tabloid. "Writer's Wife Murders Book in Jealous Fit". But that was it. Those were the typewriter days.'

'What did she do to it?' Buddhoo asked, hesitantly.

'She burnt it. That last chapter was never written. Nor, between Pragya and me, written off.'

7

Sravan often felt that the book he was writing was something pre-existent. All he was doing was intuiting its outlines, as one would unveil a statue. He wasn't inventing Devyani—he believed that Devyani existed, an entelechy summoned out of the past or the possible. She had probably existed exactly as he conceived her, in an earlier time. Equally possible, she lived somewhere in the spacious present, in silent accord with his imaginings. And in another time and place, he himself might speak in the fictional script of another.

He found Devyani so easy to visualize. She was pliant, unformed, a non-person who achieves personality in two rapid strides—the moment she discovers her adored elder sister, Mondira, in her husband Mihir's arms, and the moment she decides to jump into the well. She might be fifteen or seventeen.

> Her face round, her nose and chin small and moulded, her eyes unsure and shrinking. She smiles in little flutters, with tiny darting glances for signs of disapproval or offence. She flushes easily and is apt to grow speechless for long spells. Her figure is slight to the point of being emaciated. She is good with her hands and when she is all by herself, she hums. The humming ceases abruptly upon a little tremor at the first sign of an intruder. And she likes sitting facing the door, as though she fears that an assailant might steal up from behind and strike her unawares.

It was funny, thought Sravan, this inverse relation—simplicity expressed in complex ways and complexity in the simplest. In the total sweep of his book, Devyani was a minor character, part of the scaffolding, but she seemed the most readily invoked, the most accessible.

Sravan still chose to do initial drafts in pen. For the first draft, he preferred the legato glide of the pen to the staccato notes of the keyboard. (He compared the two to the sitar and the piano.) The second draft he fed into his computer, transforming, amplifying, shading, enjoying the float of words beneath his fingers. Pen and computer together created this delicate illusion: paper and pen for anchorage, the monitor screen for flight.

The present chapter described, in her child's voice, Devyani's shubh-drishti, the viewing of bride by groom and groom by bride beneath a cloth canopy. Sravan had chosen Bengal as the suitable setting, largely in view of the Partition sequences, the necessity of keeping the action in the Calcutta hinterland. Still, he was determined not to let the story get culture-specific.

Devyani is charmed and awed by the devastatingly good-looking young man her sister has thought fit to choose for her. She has never met him, but she has always put complete trust in her sister. Didi accompanies the bridal entourage back to the groom's village, a protective presence for the nervous little bride. And Didi brings the glass of milk and the sweets to the bridal chamber on the wedding night. The next morning, when Devyani emerges, tired and bashful, she finds Didi already waiting on the veranda, and wonders why she looks strange. She weeps more bitterly than the little bride has ever known her to. Devyani is overwhelmed that her sister should feel so deeply for her.

There were times when Sravan felt oppressed by his artistic scruples. His taste in language had grown impossibly refined. No phrase pleased him. Everything seemed excessive or inaccurate, rough-edged or improperly turned. He took too long to limber up each sentence, file its edges and buff it into shape. He suffered and fretted and envied young writers whose headlong prose came bounding out, indiscreet and awkward and scalding to the touch.

> Did Devyani never suspect?
>
> Did she never look closely at her sister and notice, behind the smiling gentleness, the spectre of vicious enmity? How is it possible to stay unaffected in the presence of someone who violently wishes one ill? But Devyani never sensed the waves of hostility crossing the narrow space between them.

The big scene in which Devyani sees Mondira astride Mihir could not possibly be narrated in Devyani's voice. Devyani had few words to begin with and was left with none at the end of her brief life. No, her big declaration was her death.

> She looked on them, her sister and her husband, her face charred with horror. Her eyes unblinking, pupils pulsing with shock. In the shaded summer afternoon, the cowshed was dark as a well.

So Devyani grows great with both child and secret. She fears that she will confess her discovery; there are times when she is on the verge of telling someone. Suitably, she chooses to die in a well in an orchard.

Sravan stopped to indulge in one of his mid-script reveries. Devyani was terrified that she would spell things out, so she died in full understanding, while he was anxious to spell out everything, afraid of dying without having said it all.

He wished Pragya wouldn't barge in with his eleven o'clock cup of tea the way she always did, brisk and bursting with news. She usually apologized loudly for disturbing him and then stayed on to chatter inconsequentially, wasting a whole precious hour.

'Uf, these Sundays! Should be banned, if you ask me. I've had an absolutely mad morning. MAD!' She fanned her face. She put down two mugs of tea on blue mica coasters and pulled herself a chair. He sipped, wary. She waited for him to ask after her mad morning. He decided to vex her by not asking. She waited, then gave him the full account.

'I gave that dratted kid a tight slap. You know what he and Haider have been doing? Putting a dead lizard on a sheet of paper and shoving it under Banwari Lal's front door. Banwari Lal's wife complained. She also told me of this other atrocious prank they've been playing, shouting, "*Chamar! Chamar! Chamar*!" behind her when she goes out shopping in the bazaar. I called them and gave them a shout in her presence and our Ashu a good, hard smack. He's been fighting with me all morning after that. The only place where there's a bit of peace and quiet is this study.'

There won't be much left of either if she stays long, thought Sravan wryly.

'Have you noticed how clannish kids have become? It's a recent thing. In school and on playgrounds they divide themselves into teams based on caste or religion. I don't like it. It's bad for them. Oh, I must share this funny thing with you. The other day Ashu and Haider were playing in the sitting room. I've warned them dozens of times not to play ball indoors, but do they listen? Something had to break—I knew it all along. So of all the ironic things to happen, Haider's ball went and hit that little glass Shivlinga on the sideboard. Knocked it over and left it in a hundred pieces on the floor.

'Later Ashu comes running to me and says, "Hey, Ma, something's gone wrong with Haider. He's hiding under the bed and won't come out." I thought it was a kids' game and I went down on all fours and called, "Haider, come out." And you'll never believe this, Sravan, the kid began to shake. He was huddled up like a tiny dog under the bed, and when he saw me he started crying. I just couldn't understand it. I called him out, coaxed, tempted, said okay, I'll send for some Vadilal's ice cream—why don't you and Ashu bring home a brick? Then, the kid says—just hear this, Sravan—the kid says: "I didn't know it would break, Auntie." I asked Ashu, "What's he mean?" Ashu shrugged and went on chomping at his gum. "What's broken, Haider?" I asked. "Your god," said the little mite. Hell, Sravan! The kid thought I'd bash him up or something. I persuaded him to come out, asked him what had given him the idea that the glass toy on the sideboard was my god, he said his ammee had told him the stone bull near our front door was our god and also the lady monster on our wall with her tongue out and also the long cylinder-like thing made of glass. I hugged him and told him they were only toys to decorate my rooms with, that he shouldn't worry, that Ashu himself could have smashed one of them. Guess what he said? "But I'm a Muslim, Auntie."

'So what happened?' interrupted Sravan.

'God bless the name of Vadilal. I sent for ice cream and relied on it to make everything cool and smooth again. I only wish that could be possible with grown-ups. Banwari Lalji and his wife are very touchy about the caste issue after their daughter-in-law abandoned their son.'

Sravan was in no mood for neighbourhood politics. But he knew from long experience that there was no silencing Pragya when she'd come to his study with a scoop.

'Actually that was a smart girl, Suchitra. Remember how they carried on about their son having disgraced the family by marrying a Brahmin girl? The old folks wouldn't touch food or water touched by her. After the wedding, when Satish brought her home to meet his parents, they refused to let her touch their feet! This bit of vanity I've never understood. What great deprivation do you inflict upon another by not letting him or her touch your ugly feet? The girl came to live with them and they outdid themselves in general nastiness. Funny, isn't it? This reverse snobbery. Not only has the practise of demanding huge dowries been acquired by people on that side of the great Indian divide, but they're coming to mimic the obnoxious things common to the caste folks.'

'Look, why don't you write an article or something?'

She didn't catch the snipe. Instead she took him perfectly seriously. 'D'you think I should? I'll think about it. But, yes, Suchitra's gone and outsmarted everyone, her own furious family and her in-laws. See what happened? She appeared in the civil-service exams. Got selected for a reserved vacancy—which she'd never have done had she remained technically a Brahmin. Now, very coolly, she's filed a divorce suit against Satish. Point is, does that cancel out her selection? No, say the rules. It's our very own indigenous version of the green-card-marriage syndrome. As for

Satish, I'm sorry for him but he did precious little to protect her from his parents when she was staying here. I guess it is a bit unfortunate that neighbours keep stopping Mrs Banwari Lal and congratulating her on her ex-daughter-in-law's selection. One of them even wanted to know if a man marrying an SC girl qualified for a reserved vacancy and if a girl married to an SC man could be given that facility, why not vice versa? Then these brats had to go and call out rude things . . . And look at Ashu's cheek! He waited for Haider to leave and picked up a fight with me. Said: "Why did you say our Nandi bull and Kali-Ma and Shivji are toys?" I said they stand for powers but in themselves they're there to add to the décor of my room and not for puja. I said these powers aren't only Hindu powers but belong to everyone else and have other names. He said, "No, why did you call them toys? Because they AREN'T TOYS!" I said don't bother your head over all this nonsense. He said, "It's not nonsense. They AREN'T TOYS." Did you know, Sravan, that you have a fundamentalist eleven-year-old son and there's nothing you or I can do? I said Look, it's time for your papa's tea and I'm off. And here I am, seeking shelter from the little fanatic.'

She sighed, sipped her tea, looked meaningfully across at him. 'And there's this other thing bothering me. It's about Malini.'

He mastered his face. 'She came?'

'No, she telephoned,' said Pragya. 'Told me something very upsetting and I want to discuss it with you.'

Above all, he had to unhitch her eyes from his face.

'I asked her what she wanted me to do about it. I mean, how did she expect me to react? And how should I pay her back?'

Slow, this masterful knife-twisting. He had to shake her eyes off his face before they drained him of all his poise. All he could utter was a guarded 'Uh-huh?'

'I gave her the choice. Since the amount concerned was only three thousand, I could repay her in cash or in clothes. She chose clothes. Three outfits out of my summer collection. A lovely pale-lemon Dhaka cotton . . .' She was still studying him too closely, thought Sravan. He busied himself with the last dregs of tea in his cup. 'The point is, Sravan, that bank account is depleted again.

You'll have to put something in soon.'

A sick feeling gaped in his stomach. His voice was curt. 'When did she visit him?'

'Last Friday. You were out.'

'She didn't tell me.' Oh hell, an involuntary slip.

'No? Did you run into her somewhere?' Again that large-eyed innocence, that trusting voice.

'She phoned.' He went on, frowning to give his unsure face a focus. 'Pragya, you've got to speak to him again. Tell Babuji enough is enough. He can't go on embarrassing us this way. Taking loans from our friends and repaying them in cheques that bounce! What sort of senile mischief *is* this?'

'And I'm worried about these kids of ours. Take Rina.' Child psychology now, groaned Sravan. 'Only nine, and broken-hearted that she can't grow up to be a model! Depressed. Why'm I so ugly, Ma? If you please! I tell her Rubbish, you're not ugly, you're a very cute little girl, but she won't be consoled. I can't get this nonsense, out of her head. And it's funny—it's what I used to ask as a child. I used to think of myself as the most hideous creature around. The most unpresentable and absolutely unlovable.' Her narrative slowed down.

She added in a wistful voice, 'There are times when the feeling comes back. That I'm growing old, the best is over and didn't amount to much, that the years and hopes were wasted, that I'm finished, with nothing left in me.' She waited, gazing silently at Sravan. Hoping for reassurance, refutation. But Sravan refused to be stirred by this appeal to his gallantry. He kept a non-committal silence.

'One can't share these moods with anyone. I have just you and Malini—the only two people I'm close to. She told me it was the midlife blues coming on.'

Sravan became uncomfortably aware that she was watching his reflexes with peculiar alertness. He felt the scrape of her searching gaze upon his raw skin and he tightened his will in resolve. He wouldn't flinch. Wouldn't be outmanoeuvred. He looked away and yawned.

'Pragya,' he said in a deadpan voice, 'there's something I've been trying to write all morning. If you don't mind . . .'

'Oh, sure.' She jumped to her feet, crestfallen. 'Why didn't you say so? Okay, I'll be off—sorry for wasting your time.'

With Pragya gone, the density of stress fell, the oppression instantly lifted. Sravan turned to Devyani like a lover long denied and found, to his dismay, that now he couldn't fix her in his mind. She kept disintegrating in flakes of clichés. Devyani had escaped through the slats of his description, and the closer he knit his sentences the more insubstantial she grew. Then, just as he was managing to retrieve some of her with a few magnetic syllables, an irate voice in the next room shattered the spell entirely.

'This country! They should have the flag hoisted by a beauty queen or a cricket player and train the bureaucrats to give a PT display! Independence Day parade, ho! Saala dogs!'

His father's strong, subjugating, supremo voice. A voice that dehydrated the words it uttered.

Years back Sravan had begun avoiding looking his father in the face, but he had memorized each line of it. The loose mouth—who could tell that the slack muscles of that lubberly snout could squeeze out such an uproar? For years Sravan had carried the blurred blueprint of that laxated mouth movement. The soft, nude slope of the upper lip, the elastic flex of the corners, the pliant sphincter of lip tightening round its roaring gush. So many shades of deprecation in its repertoire. One side curled down in grimace, the other twitched up in withering scorn. Or both sides plastered flat in a long-suffering, malevolent stretch. Now, in old age, that mouth lay lapsed in a crumpled sponge of flab, but it needed only the whim of a moment or a stray irritant to make the man unzip his lips and piss poison over them all.

'Uf! You say such crazy things, Babuji,' came Buddhoo's laughing voice. But the old man cut back.

'That big freedom-at-midnight binge in '47? I'll tell you what happened to me. I went with my wife on a tonga to the chowk bazaar, where a massive celebration was on. An August night, so I carried my new umbrella. The first thing that happened to me after midnight struck and we made our tryst with destiny was that my umbrella got stolen! Don't laugh—I see nothing to laugh at.

Now let me tell you about my friend Kishori Lal Haldar's ancestry. He's the one who owns a couple of prime guava groves on the Manauri road. That and the massive haveli in Begum Bazaar. His grandfather didn't build it, as he claims—what did you think? Ji nahin, ask me who did. Well, that property belonged to the Kunwar Sahib of Kanauj. In 1857, when a lot of Kunwar Sahib's kindred were hung from the roadside pipals, a handful of British soldiers stormed into Kishori Lal's grandfather's outhouse. He was the Kunwar Sahib's munshi. They hauled him up, quivering like jelly. They produced a scrap of paper with a garbled Persian message scrawled across it, and thundered at our friend to translate it. He said he couldn't, and they'd have strung him up as prompt as you please but he begged for mercy, pleading that his wife lay ill in the inner room, with the pox, the horrific maata. That hit them in the arse. Off came their caps—they'd developed a healthy horror of the maata, the bastards, and all its native offspring—malaria and cholera and dysentery. They spared him out of sheer dread. The pox proved his fairy godmother. The message he decoded for them turned out to be half correct, and taking him for a faithful collaborator, they granted him the Kunwar Sahib's property. On the condition that he permit them to go on hanging rebels from the big pipals in the grounds, which demand he readily granted! They granted him a title as well—Haldar, for Havaldar of the Company's Forces—which turned him from a Gupta into a Haldar, ha ha!'

A blast of laughter. Like a handful of sand smarting in the eye.

'Freedom! And now allow me to tell you about how my friend, Kishori Lal Haldar, turned summarily into a freedom fighter in '42. Today he enjoys all the freedom-fighter perks. Wears only khadi. Has jaggery in his tea, no mill-refined sugar—he's for the cottage industries, the humbug! Cuts ribbons and lassoes garlands around Gandhi's portrait on Gandhi's birthday. Remembers those glorious days with tears in his eyes. Travels AC. Freedom fighter—hish! I'll tell you how he became one. Boarded the Upper India Express one day. He never bought a ticket—always travelled without one. Was nabbed at the next station and arrested. Consider the rascal's presence of mind: He started shouting *Jai Hind* and *Bande*

Mataram! I refuse to buy any saala *railway ticket from any* saala *British sarkar! Jai Hind!* Flung his tweed coat on the ground, struck a match with a flourish and tossed it on the coat! Turned into a freedom fighter overnight!'

This time a low, vicious snigger. His father's brand of humour—mustard oil and gastric juice. A special hyperacidity. Bilious memories soaked in gall. The crumpled old Jeremiah sat with blight on his tongue, scourging past and present.

'Shocking,' exclaimed Buddhoo.

'They sent round an ad just after your precious Independence. Asked, *How many times has the candidate been to jail? For how long? How many times beaten? How many lashes?* Fellows made ten into twenty and twenty into hundred. Me? I refused, Sahib, I refused with good reason. I wasn't going to trade the batons on my stinging rear for the pleasure and the privilege of sharing an AC compartment with haramzada scum like Kishori Lal Haldar–sometime–Gupta! I spit on the lot! Saala swine-born curs!'

Sravan wondered how this squared with the Ha Ha Hi era, when his father was avidly serving the British Empire. But he allowed him a bit of fictional licence.

Buddhoo had a technical objection. 'Swine-born cur? That'd be a creature that our best zoologists . . .'

'Be quiet,' crackled the old man.

Buddhoo would not be suppressed. 'As for haramzada dogs, Babuji, bastardy's the pucca convention in beast circles.'

'What more?' continued the old man's gravelly voice. 'I'd composed a very pleasing melody for the national anthem and sent it up to Delhi for consideration. Later a perfectly ghastly tune was selected for the *Jana Gana Mana*. Yes, it's totally appalling and I wrote to the editors of hazaar newspapers complaining, but did the ulloo ka patthas ever dare to publish my letters? Nah! I'll go on calling it execrable! When the tricolour soars across the movie screens at the end of a film . . .'

'It doesn't anymore,' put in Buddhoo.

'It did twenty years back. I never stood up, as others did, when the national anthem played. My democratic protest. What have I to fear? I'm going to die soon.'

'Nonsense. You're getting better and better,' came Buddhoo's soothing voice.

Sravan could hear the sparks snap in the old man's voice. 'Don't lie to me. I can't stand liars!'

There was an uncomfortable pause, and then the old man husked on: 'I don't mind dying one bit. I welcome it.' His waspish voice turned pontifical. 'There're only two things one must hope for. A life of honour and a death with dignity. I'm ready now.' A resounding line like that needed a significant pause to round it off. The old man observed a two-minute silence in honour of his utterance. Then he picked up the thread again. 'You can celebrate fifty years of independence in this benighted country, but I'm the only one in this house who's going to enjoy real independence. None of you. All I've got to do is wait for my personal independence day to approach. Then I'll be rid of this world and the world shall be rid of me. Good!'

Forgodssake! fretted Sravan. Why did everything have to find a dramatic connection with his father's own death? For years the old man had dangled his death over their heads like a baleful threat. There he sat, coddled and pampered, recovering from his stroke, with nothing worse to impede his normality than a fall in the bathroom and a fracture of the hip. Even the bedsores had healed now, and Buddhoo gave his back a diligent powder-and-spirit massage every day. His speech was unaffected, the physiotherapist came daily, a walker was used to coax him out of bed, but the old man had set his teeth against all chances of recovery. He'd always been proud and possessive of his illnesses, peevish at his recoveries. A man who in former times had lived to eat, who'd fly into a passion over a piece of fish or one chapatti less than what he was used to.

'I'm not afraid of death,' he repeated in his most pompous tones. 'So many sister-fucker fools have managed it—why can't I? If Badrinath Gupta could manage it, why not me? I always did everything he tried to do much better. And Mahendra Singh Chauhan, who always surrendered to me in argument. And Raghupati, Vishveshwar, Jagdish Prasad . . . If they coped with death, I'm sure I'll cope ten times better.'

'Funny thought,' mused Buddhoo. 'I wonder if God awards trophies for excellent death performances. You seem to have quite a social circle among the deceased, Babuji. It sounds like a law-abiding, tax-paying, urban middle-class colony.'

Another serrated laugh from the old man. 'That's right, Prabuddha beta. I know more people there than here. My only regret . . .' He lowered his voice. 'My only regret is that I'll die in this swine-ridden hell-hole city—I'll never get to see my Etawah again. In the last week, there hasn't been a single night when I haven't dreamt of Etawah. Wandering down the old bazaar . . .' The vinegar in his voice blackened with longing. 'Through those old winding lanes and plunging roads, those sudden staircases. Going down deep troughs, up the steep climbs past the ruins of Jaichand's fort, towards the big temple on the hill. Tixie Temple, it was called. Like a massive fortress, flags flying, ravines stretching away as far as Gwalior. The two highest points in the city were the railway station and the Tixie Temple. The city nestled in a hollow between them . . . and beyond . . . the ravines of the Chambal valley. If you dropped a coin into the Chambal, you could see it gleaming on the riverbed—that clear the water was.'

Buddhoo ventured, 'I'm from those parts myself, Babuji. I know the city. Went to Government College there . . .'

A sudden squelch of emotion in the voice: 'Ah, did you, then? How did it look in your days?'

'Muddy yellow walls. Vast dusty grounds. British Normal School architecture.'

'Doesn't change, that sort of structure. Until it caves in and sinks like a toothless mouth.'

'Or is pulled down to make way for a glass and concrete box.'

'And d'you remember my college? Islamia College? With the carved, mosaic-crusted arch and minaret?'

'Part of it was damaged. Maybe by an earthquake? I'm not sure what made the dome crack through. Looks like an overturned china bowl.'

'Sometimes I find myself in one of those twisted lanes behind the main bazaar and there's a low muezzin's call in my head, shivering all the way down my spine . . .' The old man had a sudden fit of coughing. He coughed as though the words annoyed his throat, hooked themselves to his larynx and he had to cough to clear them away, wheeze to spit them out. A sound like *Haaaakkkhhh*! Sravan knew it well. *Haaaakkkhhh* was catarrhal and cathartic both. It deep-dredged stubborn phlegm and buried pain in one spirited interjection.

Sitting at his desk in the adjoining room, with the door slightly ajar and every sound clearly carried by some accident of acoustics, Sravan found his attention ensnared. His father, he reflected wryly, always spoke of himself and his history in a stilted narrative mode as though he were reading passages from a future autobiography.

'There used to be mangoes in season, piled roof-high in our house, mangoes from our groves in the village. My mother owned a huge, iron chopper blade hinged on to a dark wooden block. Like a hand-operated guillotine—I remember her putting a mango on the block and hacking it precisely in half. There used to be loads of jaggery and earthen pots of cool cane juice. Outside was a little mud-plastered hearth backed by a sooty wall. A narrow staircase led to a larger room above, which held a massive carved bed. A Moradabad brass bed. My grandfather's. There were balconies on either side of the room, with ancient, rusted cast-iron grilles. Above was another unrailed terrace where we flew kites or watched swarms of homing pigeons. D'you know what old houses turn into? When father and mother are dead, what do old homesteads become? I've discovered that old houses take on parental identity. I don't think you understand this.'

'I do,' said Buddhoo.

'Now I look around the room in my dreams. And there, on a peg, hangs the same small coat. Ah, the sight of it! The weave of that faded black serge! I seem to have journeyed across all that time and distance . . . only for a heart-wounding glimpse of that coat.'

The voice was now scaly with emotion. 'Listen to this. I had a brother. Two years younger. He was three. A pale, snivelling child with a runny nose. Thin legs and a whine. I hated him with all the intensity of my five years. I fought him over food, over kites, over the pup in the yard, over my mother's quilt . . . I thrashed him black and blue. He cowered from my blows, pale and whimpering, and when my father returned, he'd sidle up to him and say, hiccupping with tears: 'Bhai Sahib thrashed me again. Take me with you tomorrow.' My father'd grab me, cuff me, deal me a rain of blows, send me flying. So the next day I thrashed harder. He'd piss in his pants when I thrashed him good and hard. He was in mortal dread of me.'

An uncertain, numb silence. What sounded like a sniff turned into a *haaaakkkhhh* and a resounding rattle and split.

'Then there was a cholera epidemic. My brother looked so small, laid out like that, with joss sticks burning round him. I ran into the upstairs room, didn't go to the ghat, didn't come near the bamboo ladder they'd tied him on. I hid myself away with this coat, babbling into its folds. All night I buried my head in its lightless cave . . . Hell cannot be darker, son.'

Another long pause.

'My father is dead. My mother is dead. That boy, my brother, is done for as well. Much after his death, my third brother was born. Then my two sisters. None of them ever saw that boy. His name means nothing to them. There's no photograph. He's lost. Wiped out. But to me he has a name. It brings up a face. It's like a face you see in water—it floats away from itself, comes together, floats off, joins up again and suddenly you see it whole. I can't bring myself to speak his name. Ever. To a single soul.'

A charged silence. Then Buddhoo spoke in a dilute sort of voice. 'You have to get that coat off your back, I guess. Maybe you can just write it all off.'

'Write it off? I wrote off that house years ago. Sold it. Signed it off. Like that. Court fee. Stamps. Signature. A dismal ritual. I sold it off and visited a temple in expiation to my grandfather who'd laid each brick.

'I don't mean that way,' said Buddhoo when he managed to break in. 'I mean write . . . of that experience. WRITE . . . like Ravan does.'

'WRITE!' He sniffed at the word like a dog at a scrap of garbage. 'That kind of saala four-twenty thing! No thank you. We've had more than our share of writers in our family. It's an evil karma.' He munched on his anger. His next words were chilli-hot.

'I'll tell you about a couple of old-timers in my family. My maternal grandfather, poor fool, came jolting and juddering down from Mathura—must've been the late nineteenth century. He had prime land outside Mathura and custody of a temple or two. He came with his family, fleeing a riot, the Muslims on the rampage in one of those periodic bloodbaths. So along came my ancestor on the run, with chadar-draped wife and a gaggle of daughters, among which number my lady mother, and never a brass pot or a gold belt picked up in his haste! Well, he'd all but reached Etawah when the demented fool remembers something he's left behind. He sends on his wife and daughters, all protesting, holding him back, appealing shrilly, but did he listen? Nahin, Sahib. So the fool goes scuttling back to pick up something so precious that he's willing to risk his life for it. He goes all the way back to his burning village . . . And he never got away alive, hah! They hacked off his turbaned head. Probably his penis as well! Threw him to rot in the dust. And you'll be wondering, my lad, what the fool went back to fetch?'

A long pregnant pause.

'What?' breathed Buddhoo, timorous.

'Not a pot of gold mohurs buried in an orchard, nor the family jewels in a hollow in the wall. No, not title deeds to groves or acres of land. No, huzoor. He went back to fetch—if you please—the manuscript of a wretched book he was writing! Ghazals, it is said. Ach! Ghazals! Dripping, drooling lyrics on springtime and monsoons and grief and women, hah! Women he had aplenty on his hands—he'd fathered eight daughters—and he came to grief right well with his folly.'

'Bud did he manage to recover his book?' asked Buddhoo weakly. 'I mean, it'd be some consolation to think he . . .'

'Book?' The old man laughed in sharp-toothed malice. 'Who cares for saala books when men are letting blood! And that was only one idiot in our family. A writer, mind you. The second idiot . . .' He stopped for rhetoric effect.

'Yes?' prompted Buddhoo.

'The second was an uncle on my father's side. Went mad. Stark, staring mad. Said to be uncannily bright once, with a photographic memory. Went to mushairas and came back with every poem recorded in his mind. Went to kirtans and made up hymns on the spot. Complicated rhymes. He was a legend in his time. Invitations came from distant towns. There were no tape recorders then, so men learnt his stanzas by heart and taught them to their mates and went home and wrote them down. Well, this uncle wrote a Sanskrit book. It was whispered that he took dictation from some yaksha or gandharva. He used to be seized by paroxysms when his head was engorged with lyric and melody and he'd be singing away like crazy. Hours and hours. What came of it, eh? Fellow completed his Sanskrit book and went barmy! The gandharva's parting gift, see? Too much truth and beauty aren't good for the human brain, see?' He took a razor swipe with his wickedly joyous voice.

'And the third writer in my family . . .' he resumed with a grandiloquent flourish.

'Ravan?' anticipated Buddhoo.

There was an uneasy break in the flow. When the old man spoke again it was in gruff, injured tones. 'You're wrong, Prabuddha beta. The third writer in my family—though few people know it now—was myself.'

'You!' cried Buddhoo.

'Yes,' admitted the dusty voice, as though it were unearthing an old, shameful misdeed. Sravan knew what was coming. His father always spoke about his erstwhile writing first with fake condemnation, then in solemn and vengeful tones, as though by not allowing it to see the light of print he was denying the world a treat as a penance for its sins. When Sravan had dedicated his first novel to his father, there'd been a peculiar scene at home. I've dedicated it to you, Babuji. Why? Silence. Sravan had waited for what he'd craved all his days, a word of approval. But his father, lips pursed, had turned the pages with a look of long-suffering scorn on his face, then said acidly—Well, I suppose I have to be grateful for the honour, thank you very much, I am much obliged to you. Every word a whiplash. With his first royalties he'd bought his father a pair of leather slippers. Not to be embarrassed into approval, his father had said—What an abnormal colour. Couldn't you get me something in black? The black ones were very expensive—the sari for Ma cost quite a bit—I didn't get all that much. Pat came the observation with a thorny laugh—I'm sure I earned more from my honest desk job than you'll ever do as a writer then, Badshah-salamat! Sravan had been stung. Hurt. Inveigled into losing his temper. He'd begun shouting. His father, triumphant, had shrugged and said—Why are you shouting? Who asked you to give me anything? Did I ask you? I'm doing very well for myself, thank you. Doing very well for himself, thank you, and lashing out with fangs bared and nostrils flaring at all those others who presumed to write. Once, when he was small, Sravan's mother had called him aside. From the interiors of her bodice, where she kept her coin purse, she had fished out a folded sheet of paper. It was moist and had a faintly sour whiff of sweat. She had unfolded it with an expression of bashful pride as though she was revealing a love note or an advance draft of her last will and testament and leaving incalculable riches to him. She had held it out to him. It was a naïve, stumbling poem. He had tried to pull her leg and chant it aloud but she snatched it back and stuffed it into her bosom, hissing, "Chup! Your father will hear." And considering how often his father loudly pronounced his mother a damned fool, a blathering idiot, a dumb poop, he could understand her anxiety to keep her little scribbles a secret. Her only guilty extramarital flings, poor thing, all lost. Destroyed like secret love notes. Sravan wondered if his own writing was an act of lifelong vengeance on her behalf. It was that—and also its pathetic opposite, a desperate, lifelong campaign for his father's approval. A way of prising open that closed, mean heart.

'I'm not saying I'm great, but . . .' The old man brought out an old refrain. 'I'm not saying I'm great, but . . . This is how it all came about. I used to do some voluntary teaching and accounting work in a few local charity schools. That's when I began drafting letters for people. I'm not making any tall claims for myself but so effective was my writing style that I thought of writing a book. You could say I was talked into this fool enterprise by some of my regulars. Personally I wouldn't ever have contemplated the idea. Saala waste of time! No pursuit for a man of sense. But you know how it goes—start a job and you've got to carry it through. I worked at it for three years. Fitfully. Tough work. Not the writing itself—that's fool's stuff—but the making time for it. Each time I'd start, something'd crop up. Get me some green chillis from the bazaar, eh-ji, the wife'd call out. Work out this square root for me, Babuji, the son would whimper. Can you make time for a letter to the Pension Section of the AG's Office, Madanlalji? A neighbour would descend. A bit of tax calculation for the Principal sahib, Madanlalji, a phone call for you—from the house next door. Sometimes I'd just taken off and was doing just fine, spinning the sentences along like a Nobel Laureate with an oiled and battery-operated pen, when along comes the kid and pleads—Talk to me. Tell me a story.

'So the wretched thing took three years to write and I was fed up to the teeth with it, I can tell you. Then came the business of finding a publisher—a most unlovely job. It came bouncing back to me once, twice, thrice, yes, it came back to me twenty times in all, janab!'

'Shame,' muttered Buddhoo politely.

'These callow new writers—like my nawab sahib in the next room—what do they know of struggle and setback? I tell you, setback hones your spirit if the struggle is at all worthwhile. In my case it wasn't. I got the politest of apologies from publishers. All the virtues of my book were listed and applauded. My wit complimented. My scholarship extolled. My humanity commended. My wisdom exalted. The haramzadas couldn't say enough! Still, they regretted they couldn't fit it into their slots. Agh! They could stuff it up their slots for all I cared! I tried and tried—it became an obsession. By the twentieth time I'd decided—just one more try and never again. So I cycled off to the GPO with my bulky manuscript on the carrier. It was the end of the month and I was flat broke. Not a fake cowrie for the milkman or the vegetable vendors—living on credit and goodwill till salary day—just enough wangled out of the wife's emergency kitty for the postage. Then? What d'you think happened?

'I'd just reached the side gate of the GPO and was lifting my bike over the gate when who should come along but my friend Badrinath Gupta. What's up? I say. And he tells me—Shivcharan Shukla's daughter's dead. Electric shock, poor girl. Come along with me right away. D'you have any cash on you? Good—it's needed desperately. You know what a boozer he is—his wife's fainted from the horror of it—no money for the funeral—the bastard's sold all her jewellery down to her last kangan. Okay, I considered the situation. Here I was, sending my useless book off for the twenty-first time, taking my last shot at the Nobel Laureate racket, and here was this saala turning up at the gate of the GPO itself with an appeal that couldn't be ignored. Okay, I'm not saying I'm great, but one chance less or more at this blasted business isn't going to make much difference, I argue. Here I am sending off a book and there's that poor devil who hasn't got the stuff to send off his daughter to the ghat! And there's this thing you'll have to grant me—I've always been the first to arrive at a house where there's been a death. The first to help with the funeral shopping, the preparation of the body, the wood-buying at the ghat, the food-sending, the telegram-despatching, the obituary-drafting, the shraadha-arranging. If anybody tries to thank me, I say—It's a principle with me. Absent yourself from tilaks and thread ceremonies and birthdays and marriages, but never, never neglect a house of mourning. I know of a poor widow who arranged a massive thirteenth-day feast for the peace of her dead husband and nobody, nobody had the decency to turn up. There're folks that won't eat in a house of mourning, as if death's a viral infection. But I'm glad to say I'm not one of those. For me funerals and obsequial feasts command compulsory attendance—else no one'll come to yours.'

'Sound reasoning,' smirked Buddhoo.

'Now, was there any question of my refusing? Could I stand there and say to Badrinath Gupta—Forgive me, Guptaji, I've an important job to complete, I've got to send my trashy novel to the twenty-first publisher so that he can stuff it up his arse and write me a love note afterwards saying what a joy that was? The sister-fucker novel would have to be shelved, that's all there was to it.

That's how the twenty-first attempt was foiled by fate—what was that thing we recited—the moving finger writes and having writ, flushes it all down with the shit!'

'Haw, haw haw!' Buddhoo guffawed.

'I then understood too clearly that this writing nonsense wasn't for me. It wasn't what I was destined to do in life. Destiny had other important things for me. There'd been divine interference working all the way, retarding me. Because I was doing the wrong thing. Because I was going against destiny's current. I'd successfully learnt to read Fate's blueprint—my success had come of age! *Haaaakkkhhh*!'

'Wah!' cried Buddhoo in admiration.

'So what did I do, ask me? I had a way with words, didn't I tell you first thing? So I went back to drafting letters for people. What's the use of writing massive tomes on people who've never existed? Wretched things happening in your miserable little head, huh? Who's interested? You should see the letters I wrote. To governors of states, appealing for redressal of grave wrongs. To directors of education requesting transfers of poor teachers so that the poor blighters could go eat decent dal-roti with their families instead of rotting out their innards eating crap at the Hira-Moti Vaishnav Bhojnalay! To ministers, joint secretaries, even to the president of India once. I knew how to whittle away at each sentence. How to give a line the proper ring. How to tease a man's special bogey. How to graze a guilty conscience. I say with pride, Prabuddha beta, that every one of my letters gained its object. So many people actually helped! Each one of my petitions did more in its way than all your Pulitzers and Bookers and my nawab sahib's precious awards. I am a man content.' He waited. There was more. Sravan grinned to himself, wondering if Buddhoo imagined the tirade had wound to a close.

'Consider your books of literature,' his father resumed. 'What've they actually done to help the world, kyon? You sit in your armchair, you read, you're stirred by greatness, suffering, emotion, whathaveyou, your slumped conscience like a long fallen dick gets tantalized. And, huzoor, you get a tiny spiritual shiver, a saala moral erection. You feel like doing good and fucking evil but d'you actually do a thing? Never. But my petitions were the real thing. The genuine article. They changed things . . . for real folk. And it took me twenty-one failures to achieve this.'

'Still, there's that little matter of the coat,' said Buddhoo. 'And if you were to consider writing about it, I mean now that the petition days are nicely over and you have all the time in the world and yours truly to take dictation . . .'

'Now?' snorted the old man.

'Why not now?' persisted Buddhoo.

'I'm not going to last,' huffed the old man.

'Oh, come on. You'll live long enough.'

'No.' The old man sulked.

'Yes,' pursued Buddhoo.

This was going too far, but how was the fool to know you don't push Babuji beyond his patience? An explosion was brewing in the next room. Sravan enjoyed the prospect of his father ticking off his fool of a friend. But to his surprise, his father's voice sank to a low musing. 'How can I make you understand? Who should I write for now? Madhuri's dead. Balwant is dead. Raghupati, Dr Jacobs, Vishveshwar, Jagdish Prasad, Brahmadev Pundit, Moinuddin. All gone. I could count them on my ten fingers. When I wrote it was for them—people who understood the things I had done. One always writes for a handful of people. Why should I write for strangers, han? Smart-arsed bastards who don't believe or respect what we of my time believed or respected. They aren't worth the strain; buss!'

Sravan remembered old Moinuddin, the ophthalmologist. As a shortsighted kid, he'd shrieked with fright seeing Moinuddin's enlarged Paleolithic eye draw menacingly towards him in the lens of the slit lamp in an eerie dark room. His first spectacles. And his delighted cry when he put them on—Ma, do you really see such a lot? Then Moinuddin had patted his head, his trim, combed beard fragrantly close to his nose, and said—May these eyes always know how to see clearly. Moinuddin was twenty years dead now, and as for seeing clearly, it wasn't myopia that made it increasingly difficult. Sitting at his desk in the next room, Sravan felt a nebulous fear surround him. The threat of a future negation.

8

Buddhoo was jabbersome. 'Yaar, I've got a book inside me. I can feel it coming up my throat. A basin, quick! I've got to write it down. The big book of my life. Confessions of the Indian Lotus-Eater. Portrait of a Former Flower Child. Diary of a Drop-Out. The Growth of the Middle-Aged Poet's Mind. The Interlude . . .'

'Inter-lewd?'

Guffaw. 'Its going to be a book on LIFE. An approach to life. A reproach to thought. With footnotes and glossary. Its going to be called *Eat and Excrete: An Elementary Tract*.'

'Alimentary?'

'Shabash! That's a good one! I've even got the first sentence in my head. Good, round, resounding line.'

'Let's hear it.'

'*Excretion is the better part of squalor*!' Buddhoo roared. 'Ho, ho, ho, ho! Fact is, man, you're giving me an inferiority complex, sitting there perspiring at your desk. I said I've got to write my book too. The big book of my life. So I, ha, cast a merciless look at my life as lived so far, and to tell you the truth, yaar, weighing the essentials, I found I've achieved just one thing. The Great Digestive Cycle.'

'Great. You're welcome to my PC in the afternoons,' said Sravan with mock solemnity. 'Or is it to be pen and ink? My old manual typewriter is free, too.'

Buddhoo regarded him with scorn. 'None of your second-rate gadgetry. This is pure inspiration. Composed in the stomach.

Consummated in the soul. By the way, have I told you of the time when I asked a memsahib the difference between consumption and consummation?'

'Let it wait, will you?' Sravan retreated studywards in haste. 'I've got some of my own stuff to complete. No pure inspiration for me. I must say to the muse what the earl said to the nun—Go spin, you jade, go spin.'

'Which earl?'

'Pembroke,' called Sravan from the study.

'Which nun?'

Sravan bolted the door, switched on the lamp and took up his notes.

> Mondira once spent a long, lazy winter with friends at their estate. The local zamindar family owned enormous farmlands and orchards. There was a visiting nephew. His name was Mihir. An old, remembered picnic at the Shitala Falls . . . Lentils boil on a wood fire. The smoke rises. Dumplings of crisp flour baked in hot ash. Brinjals and potatoes. The fragrance of powdered gram, sharpened with pickle oil, pungent with garlic and melted ghee . . . Mondira's eyes sting with the smoke and the misery of Mihir's indifference. Sugarcane and mustard fields, gold and green, and away, in a hollow of the valley, the low, wet dark of mango groves. Guava plantations. Near the fall, the land is rocky. Deep-fretted with seams of water. Raked with massive cloven ploughs. The boom and crash of water, its wide, electric bolt blasting its way down, sparks flying. Giant vapours rise from the boiling hell-brew in the basin beneath.
>
> Five years later Mondira revisits the fall with Mihir on a family trip. The river is now reduced to a solo strum. A small pulse still beats in the rock. The cry of a solitary bird creates a disturbance in the still waters of the sky. And Mondira at last plucks up the courage to ask Mihir: Did you get my letter? That one I sent at Kali Puja, five years back? She has been rebuffed by his silence, his

complete casualness. He answers: Yes. Her heart lurches in her ribs. Then he adds: I couldn't read a word. It'd been drenched in the rain—every word washed off. She is left wondering how many words stayed legible and how much was washed away.

So Mondira's motives are complicated. She arranges a match between Mihir and her sister, the little Devyani. She believes she has resolved the question, put Mihir out of reach. Paradoxically, she also manages to keep Mihir in the family, always available to her, and she knows that too.

What Sravan wished to create was a series of overwhelming pictures. No intrusion of authorial observation. A prolonged disappearance of self. In recent years he had at last learnt this disappearing act, switching himself off and staying carefully out of the story. As though it was necessary for book and author to keep themselves at arm's length. The novel gained in direct proportion to the efficacy of his own dissolution.

He lit a cigarette. As if on cue, the phone rang. He clicked in annoyance, then realized it might be Malini and hulloed with some eagerness.

It wasn't Malini. The voice that rose from the phone in a dim fog sent misgivings through him.

'Congratulations. I read your new book.' The voice paused uncertainly after each sentence as though it sought confirmation or approval and wasn't sure of receiving either.

'Yes.'

'Saw you at Ranjana Devi's place the other day. I was going to come speak to you but the place was too crowded. You left early.'

'Yes.'

'Didn't wait for dinner. Or any of your old crowd.'

'No.'

'I was disappointed.' The tone was cryptic. The voice leaned towards him, slunk its way slowly round his throat and slipped on its coils. Sravan steadied his own voice. When he spoke it was with an air of suave interest. He asked, 'What're you doing with yourself these days?'

'Nothing much.'

'What're you writing?' asked Sravan, feeling his way warily, relieved to find himself recovering his usual poise.

'Just a textbook or two.'

'Good money.'

'Not so good, actually. Lots of middlemen. But it keeps the kitchen fires burning.'

Sravan had hit his stride by now, and the spark of a laugh ignited his voice. He put the next question with an air of jocular concern: 'What about the creative fires?'

The voice paused heavily, then said, 'I sometimes do short stories for magazines. Tried a potboiler—somehow couldn't write the sort of thing the market wants. Not much good at it.'

A span of silence.

'I learnt of this Golden Lotus windfall of yours.'

Sravan was surprised. The news had got round already! He uttered a non-committal murmur.

'I wondered if I could do a feature on you. An interview, maybe?'

This was more than Sravan could take.

The voice went on, scrupulous about leaving nothing to inference: 'It'll pay me some okay cash, and frankly, I could do with it at the moment.'

Sravan had an uncontrollable impulse to put the phone down. He mastered it and said with some difficulty, 'Sure. Any time.'

'You must let me have the full scoop. And another thing. I'd appreciate it if you didn't give anyone else the full-length account before mine sees print. Is it too much to ask? For old times' sake.'

That last awkward phrase rattled Sravan. He said, very low and guarded, 'Okay.'

There was another heavy pause. 'Tell me, is it true that the Golden Lotus means a cool two-point-five lakhs?'

'Something like that,' answered Sravan, swallowing. 'Pathetic, isn't it? Considering the megabucks they shell out abroad. All those auctions. Rights going to the highest bidder. Our Indian scale is pitiful, no?'

'I don't know,' said the voice. 'Bit like the stock exchange, I think . . . but I'm no judge. I don't belong to that club. Never understood market management.'

'Can't do without it.'

'Oh, I'm managing. Not too well, but any old how. There're two kinds of writers: macro and micro. I'm not just micro but mofussil as well. Gives you the freedom of the fakir.' An uncanny laugh. Then a changing of subject. 'I liked your new book.'

'Thanks.'

'There were things I could relate to—exactly.'

'Good.'

'Might have been written by me.'

'Yes?'

'In fact . . . in fact I suspect it was.' What was this now? The old, sick panic came blundering back. The voice had renounced its caution, begun rising in a giddy curve. 'Remember "Pravesh"? My old short story? Published in *Lekhni* ages back. No, I thought you wouldn't. Considering that you've made quite a nice novel out of it, with a few changes here and there. And glib. Your special sort of glitter. Your uncanny way with words. Your ingenious way of hacking up an original and rehashing it into something new. Exciting. Your award-winning best-seller . . .'

He was clearly raving. There were rumours that this man had turned alcoholic, and hadn't altogether recovered after that disgraceful breakdown. Another minute and he'd be lapsing into abuse. An old scene replayed so many times. Sravan tried to interrupt with contempt. Dignity. A confidence he did not feel. 'What are you suggesting?'

'Exactly what you make of it.'

He decided to make light of the whole thing. Affect a bantering tone. 'You're imagining things, yaar. Come over one of these days for a drink and tell me my misdeeds in detail. I'm interested.'

There was now a distinct slur in the voice. 'If I do, you'll probably leave a message that you're out. Well, maybe we'll put together that feature on you. It's one of the few things I can still manage.'

'Oh, come on,' said Sravan appeasingly. 'You've managed to stay afloat.'

The voice turned suspicious. 'What d'you mean?'

'You aren't writing in any prefigured frame. The dispossessed Dalit, the woman, the tribal, social violence. Not even those all-purpose evergreen clichés, sex and death. So next time you do a short story for a magazine, feel free to help yourself to a novel of mine. Take your pick. Snip it up. It'll give you a dozen good stories. Good luck to you.'

Then he summoned his laugh. Sravan had a special thunderclap laugh, its sheer volume designed to silence opposition and put an end to inconvenient conversation. It worked specially well on the phone. That done, he slammed the receiver down. He noticed for the first time how dry his throat was, and how tight his head. His legs felt a desperate compulsion to walk. Up and down the study, round the desk, along the window overlooking the park, up to the bookshelves and back he walked, overcome by an old nausea.

But instead of working off the disturbance, the walking only recharged it. He looked in at the room next door. A biggish crowd was piled on Buddhoo's mattress, on the chairs, on the Mirzapuri dhurrie. The kids, their friends, some neighbours, Pragya, even the maid. They appeared to be enjoying themselves hugely. The opening lines of Buddhoo's literary venture had plainly captured an enthusiastic audience. Sravan stood a moment at the door, still a bit shaken by his phone conversation. Buddhoo caught sight of him.

'Ah, there you are, Ravan! Just the fellow I need. Emergency! A ticklish point of poesy.'

'It's in verse?' Sravan forced himself to speak in a hearty voice.

'Reverse verse.'

'What's that?'

'Wait and see. Can you tell me a word that rhymes with *analysis*?'

'Paralysis.'

'Won't do.'

'Dialysis.'

'You're getting too bloody medical, yaar. No others?'

'Sorry. Not at my best and brightest.' Sravan renounced the effort at merriment.

He went back to his study, called Malini, changed his mind before her phone rang twice, and resumed work with a sour heart.

> Their first meeting, when Amalendu came to 'view' Mondira, was in a large guava grove. He offered her a ripe guava. She took it, grimaced, lip curling. She was lovely, he old for his age, gangling and gawky. The match was settled. She hated the sight of him. Their marriage has been a lifelong pact of hatred. She defies him. He beats her up, a surly man. All the same, Amalendu desires Mondira not from any love but from bitter detestation. For no other woman can he feel this exciting repugnance. He can stab her into silence with his thrusts. He keeps one hand firmly on her mouth till his climax resonates with her chokes. They only sharpen his pleasure. She seethes and plots. When he tries other women, he finds himself cold. Almost as though she has cursed him with impotence.

Sravan stopped. It just wasn't coming right. Almost as though he shared Amalendu's impotence, and it was happening with disquieting frequency. He found himself dragging the numb words across the floor of his mind like inert furniture. He could shudder at the grate of them, the nerve-distressing creak. This wasn't what writing used to be—this hoisting words into position like ungainly weights, this strain. That's it, he thought. It's no longer what it used to be, an effortless emanation.

The journalist scene was proving specially stubborn. It had become a kind of bogey with him. He knew from experience that there were these bogey sequences. No matter how hard he strained, the form of the journalist who came to inquire about Mondira's runaway kid just wouldn't take shape. The dialogue wouldn't move. There was an expression jam somewhere inside him. The policeman sequence was no better; those two scenes had become tests of some kind, and he was failing in some way.

His reflections were interrupted by what appeared to be muffled singing in the next room, accompanied by gusts of laughter.

Buddhoo was giving a recital. Devilish, sing-song words. Suddenly Buddhoo's vast vocal range displayed itself. Sravan felt the vibrations jangle unpleasantly on his edgy nerves. Tense as he was, he flung back his chair, stormed across and banged on the door to tell the bastard to pipe down.

The crowd seemed to be in splits. As he stopped at the door, Buddhoo's eyes challenged him across the floor:

'Presented herewith in your service, dear Ravan, my second songlet!' he announced gleefully, and patted the mattress beside him in a motion for Sravan to sit.

I have two pairs of cheeks, you know.
One up here and one down below.
Betwixt the twain I have my lips.
The other dwells between my hips.

I use one set to smile and kiss.
I use the other to snort and hiss.
Don't be surprised to hear me, friends,
Blowing my trumpet from both ends.

Sravan pulled a disgusted face, but all the others roared. Buddhoo wound up with a stagey flourish:

One speaks high words, the other low.
But they're great pals where'er they go.

Turning to Sravan with a wink, he twiddled an eyebrow. 'Like you and me, na? High and low—right?'

'So this,' observed Sravan, 'is what's called Reverse Verse.'

'Yeah. Deals with the reverse gear. The source of my emanations,' crowed Buddhoo.

Hearing the word *emanation*, and contrasting his own solemn use of it with Buddhoo's broad farce, Sravan had to grin in spite of himself.

9

Pragya sat showing Buddhoo a well-worn album. Old black-and-white photographs on thick black leaves.

'Quite a college beauty,' observed Buddhoo thoughtfully.

Pragya flushed with pleasure. 'Also the college heiress,' she added—most unnecessarily, thought Sravan. 'I was a beauty, yes. I'm just an old woman now.' For some reason she shot Sravan a sharp look.

He had always marvelled at her superb gift of equivocation, which could turn a simple sentence into a loaded accusation. The right stresses, combined with the appropriate body language—a bleak look or a bitter sag of mouth—could carry an enormous weight of reproach. What had begun years back as a hairline crack of disquiet between the two of them had grown into a sharp wedge of nastiness.

Sometimes he itched for a quarrel. He confronted her with that heiress bit as soon as Buddhoo was out of earshot. 'Just what were you trying to put across? My great good fortune in marrying you?'

She looked straight at him, ready to take him on. Their eyes collided so hard that the impact hurt. They winced, and it was some time before they dared look at one another again. Both had proved masters at this guerrilla warfare. Then she laughed in his face. Her flawed laugh. Tarnished silver that had darkened with the years but that might still sparkle if polished.

'You've never been ashamed to be indebted to me before.' She spoke ironically, but there was a small mote of apprehension giddying about the air. 'So what're you so cut up about? He's your friend, and I'm doing my best to amuse him.'

The doing-my-best line always irritated him. This achingly earnest act was a tactical strategy to put him at a moral disadvantage. Still, he knew that she strained after his approval, which he'd forever withhold—for the pure joy and power of denial. The truth was that he didn't know what she was really like now, beneath her tumbling chatter. He knew her slack, cold body with its untended pubic hair, its flaccid, brown belly muscles, its formless pancake breasts. He'd watched it age and lose its proud cohesion. But he now knew nothing of her devious mind.

Her next words sounded an alarm in his head. 'By the way, I spoke to Malini on the phone yesterday. I suppose it's time to congratulate you . . . You didn't think of telling me anything about it, but I guessed. Long ago. A wife always gets to know. As I told her . . .'

Her voice halted over each innuendo. Weighed the air. Checked his face. He studied her with distaste. The patch of sweat highlighting her armpits. Her stocky arms encased in the creased cylinders of their sleeves. The wad of flesh supporting her chin. Her broad, grooved neck nestling on squat shoulders. He let his eyes scrutinize her in open and intentional disapproval. Her classic good looks had gone. She'd softly ballooned with time, her eyes grown bulbous, and a strange air of unresigned ruin clung to her. Classic Indian sylph turned classic Aryan cow! Big, white, dew-lapped, big-teated but liable to kick you in the face, he thought.

'I suspected something was on, but I thought, If he wants to hide things, it's his business—and his karma . . .'

Oh, hell!

Her face and voice had gone into their act. A little coil of pain came into her eyes. A sweetly contrived furrow of despair strung along her voice. God! He hated her! Her sad-caring, sulky-sneering, reproachful-righteous ways.

'I mean, look who's sponsoring this award . . .'

With a boom of relief he realized that she was talking about the Golden Lotus!

'It's a shame—how could you consent?'

'What d'you want me to do?'

'Can't you turn it down?'

'No.'

There was a shrill peal of rage in her pupils. 'I don't see why not.' Her voice had risen.

He put on his special, maddeningly patient tone. 'I don't expect you to.'

'You know what? You've sold out. To this hype, the attention, the sales figures, the cameras popping, the journalists, the women drooling . . .' She caught herself in time, the unspoken rage rearing in her face.

'You know as well as I do that refusing would only stir up more hype. I'd have to state my reasons, and that would only rake up trouble. Attract too much attention.'

'If you ask me, it'll be the right sort of attention. A serious gesture doesn't go waste.'

'I have no faith in gestures, Pragya. They don't achieve a thing.'

She stared at him, simmering. When she spoke again it was in a dramatized mock wheedle. 'Don't worry. There won't be an embargo on publishing your work. It'll only mean greater dignity.'

Fuck-all, these words!

'I don't want to carry on with those crusades.'

She persisted. 'You don't have to explain anything to anyone. No public statements. The reason you give need not be the real one. Say you've changed your mind. Say you don't believe in awards or something . . .'

He laughed a hollow laugh. 'After having received so many . . .'

She ignored him. 'No one obliges you to spell it out. But everyone'll know why.'

'No, Pragya, I've decided.'

She fell silent. He knew there was more coming. She wasn't one to give up easily. 'I'm ashamed,' she said at length. 'I was so proud of you that time. You stood out in a crowd of literary mercenaries. Among the callow stars, you seemed the enduring thing. I'm proud of that period, in spite of all the risks and the threats and the tension and everything. And now you're ready to undo it all.' She searched his face. He looked away, sickened. 'And what hurts most is that my opinion just doesn't count. It isn't important. It's as if I don't exist . . .'

Oh, go to hell!—he swore to himself.

'I'm of no consequence whatever. My words don't matter. As far as you're concerned, I'm just a shrew, a nag, a bore, a fool! Or is it because of that old issue? Is it that you hold it in your heart against me? When I was so genuinely sorry after I did it . . . you knew how sorry I was . . . do you have to go on punishing me all our life?'

She spewed out the words in a bitter gush. Her wet gaze swabbed his face, slobbed all over it in sticky pleading. He wanted to mop his skin clean. It revolted him, this slovenly grief. He forced himself to look at her. Tears ran down her face like rain down a grimy windowpane.

'What are you carrying on about?' he asked impatiently.

'That my opinion doesn't affect you one way or the other,' she blubbered. Her words sounded like the glushing of rainwater in a gutter, he thought, and he liked the simile instantly. He'd jot that one down. The glushing of rainwater in a gutter . . .

'That you should carry that old matter in your heart and go on punishing me like this. That you should think me a shrew, a fool, a nag, a bore, a drudge.'

'I never said those words,' he said wearily. 'You did.' Then, with a cruel flash of vengeance, he added, 'I merely agreed.'

All of a sudden she was absolutely calm. 'Okay,' she said. 'Go ahead and accept the wretched thing. I expect you're apprehensive of letting anything go—insecure.'

This was another remarkable thing—her lightning switches from hysteria to composure. They'd been having these see-saw quarrels for years, he and she alternating their tactics. When one became calm, it was a cue for the other to turn hysterical. He knew now that their marriage had outlived its span. In better moods he found himself adding up reasons for gratitude, all the good things they'd once shared. But better moods came less frequently. All too often their dislike surfaced in trifles, and this feeling of fatigue had come to stay.

Now she swallowed, studied him in quiet triumph as his own voice rose. She nudged him, said in a strained voice: 'Ofo! Don't get excited. You can do as you wish if it gets you into such a state. I've nothing more to say.'

At the door she turned to have the last word. 'I'm only terribly sorry you're being bought over like this.' He wished he could knock her jaw in.

Half a minute later Buddhoo appeared on the scene, a look of benign interest on his face. 'How now? Bought?' he asked. 'Sorry to butt in, yaar, but that was quite a domestic jham, na? Small difference of opinion betwixt man and wife?'

'Well put,' said Sravan drily.

'Couldn't help tuning in.'

'Your pleasure.'

'Kindly explain this to me. Unless you'd rather not. I understand from what she tells me that you're just about to disgrace yourself by accepting that award—that Golden Phallus, sorry, Golden Lotus, right?'

'That's how she looks at it.'

'How're you looking at it?'

'Look, I don't mind telling you the whole messy history, but in case she's sent you pimping for her, you can just fuck off!'

'Relax, bhai. She hasn't sent me. She hurtled past me and locked herself in her room.'

Sravan twisted his face into a grimace of a smile. 'Good. Now you're in time to see me hurtle past you and lock myself out. Not to worry. All in a day's work. I've got to get out of this hell-hole—take a walk round the block. You can come with me if you like. I'll tell you everything.'

'The award's been sponsored by the Katrak Group. Know the name?'

'Newspapers?'

'That's right. Bunch of high-profile, hard-hitting, multilingual tabloids. *Azad Hindustan*, *Bengal Bulletin*, *The Voice*, *Southern Cross*, *Sportovision*, *Life and Letters*, all those.'

Buddhoo nodded.

'About six years back I had an unpleasant brush with J.B. Katrak, the media baron. It was just after my book *Vipreet Karma* was banned. You know about that?'

'Actually, I don't. I was—underground six years back.'

'Ah. Well, *Vipreet Karma* is my favourite—my best, my only real book, I sometimes feel. Ten thousand copies of it were burnt in a single week. All over the country. It continues to be read—in private. And discussed. But the ban hasn't been lifted. Bookshops were looted, windows smashed. I was attacked at an inaugural reading organized by the *Vakya Sammelan*.'

'How flattering.'

'Sure, when it wasn't terrifying! The surreptitious sales continued. No profit for me, of course. For me there was hate mail and threatening phone calls. Pragya and the kids were house-bound. Even my servant got threatened. Too much attention for my liking. Yet that's the period Pragya's so proud of. It gratifies some funny moralistic gloating in her. Even after it had all blown over, whispers followed me—at conferences, parties, readings. The sodomy scenes were widely discussed.'

'Details?'

'There was one sequence about caste war. A Brahmin boy in a college hostel is sodomized and killed by four Dalit seniors during ragging. He's made to pedal a rickshaw round campus with the seniors sitting behind, lashing him on with an improvised whip—because he happens to come from a village where ten years back a Harijan busti was torched. When his elder brother abuses them, he's beaten and reported for misbehaviour with a Dalit. No one will record his complaint. There's no chance of justice for him or his brother. The class war in the hostel spreads to the township. I'm proud of that book. It's the whole truth, not a partial or expedient one. It's never a class that history punishes—it's always an individual. The individual's trapped. That's my abiding concern—the captivity of the individual in the history of his time. Classes are abstract things. The boy in my book begs for mercy, protests—I and my family had nothing to do with that Harijan busti—I was only seven years old then. But he's taunted by his tormentors—You're a Tripathi. You're one of *them*. Is it a human-rights issue or a retributive vendetta? Is it ever possible to rise above this caste complication? Those are some of the questions I tackled.'

They'd reached the end of the last lane in the block. The failing light dribbled into the ashoka trees in small runnels. Buddhoo produced his wallet, upturned it on his palm and, under the street lamp's faucet of sodium light, counted the coins. Sravan understood, turned right and chose the lane leading to the corner cigarette–bidi–paan–masala booth. They bought their fags, lit them, and turned back across the park's overgrown quad to Sravan's house.

'Shortly after that, when the pandemonium was wearing thin, I got a phone call from J.B. Katrak. You know—mega-journalist, political power broker, unofficial Opposition activist, general dicey character. Applauded me for my "bold" upper-class partisanship, as he put it. I said I spoke for myself and no class. He wanted to discuss a biography of his grandfather, B.K.G. Katrak. Wanted me to do it. My banned-book fame was just the sort of publicity he needed. B.K.G. Katrak was an exemplary man. Freedom fighter, social worker, human-rights activist, philanthropist, you name it. I told him biographies didn't interest me. He said—Come over all the same. I went. He started off politely enough; said there was also a column he had in mind. We want a responsible and recognized author to cover certain under-exposed events from a class analyst's angle. I asked what events. He said one of them was the Madhavgarh immolation riot. Fifty young men and women had set themselves alight; twelve had died. But that wasn't a caste issue at all, I said. It had to do with a labour complication in the carpet belt. He said—Never mind what you know; the six who died were Dalits. I said the issue for which they died wasn't a caste issue, and anyway the remaining six were a mixed lot. And the surviving forty-four? They were largely Dalits, he insisted. I said I knew for a fact that they weren't. You can't have a headline screaming, "Six Dalits Immolate Themselves" and suppress the thirty-four others. He began to laugh, and said—Ah, I've got you now. You're an upper-caste partisan after all. I retorted—What's upper-caste about citing the facts? Ah, but it's the particular facts a man chooses to cite that betray his affiliations, Mr Kumar, he sniggered. I said—You're a psychologist, Mr Katrak? Then you'd do well to read my earlier novels, all, without exception, citing facts to support the Dalit cause. So if you don't mind, about that column you proposed, I don't think you and I shall be able to see eye to eye, and biographies are not my line. He said—You're perfectly within your rights and I have faith in your astuteness, Mr Kumar, but I hope you'll reconsider. I said I'd get back to him in a few days. That's how we parted.'

'Did you get back to him?'

'Of course not. That matter rests. The biography hasn't been written, the column didn't find other takers. Somehow Katrak's offer and my reluctance became public—a literary rag carried an account. But meanwhile there's the Golden Lotus, funded by the Katrak Group. Okay, I've accepted it—and why shouldn't I? I turned down Katrak's offer as an independent individual, and it is as an independent individual that I've accepted the award. But try explaining that to Pragya—the opinion of others has always mattered too much to her.'

If he expected comment, he was disappointed. Buddhoo kept a guarded silence.

Back in his study, Sravan worked off his disturbance by rewriting a chapter. But a low hum crept into his room, like the distant surf-roar of traffic. 'It *can* be done. The portable automobile is practical, non-fuel, lightweight, collapsible canvas body, aluminium frame. Lift your car, pack it in a shoulder bag. A price low enough to beat the price wars. The Great Indian Dream come true. I resent this attitude: if a Japanese company does it, it's the rage; if yours truly announces it there's ridicule . . .'

Buddhoo shifted gears.

'Wah-re-wah, my little tomcat! Scratched the bloke's face with a razor, eh?'

'Ya.' A child's sullen voice. Sravan's eleven-year-old, Ashvin, was a snub-nosed kid with narrow eyes in an intent face, and a stubborn knot of muscle bunched between his eyebrows.

'What were you up to, yaar?' persisted Buddhoo.

'Murder,' was the crisp answer.

Buddhoo sounded impressed. 'Eh, shabash! How many murders you completed, bhai-jaan?'

'I've murdered him four times before,' announced the kid with pride.

'Satyanash! And has he managed to murder you yet?'

'Only once.'

'Anyone else murdered you so far?'

'Two small-small times. Rahul Gupta murdered me once,' admitted Ashu, voice lowered. 'He's a bania. And Sanjay Soni did it once. He's a Punjabi. But that was when I was so high.' A pause. 'They don't even try it now—I don't let them.'

'Wise.' Buddhoo approved of such prudence. 'But that business with the razor—your Ma was called to the school, you know—what were you murdering him for?'

'HQ said to.'

Buddhoo began to laugh. 'I see. Urgent message from Police Headquarters.'

' "Shoot to Kill," ' completed the kid.

'Okay, why did HQ order his killing? Had the guns landed by parachute on his farm? Was the bastard refusing to give them up?'

'No. He called me bloody motherfuck chootiya. So I told him to go bugger himself. He told Madam and Madam hit me—with a ruler—here.'

'Ah.'

'How did HQ's message come across?'

'Wireless.'

'Why not your mobile phone?'

'Top secret.' The kid had the fantasy completely ordered in his head.

'But have you got enough arms, brother? Bombs? Bullets?'

'Not yet,' confided Ashu. 'Rakesh Pandey—he's in the Senior Section—he's a Brahmin—he said he'd teach me after Diwali.'

'Teach you what?'

'How to make a bomb.'

'Arré baap ré!' Buddhoo gasped. 'But why after Diwali, yaar?'

The kid clicked impatiently at this display of adult obtuseness. 'Because we have to collect the fireworks powder from the park.'

Buddhoo uttered a low whistle. 'Have you made bombs before?'

'Once. Clinton, Rakesh Pandey and me.'

'Clinton!'

'Clinton Peters. He's in my class. He's a Christian.'

'He's actually called that? Arré baba! Yes. All the kids in the class followed him round the playground singing, "Monica, My Darling" and he cried and cried.'

'Stop! You're going too fast for me. Why did they sing "Monica, My Darling"?'

'Because of the blow job,' said the kid disinterestedly. A splutter from Buddhoo, who appeared to be choking. In a distinctly shaky voice Buddhoo asked, 'How did you know about that?'

'I saw it on the Clinton Web site,' said Ashu professionally. 'Shekhar Suman says Clinton wears purple underwear . . .'

'Shekhar who?'

'Movers and Shakers.'

Buddhoo's aplomb was plainly baffled.

'A postmodern Indian child,' he observed.

'Look here, yaar, anyone told you about Mr Bankim Nath Chakravarty?'

The kid perked up.

'No, tell.'

'Ha, the postmodern child wants a story as badly as the medieval one!' laughed Buddhoo. 'Okay. There was this crazy Bengali gentleman in Calcutta who went to the Eden Gardens to watch a cricket match.'

'Buddhoo Chacha, stop,' begged the kid. 'I'm pissy. I'll just piss and come.'

Buddhoo laughed. 'Do that. We'll keep Mr Chakravarty waiting till you return.'

A brief pause. The kid came scuttling back in a flurry. 'Buddhoo Chacha, come with me—I'm scared.'

'Scared? A mafia hood like you! What're you scared of? Okay, let's hoist you up.' Sravan heard the creak of a door, a squeak of hinges. He hoped the story wasn't going to continue in the corridor. He was keenly interested in the Bengali gentleman at Eden Gardens.

When the door squeaked open again, the story was far advanced. 'After fifty years, Sri Lanka made 251 runs for the loss of eight wickets. That year India had beaten Pakistan in the quarter-finals. You remember the crackers going *dhoom-dharam* in the night? And the rockets whooshing up? Fine. When Azharuddin won the toss and decided to field, Mr Bankim Nath Chakravarty was moved to strong emotion. Tears, poetry and song welled up in his soul . . .'

'What was his name?' asked the kid, thrilled but confused.

'His real name—the one his father and mother gave him—was Bankim Nath, though in those parts they call it Bong-Kim Nath. But Mr Chakravarty was an Englishman at heart. He loved cricket, he played the piano, he spoke a resounding English and he wrote nature poetry that began with lines like "Hail to Thee, Glorious Mother Mine" and "Tears Drop From Mine Gloaming Eyen." He encouraged his friends at the Calcutta Club to call him Bonkers or just Kim, and he began spelling his name *Chuckerverity* to accommodate his plummy mates. They started calling him Chuck. Finally he changed the name officially to Bunkum Not, and he was pleased that it even made some kind of sense.'

'What's it mean?'

'*Bunkum* means—you know—rubbish, faltu, nonsense, shit! *Not* means—well, you know what it means, so Bunkum Not means No Nonsense. Get it? So now he was being slapped on the back on the golf course at the Tolly Club and called "Bonkers, old chap!" Where was I? Ah yes, I was telling you how thrilled Mr Bunkum Not was when the match began. Especially as the Indian team was playing wonderfully. But then, he became a little worried. You see, the Sri Lankan batsmen played still better. They thrashed every Indian bowler in every corner of the pitch and piled up a huge score. And then . . . and then the pitch began to change. The dew. Only, the Indian batsmen didn't realize it then. Now the Indian score was 120 runs for eight wickets and Mr Bunkum Not was frantic. He couldn't stop himself—hopping mad he was. Like he felt when Subhash Bose disappeared, like he felt when he read the history of the partition of Bengal, like he felt when he heard of those mealy-mouthed east-country rustics pouring into his golden

Bengal and bagging all the coveted positions. He wanted to do something, either write a poem of passionate grief or tear his hair and scream. It was, unfortunately, not possible to write a poem in a crowded stadium on a muggy day, and when his hand closed on his plastic water bottle, he flung it with all his might into the field.'

The kid tittered.

'Well, that did it. Mr Bunkum Not had always dreamed of being a leader of men, a man whose slightest word and act could fire multitudes. And now he saw it happen. All at once he saw his fellow Calcuttans slinging bottles, papers, magazines, sunshades, even chairs on to the field. The police appeared with their lathis and cracked a few skulls and wrestled briskly with a few hundred maddened fans, but they could do nothing. Until the referee, Clive Lloyd, stopped the match and announced that if people didn't behave themselves immediately, the match would be stopped and Sri Lanka declared the winner. The public quietened down a bit, but again the flinging match began. By now burning paper was being thrown, too, and a fire broke out. Mr Chuckerverity was capering about the pitch when he suddenly noticed something funny—his bottom felt hot. It was smoking. Burning. "Gosh!" he cried, and "Good grief!" and "Bless my Soul!" and "Upon my word!" But when your bum's burning, smoking like the chimney of an Olde English cottage on a Christmas card, you need a fire brigade, not Victorian English. His dhoti was on fire!'

The kid shrieked. Sravan had the impression he was rolling and thrashing about on the mattress.

'Now, one thing Mr Bunkum Not hadn't abandoned when he turned sahib was his dress. He loved his dhotis. Light and airy—they allowed the breezes from the Bay of Bengal to sweep into his interiors. Nothing could induce him to give up his dhotis—except a fire. Mr Chuckerverity was appalled. To stand before the world in scorched, striped underwear—nay, he thought. Is it for this that I have spent the flower of my youth and the prime of my life writing nature poetry, reciting Burke and playing the piano? But there's no arguing with a fire, even in Victorian English. The long and short of it is that he had to go home without his dhoti, in his ripped and fretted underwear, and suffer the shame and sorrow of meeting one of his "Bonkers, old chap" friends from the Tolly Club on the way! And when all the Calcuttans sent a letter saying sorry to the Sri Lankan team, Mr Bunkum Not's name was among the thousands who signed. The neighbours laughed at him for weeks.'

'Oh, ya,' chuckled the kid, impressed.

'Now, have you heard of Purushottam, the Ambassador Dog?' continued Buddhoo, almost in the same breath.

'No!' cried the kid, panting with laughter.

'Then listen to this one. There was once a virtuous man named Purushottam, who ever strove to be righteous, who examined his conscience with tireless scruple and lived a life without taint or blame. Still, there came to him great suffering. Fed up with his lot, he fixed an appointment with God, met Him and said: If you don't mind my saying so, sir, there's something wrong with your system. Fatal error. Evil gets comfort, good is battered.

'God pondered a while. Said, "To tell you the truth, I too am vexed. It's a troubling thing—something wrong with the programming. The Evil One is the Arch Hacker. He's squeezed in a cosmic virus, and now there's something wrong with the hard disk of the world. My universe grows bigger and bigger, with every star racing away from every other star and every creature from every other creature."

'Till it'll all go bang!' interrupted the kid.

'Exactly,' said Buddhoo. 'God went on—"I'm now informed that there aren't any straight lines left, no *time*, and everything is both this and that and neither this nor that. My laws all seem to get reversed. It's a management problem. What's worse is that some men are such hypocrites. They come to me at my various camp offices laden with coconuts and milk and sweets and coins and pious assurances. How am I to distinguish the wolves from the lambs? I've been thinking of downsizing the world—I've done that before when things got unmanageable. If I could be sure of only one man . . ."

'To this the virtuous Purushottam said, "You can count on me, sir. Ever your devoted employee."

"Good," said God. "Then you, my friend, must assist me. If

you're indeed the righteous man you claim to be, you must prepare to suffer a little more for my sake.'

'Purushottam wasn't happy to hear this. "But haven't I already suffered enough?" he protested.

"Just this once," God pleaded gently. He'd just read a book on human-resource development and was now trying to get the most out of his creatures.

"If you say so, but what incentives, sir, if I may dare to ask?" Purushottam murmured.

"A speedy promotion—from dog direct to angel, superseding the entire human race in record time. By the time you're ready to retire into salvation, you can hope to be an archangel at the very least—a GM-level position."

'Purushottam bowed in humble assent. So God transformed him into an ugly, ailing dog, covered with running sores, crawling with ticks and fleas, stinking with the mange and carrying a crazy glint in his clouded eyes. "Go ye and watch men closely," are God's instructions. "Learn the names of those who spite and spurn you, those who despise and injure you. Learn the names of those who hurt not but look with abhorrence in their eye. Learn also the names of those who can't help you but look on you with compassion. And those who, in passing, toss a scrap or a morsel. You shall be my personnel man to test mankind."

'And so sits that sleepy dog, flicking away at the flies, awaiting promotion. He sends God detailed accounts. Writes confidential reports. He's known to the angels and spirits as the Ambassador.'

Buddhoo's tone changed swiftly to one of informal enquiry. 'Speaking of dogs, I saw you throwing stones at that lame brown dog by the colony gate. The sentry told me the other day that you lit a candle and burnt his whiskers.'

An embarrassed giggle. 'Sanjay Soni's idea. Actually we wanted to brand him for our ranch.'

'Eh? Why?'

'To tell others he's ours. For Diwali. To tie the crackers to his tail and blast them off.'

'And what d'you think he'll write in your report?' asked Buddhoo grimly. 'You'll probably be demoted—be born a snake or a pig in your next life. Better to adopt him without branding—feed him every day so that he sits waiting for you and gives you a toothpaste smile when he sees you.'

'What was the Ambassador's breed?' the kid wanted to know.

'Pariah. Cur.' Buddhoo ventured. 'No, that doesn't sound nice. Come to think of it, yaar, our native dogs have been shamefully neglected by zoology. We must give our street dogs a nice, Indian zoological name. Let me think—let's call them Margvasi hounds. Margvasi—get it? *Marg* means road, street, *vasi* means dweller, inhabitant, so Margvasi would mean . . .'

'Who lives on road,' said Ashu, pleased.

Buddhoo raised his eyes and saw Sravan standing at the door. Ashu slipped out.

Sravan entered and stretched himself out on Buddhoo's comfortable mattress. 'Quite a marathon yarn session.'

'You've been eavesdropping?'

'Your voice isn't exactly a whisper. Couldn't work all morning. Where the hell does this nonsense spring from?'

'Oh, just like that. Out of the juice of the moment,' said Buddhoo airily.

Later in the day, Sravan was still idly trying to figure out what Buddhoo had meant by 'juice'. Unless the fool meant *rasa*, he thought, and the idea slowly magnified in his head.

10

'The ladies decided to raffle me. Flattering, no? That'll give you an idea of my popularity. Some of it I owed to my sari-lending business, the rest to my dedicated service at the shop.'

'Selling what?'

'This was a brand-new concept. A high-brow shop.'

'Books?' asked a voice which Sravan recognized as that of his neighbour, Pawar.

'No. This was an argument shop.'

There was a moment's silence.

'Argument? For sale?'

'Ji han,' Buddhoo replied joyously. 'I'll tell you how it worked.'

'Where was this shop?'

'I'm coming to that. I was the shop. A walking shop. I sold the joy of argument as a sport. An abstract sort of commodity but quite the rage, as all my old customers still confirm. The Greeks would have appreciated it.'

'And they actually paid cash for it?'

'Bilkul! They paid and gladly. Those desirous of indulging would deposit a small sum of money, then argue with the proprietor. I had a sort of menu card of possible subjects, but I was perfectly willing to engage in any subject of the customer's choice. If the customer won, he got a refund plus a handsome percentage. If he lost, he forfeited the deposit. Onlookers were free to bet on the victory of either party. If the proprietor won, fine. He scooped up the moolah from several quarters.'

'What kind of questions were on your menu?' Sravan recognized the amused voice as that of Pawar's wife. Apparently Buddhoo's fame as a raconteur had spread outside the immediate family.

'All sorts. Great range and variety of choice. We catered to every sort of taste. There were classical philosophic questions like: How does the rope appear as a serpent? How many angels can stand on the head of a pin? Which came first, the lingum or the yoni? I had my own set of logic-breakers—Buddhoo's Indeterminate Questions, they came to be called. There were also funny questions like: Why, in Hindi grammar, are items of male dress feminine and items of female dress masculine? But one of the most perplexing questions I came across—a customer's idea—was Why is a rickshaw? Now, for heaven's sake, consider a question like that. Does it make sense to you? *Why is a rickshaw*? I'm proud to tell you that I won that round hands down, through sheer ingenuity and unstoppable bluster.'

'How?'

'I'll explain my technique. When a question boggles my mind, I usually look twice at the sound of the words, and a kind of half-witted sense sometimes emerges. Then the trick is to take the bull by the horns, speak very fast so as to confound the other fellow and get him to lose the thread. Use every method of distraction and bafflement at your command. Taking the offensive and adopting an offensive manner is one. You annoy your opponent into fallacies of reasoning. I repeated the question in great outrage—as though it was a silly, self-evident sort of thing worthy only of the greatest nincompoop.'

Suddenly Buddhoo began speaking in a stilted street-hawker's voice, a VJ's voice, a pontificating sadhu's voice. ' "Why is a rick sure? A rick is sure because it has three wheels, two for balance and one for support—which is more than can be said of you, who stand on two meagre legs. The third appendage, if in the ascendant, may achieve a tolerable stature and substance, but never shall be a support in respect of length or firmness. The fourth, the tail, dropped off in your simian past, and though you may bear a reliable likeness to the anthropoid ape, you have not the privilege of all its perks." I'm sorry to have to reproduce this argument uncensored in the presence of old ladies and small girls and I hope you'll pardon me, but it remains one of my record-breaking performances.'

The audience didn't object.

'And don't run away with the idea that it was a mug's game for the idle and irresponsible. No, sahib, it had lasting practical benefits. Honed your analytical powers, practised your speechifying, entertained you in a new way, built an intimate connection with another person (what's more intimate than a good, loud argument?), exhausted unpleasant combativeness, drained away pity and terror, in short made one an agreeable person to have around and conferred domestic peace and harmony to many stressed souls.'

'How?' chuckled Pragya.

'Simple. You attacked your opponent without pity, you lost your terror of defeat. But,' Buddhoo went on, 'there were difficulties. One, an insoluble argument led to a long waiting list. Two, when an argument proved invulnerable to solution, who won the cash? Lots of unpleasantness. Who was the referee? Nobody on the poor proprietor's side except the guys who'd betted on him. But, pitted against the guys who'd betted on his opponent, an explosive situation, believe me. Fists coming into violent contact with my collar. Three, even the meekest customer turned amazingly warlike when cash was involved. Result—the proprietor lost more cash than he earned. Therefore he closed shop. Finally, a cop came along and argued over the cut I owed him for the freedom to run a gambling business on the pavement. I reasoned that it wasn't gambling by any means, it was an intellectual sport—if you can have street plays, why the hell can't you have street debates?—but nobody can argue with a lathi. So that was it. My argument shop downed its shutters.'

Late that night Sravan cornered Buddhoo.

'So,' he challenged. 'You've been a sign painter, a fashion designer, a nameplate collector and conceived a psychospiritual text called *Eat and Excrete*. You've run a school, an animal restaurant and an argument shop. You've been in jail on charges of imposture.'

'You've forgotten the urinal-attendant stint,' reminded Buddhoo.

'That too, yes.'

'The one dream I haven't realized is being an effigy maker.'

'What?'

'See—lots of effigies are burnt daily. There's money in the thing. But no one's going into it systematically, with the right market sense. I'd like to make good, artistic effigies. Hire a cartoonist, maybe. What *is* an effigy? A three-dimensional cartoon, a voodoo object, a receptacle for popular wrath. I'd like to make protest visually pleasing, turn a useful art into a fine art. This'd be a true reflection of social reality, an authentic testimony of . . .'

'Which of these yarns has a single grain of truth in it?'

Buddhoo looked hard at him and began to laugh. 'Applied Mayavada, dear boy. Chapters from my *Mithya Sutra*.' He put on a lofty mantric voice. 'The mind clacks away by itself, O well beloved. Like a pair of birds upon a branch. Like a pair of knitting needles in the hands. It needs yarn, any sort will do—to knit with, the knit-wit (sorry for the pun)—you've got to keep the saala busy. Every life can support a book, there's content enough; all it needs is a chronology and a commentary, to decongest the head and expectorate the stuff. Know, O Shvetaketu, real stories and imagined ones are equal, see? There isn't a life at all, only a narrative, and thou art that.' He changed to a normal voice and added, 'The thing to remember is that it's all to be swept away with a broom, like rangoli on the floor. That's what the ojha fellow did. Cleared my head of the goblins, see?'

11

Half an hour of false starts. This had to be a personal letter, for God's sake! Preferably handwritten. The putting-things-right tone. Malini set store by such gestures. He'd drafted and redrafted but discovered, as he had sometimes done before, that personal letters were beyond him. Novels he could plot, poems he could craft, but personal letters, no. All his writing powers deserted him. How did one start? Dear Malini? Hullo Malini? Rubbish! Better to begin briskly with a simple—Malini, when do I see you next? Wrong somehow. Undignified and unsuitable. Too eager. He crossed it out. I look forward to seeing you soon? A summary, officious note in that one. He'd sometimes wondered if human contact was something he couldn't achieve through words. He could only hope for contact with the page. He put the half-scrawled letter aside. There was that speech to draft, too. No better than the letter.

Drafting this particular speech was proving far more complicated than Sravan had thought it would be. He found it hard to explain himself. The right tone wouldn't come. This speech had to be well whittled, with a subtle inlay of humility. Conviction. Concerned humanity. Something like: This award is made not merely to me as an individual artist but to my language, my people. (But would it be better not to sound quite so separatist?) I'm happy—but also embarrassed that others equal or superior to me have been overlooked. (But did that sound fake?) I dedicate this award to all anonymous and committed writers who've died unrequited. (Sounds fine but somehow phoney—I mean, abstract dedications are fine, but pocketing what they amount to makes it suspect. I'll be expected to donate something to some wretched cause or something, and there is no Hack Writers' Charity Foundation that I know of.) No, all this self-abnegation sounded out of character. He could just hear the press crow.

When he was alone in the flat, with his father snoring next door, Sravan sometimes stepped across the invisible border which divided his study from his father's territory. A curious, prohibited satisfaction. At complicated moments of expression, what he most wanted was to go to that room and sit by his sleeping father in a simplified relationship.

His personal paranoia sometimes reached such a pitch that a cry erupted in his head, his father's voice calling for help, piercing his sleep. And he couldn't bear to sit in a place where his father could see him. Deeply disturbing currents came through the air. He felt himself being studied with venom and mockery, and an iron clamp closed round his throat.

Now he stood above the old man, head crammed with angry confusions. His father slept with his slug-like eyes half open. They looked spectral, those faded eyes. Filmed over. Opaque bubbles filled with slime. Gone was the piercing glint. His waxen face puckered up in permanent distaste.

Sravan felt an old hurting twinge of compassion in spite of himself. Watching over his father's sleep, peering into the abysmal interiors of his murky plight, he experienced something of the man's isolation, and something of his own fascinated panic over the impending absence.

The silence thickened around them like a fog. The clock ticked. A runnel of terror cut across Sravan's thoughts. He didn't know *why* he wanted to pry into his father's sleep, what he hoped to tease out. Some guarded secret of that mean mind. Some redeeming vulnerability. A trace of mutuality. He was a timid thief. Hell, he thought, one day I'll probably look like that. Face scraped of flesh into a fretful mask. Scrawny cheeks sucked in, skin worn thin. Tangled veins trapped in a web beneath the sheer membrane. And that piqued look of insatiable discontent—a child that's howled itself to sleep. I won't be as pitiable as that!—he swore. I must write. But he also knew what became of the written word.

He remembered the unaddressed sheet of paper he had found in his mother's trunk long after her death—the trunk in which she kept her wedding saris, her bits and pieces of jewellery, her parents' letters, her small leather wallet of saved pocket money . . . The sheet was a detailed catalogue of every wrong and injury. It wasn't a diary, more of an inventory, a small testament to suffering. She too had needed words to ensure that her suffering wasn't lost. And when he had chanced upon it, he'd been relieved—it had muted his own guilt.

At the age of eleven he'd begun to resent his mother's disappearances behind the closed doors of her room, sometimes with his father and sometimes alone. He'd been vindictive—had rummaged in her cupboard and found a notebook of small poems. He'd carried it out, like the corpse of a deadly enemy, and flung it into the well in the yard. He still remembered this vividly. The fragment of his face telescoped in the sleek lens of the water. Sparks of light slithering along the surface. The little notebook had been sucked into the well's cold, black maw. And all his life he'd spent expiating, recovering those drowned words. She'd had nothing to fall back on except those. Discovering their loss, she'd flown about the house, her grieving face aflame, searching. Her doors were seldom bolted on the family again. And Pragya had done the same to him. He marvelled at the neatness of it.

The mind clacks away. Real stories and imagined ones are equal, see? There isn't a life, only a narrative. Goblins in the head. To be swept away, if one only knew how. Hard to exorcise a father's voice.

That voice—he knew each note in its scale, each octave of wrath, each tone and semitone of guile and strategy. Each juicy squeeze of malice on the syllables. Nawab Sahib is sleeping. Ah, lucky are they that can sleep in sloth. Sahib Bahadur is too busy writing—too busy for mean jobs. Do spare this garden your attentions, Nawab Sahib, and do something worthwhile with your time. By law, it's *my* house, Sahib Bahadur, not yours.

Those great knotted, knobbly hands. And the frozen shoulder Sravan had had to massage every evening for three months. Almost as soon as it was cured, the arm had dealt him a violent blow.

The eve of his Class Ten exam—summoned imperiously from his room, sent on a complicated errand. The plight to which that voice could reduce him by a single word, a look or a jibe. Wave on wave of bitter mortification, till, exhausted, he would fall asleep. Sometimes the voice chased him far into the interiors of sleep, calling him by name. Making him explode awake, strangled by his haste to rush. Still, after thirty years of conflict, so much residual poison.

Not just goblin voices in the head but impish optics in the archives of memory. His father at forty-five, in filthy pyjamas and a singlet. Scratching his armpits, planted on a divan in their small sitting room. Please, Babuji, my friends are coming. Well, what if they are? We'd like to sit here. Who stops you, laat sahib? If you would . . . What? Ordered out of my own sitting room? Are they coming to mark my examination scripts, eh? If you'd change your clothes . . . Listen here, laat sahib, I've every right to be as I wish and by law it's my house to live in as I please and no saala English-chewing lads can order the pants on to my backside if I settle against it. Sravan had kept his friends chatting at the gate for two *hours*.

Afterwards he'd rushed off to take part in a friendly four-letter-word–slinging contest between two hostels. It hadn't vented his rage. When he returned he found the house spick and span. His mother had cleaned it till it shone—that was *her* way of working off her rage. In time, every surface in the house gleamed. The neighbours exclaimed over its artistic care. His father finally gave his mother the attack that killed her. After stormy, head-bashing drama in which the old brute pounded his head with both fists, she'd fled into the bathroom. Her shits!—his father had always scoffed when she'd taken shelter there. When she emerged, she'd gone vague. Her eyes didn't move together. She went limp on the floor. When she died it was vengeance, not grief, that claimed Sravan. He sat for hours with his head on his desk, struggling with high-voltage bolts of rage that erupted in his head, tore down his throat. There was a sore, inflamed spot within him. His teeth gritted on muttered words. A muscle in his throat strained to its ultimate tearing screech until, unable to contain its ache, it pelted out its rage in a splurge of fierce, shamed tears. Another spasm seized him, and another, and another. Sometime in the small hours his hands, clawing the sides of his forearms, went limp and he lifted his head to find his notepad splattered.

And he remembered his mother's anxiety just after her operation. She was worried about the anaesthesia. Did I talk?—she kept asking. What did I say in my swoon? Did anyone hear me? He'd felt like telling her—Go on. Abuse all you like. It'll do your worn old heart a world of good. More than this bypass surgery. You can't surgically remove forty years. But he'd only reassured her—The nurses are lying, Ma. You were silent as the grave.

His father had deprived her of every moment of her spare time. All her life. She had only to sit down, savouring a quiet moment, and he sprang some fresh job on her. He was the poor, suffering patient, the perennial convalescent. Only by dying did she get away, bypass him in her own way. The old man created a weird physiology of his own, divorced from any known medical science. Days started with lengthy narrations—everyone compulsorily entertained with (a) an account of the previous night's dream, (b) possible meaning of the dream, (c) the recent misbehaviour of his kidney, heart, stomach and liver, (d) possible meaning of this misbehaviour. At the smallest sign of disbelief, the old man turned peevish, with the authority of one who had all the impunity of tragedy on his side. He spoke of each sickness with triumph. Was terrified at each symptom of recovery, relieved at each portent of illness. As if he confronted the world with a decrepit gloat—you can't hope to win against me. I shall extort your concern by the sheer force of my suffering. Even his self-engrossed silence was shrill with resentful charges.

Sravan forced himself to return to his study, direct his mind to the speech he had to draft.

I wrote because it fulfils a power motive, he admitted. But you didn't have to say that in a speech. He scribbled a few more trite lines. This is how the author reaches his public. The utility of these awards is publicity. They help to direct public choice, instruct the public in discernment of quality. Then abruptly he came face-to-face with an unexpected truth: he'd come up against the limits of his own personality. He had either to grow beyond them or stop what he was doing for good. And growth of this kind wasn't a simple vegetative thing. It wasn't to be simulated or chosen or commanded. It was to be purchased through error, adversity. He wondered what price he'd be called upon to pay, whether the terms of the deal would be worthwhile. He strolled unconsciously back to his father's sickroom. Caught himself toying with a guilty death fantasy. Doubtful if the two of us will ever fight to a finish; one of these days he'll die, and have the advantage of moral victory. Maybe it'll be a relief—but I'll probably never be free. He'll go on haunting me, all the burden of self-reproach my inheritance. Will I suffer some kind of creative inertia—seeing that his disturbing presence was the provocation I worked against—to spell myself out? Maybe his death shall enforce a new self-definition.

Sravan caught himself in the middle of his cold calculations and was shocked. And quite suddenly, as if jarred by the vibrations of destructive thoughts, the old man awoke. For a while his eyes didn't focus. They rested on Sravan, unblinking. Impenetrable. Then they began burning with their old animosity.

'It's you, is it?'

'Yes.'

'What're you doing here?'

The blood rushed to Sravan's face, drained away in recoil. He shrugged.

'Any problem?'

The old man lay seething in his bed and said nothing. Sravan, striding away, became sensible of the air, charged with captive rage. The nerves in his jangling head twanged like high-tension wires.

There was just one antechamber of self to seek asylum in—the empty page. That's where he could lock himself in and sit, snow-bound in an enclosed white space, rigorous lest any phrase or thought betray him, leaving no breach in the fortress wall. A world he fathered and dictated. Controlled, altered, rearranged.

He wrote—As for accountability, I've felt answerable only to one thing: the page. To rise above awards poses a major challenge to the artist. Some precious inwardness is always threatened. But I've tried to preserve the independence of my concerns and the privacy of my experience in defiance of every glaring exposure, mindful that it might destabilize my future work . . .

He stopped. Something had happened. A sound. A stir. It happened again. A feeble moan, then a quavering cry for help. It wasn't his old delusion—this was real. He sprang to his feet. Rushed to the door. Into the corridor. Was stopped by an intangible barrier. With his father awake, the consistency of the air between the two rooms changed. A stubborn reluctance had to be conquered. The old man's voice seemed to be coming from the loo.

'Arré bhai, Prabuddha! Kaun hai? Koi hai? Arré Pragya! Ashu? Rina-beti? Arré bhai, Shoma? Koi hai?'

With a pang Sravan noticed that his own name was missing.

The old man sat on the pot. Locked, knobbly knees, naked shanks, bamboo-pale thighs. Between them, like old clothes on a peg, his withered, shrivelled penis lapsed over the crumpled bag of his balls. He couldn't rise to his feet. He stretched out an imploring, hand, then drew back on seeing Sravan. Senile indignation suffused his mottled face.

He continued quavering in his high-strung voice. '*Arre bhai*, is everyone dead?' Slighted, Sravan moved to help him, but there was agitation enough in the old hand to shrug him off. A second later Buddhoo came bounding in, followed by Pragya. Together they heaved the old man to his feet, his knees cracking noisily, and Shoma fetched the walker.

'I told you never to move around without the walker!' scolded Pragya. 'Suppose you fell and fractured a hip? You might have called us!'

'A curse upon all you swine-born saalas!' the old man grumbled. 'To think I shouted and shouted and every haramzada in the house had turned deaf!'

Even the old man's unashamed nakedness was like an autocratic assumption of senile privilege.

'But was no one around?' asked Buddhoo, lifting the fretful old man on to the bed while Pragya dried his feet with a towel and wrapped a clean lungi round his waist.

'Not one haramzada beggar here!' Sravan turned grimly and strode back to the study.

And he found the right tone most amazingly. Those just-right words for a letter. No preamble, just—There's a Mukteshwar Barat film on at the Odeon. Saturday. You might be interested. Haven't seen you in a while. Ah, that was right. Staccato, telegraphic, sufficient. But there was still that unfinished speech. That's when he began to grasp why he stole into his sleeping father's room in times of retarded expression. It was the beleaguered feeling he sought, the anger. His natural element? No, he didn't enjoy it. More than anything, he wanted to rid himself of those goblins. Still, they fuelled his writing—creativity was conditional, for God's sake. I need my rage, he thought. Every moment of shored-up pain and the choice is suddenly stark before me: either peace or art, never both, mind, one or the other, no simple happiness for me. Or those around me, he realized with a shock. Can it be that I need to make them suffer, make myself suffer, to tune my mind to its accustomed pitch for speech?

12

No simple happiness for me, he thought. Doesn't agree with the constitution of my creativity. Now I understand why my best books emerged when my head was jammed with stress. Stretched to snapping under emotional duress. A humming bowstring. And when I was content, what came? Limp, non-functional pieces.

I understand why I scrubbed away at each syllable, my dead mother and I, straining from each an invoked, awaited glow. Had that killjoy, my father, not hounded us to it, nothing would have gleamed in my house, no sword would have flashed, no words ignited.

Which only makes Buddhoo's stupid stories more intriguing. An entirely different element at work there.

Let me watch the way my mind perversely prompts my relationships to flounder, until they turn into what? Potential reserves of unrest. And if I quit this writing, I might actually turn into a slack, peaceable being, free from this taxing pressure, this aching traction, which may well be, by default, happiness.

But, seriously, let me be clear about what I've opted for. Do I want that kind of happiness? If I discuss this thing with Buddhoo, he'll probably fish out of the cold storage of his undergraduate memory some perverted misquote like 'I'd rather be a pig satisfied than Socrates dissatisfied!' And tell me his pet tale of the Hindi-comprehension exam in which he was required to supply a title for the précis about Socrates drinking the hemlock and his thoughtful appellation for the piece, founded on sound and considered examination, was *Bewaqoof Sukrat*—Stupid Socrates.

Still, simple exuberance attracts me. Buddhoo's kind. Naïve, unsavvy. What I'm going to try doing is seriously study the stupid. Analysis and Systematic Study of Spontaneous Stories! Sounded like one of Buddhoo's projects—ASSSS! A humbling crash course in narrative.

Malini came, but not to the Odeon. She met him at a small café next door, one of their earlier joints. She came in carrying an issue of *The Script*. She pulled a chair and placed her bag and the magazine before her. Her eyes were jittery, unsettled.

'Hullo,' he said. 'Where'd you pick that up?'

'At a newsstand, naturally. I wanted an autograph of the celebrity. A souvenir.'

Uptight, he thought. He essayed a jest: 'The lovers' gallery, right?'

'Not exactly,' she answered. 'Historic documentary evidence of my place in literature.' She had a braided, multi-skeined voice. In anger it acquired a brassy clang.

'If you keep looking at me like that, with the cutlery so easily within reach, it might turn into a souvenir of the dead.'

She flipped the magazine open. Oh hell, a story of his! Translated. He was suddenly wary. There was something awkward coming.

She jabbed at the page. 'Autograph,' she insisted, threatening.

'Sure. Shall I sign in blood and chilli sauce?'

'Not here. Here.' She pointed to a paragraph. A few words caught his eye. In a flash he fathomed the mystery, and groaned inwardly. She saw him glance at the words. Her eyes narrowed to dark slits.

'Shall we have a little reading? Or, better, shall I read one of his choice passages to the maestro?'

She stood the magazine aslant against her leather bag and read:

I'm a cultured sort of person. I believe in looking after

> myself. And my home is my first priority. When I go visiting, I take in everything—the dust, the remains of cobwebs, the electric switches left grimy. I lift the carpet with my foot to see how much dust lies underneath. I examine cups and saucers closely, flowerpots left unpainted, dirt stains behind doors. I notice the rows of medicine bottles and jars, the torn silver foil of pill covers, the sticky outline of cough syrup on the tabletop. Yes, the soiled pillowcases, crumpled sheets. Her unwashed grey hair, telltale beneath the faded dye, parched hands. I say to her—You mustn't worry. If it's diagnosed early enough, it's curable. Everyone knows that. And yours is only in the second stage. But why haven't you put cold cream on your hands? They're looking so coarse. And your salwar isn't going with your kurta—what made you wear it?

When she was mad, she snapped off the ends of her sentences, as a seamstress might bite off the last bit of thread.

'Well?' she demanded.

'You're wrong—that's not you.'

'It is. You know that. So do I. Shall I tell you what I think? I think it's cheap to use your friends. To exploit everyone, anyone, anything for your rotten writing! You're faithful to nothing! Nobody! Nothing's personal. Nothing's precious. You're watching everyone like a hawk! How can one ever relax with you?'

She sprang to her feet. 'No, that film doesn't interest me.' She slapped the magazine down in front of him. Here, you can keep this! And by the way, it might interest you to know that I no longer need your patronizing promises. I've found a publisher.'

'That explains your present mood.'

She made her rebuttal a desperate retaliation. 'You've kept me waiting. I should never have believed any of your precious assurances.'

'Writing a novel isn't like having a quickie.' He spoke with deliberate offence in his tone. 'Besides, I give my support only to what I consider standard.'

He could see that this stung her. 'And who's the new broker

that's agreed to go pimping?'

She was trembling with fury. She looked ready to hit him. But she controlled herself. Spoke with effort. 'That isn't your business any more.'

His curiosity had got the better of his pretence at defiant apathy. 'And how, if I may ask, did you solicit him?'

Another two minutes of this and there'd be a disgusting scene. He half wished to avoid it and simultaneously itched to inflame it. Decided not to risk another affront.

'At Ranjana's—if you want to know.'

'You went over without telling me?'

'Do I understand that I have to seek your permission? I rang her up and asked for a copy of her poem. She invited me over. I told her of my book. She put me through to someone.' She clamped up, viciously enjoying his perturbation. 'Sorry to disappoint you, Sravan, but I can't discuss it until the deal's through. And after today . . .' Her voice trailed off. She rose abruptly, collected her bag and the magazine and stalked out with the air of someone who couldn't trust herself to remain composed any longer, her high heels clicking imperiously on the marble floor.

As usual, a scrap like that stimulated him. He went home and settled down to a nice spell of writing. His head unlocked, sped. He wrote late into the night.

A man given to cleaning things thoroughly—the yard, the old bedstead, the chest of drawers, the cook-house. Until his house is mirror-bright in its order and perfection. If there are buckets to be lined up, he lines them up along the bath-house wall with mathematical precision. If clothes hang upon the clothesline behind the house, he doesn't rest till he has arranged them in order of size, aligning corner to corner and sleeve to sleeve. He scrubs the old china cupboard, polishes the panes. Doors, tins of talcum and bottles of hair oil on the chest of drawers. Brass and silver dishes, the headboards and footboards of the canopied four-poster bed. Not a bedspread creased, not a

> chair out of position. People laugh at him. Is this a fitting occupation for the son of a landed gentleman?—they snicker. The second son of one of the first families in the pargana? The ferocity of Amalendu's cleaning increases as his marriage worsens. Until his little fling with the maid distracts him. She is fourteen years old. One day, as she sweeps the floor, he lifts her up and sets her on his knee, saying: Ah, you're as a little daughter to me, my child. She giggles, ticklish, as he presses her small breasts beneath the thin cotton of her dress, as he feels her up beneath her torn faded skirt, murmuring: You are my child. My own little girl!

Amalendu never achieves release from the strangling attraction–repulsion he feels for his wife. He soon loses interest in the little servant girl. It is only that devastating virago, his wife, Mondira, whom he desires—and with a murderous infatuation that slays her in his fantasies many times a day. On to the scene with Mihir.

> Amalendu cannot reckon up the expenses as he sits brooding beside the pond, absorbed in self-debate. A crucial financial dilemma. If he spends his savings on getting his wife treated, and if she happens to die, it will be a total loss for him. His savings are all he has. Conversely, if he invests in her recovery, will that improve things between them? That's when Mihir turns up, riding his bike down the road that curves like a sickle. One look at his wife's sister and Mihir is appalled. Do you want her to die?—he shouts in rage. And Amalendu wags his large, slow head and says—It will cost money, the hospital, the medicines, brother-in-law. Mihir's lip curls in derision. Then calculate the outlay, big-brother-in-law. The doctor, the medicines, the hospital, the bus fare. And if she dies?—asks Amalendu in a fascinated whisper. Then, don't forget the cost of the wood for the fire, the shroud, the gifts for the priest. His voice has softened to a low, menacing snarl. Consider both, big brother. Maybe the hospital shall prove

cheap for you. Not waiting for Amalendu's answer, he turns and strides back into Mondira's room. She lies, wan and listless. Her eyes snatch at Mihir's bronzed face, flushed with princely rage. Come on, Baudi, he announces. You shall go to the Panduba Civil Hospital. Damn your skinflint husband, I say! It is then that he grows conscious of her strange, searing eyes upon his face . . .

And so one thing leads to another, and a month later they come to toy with one another in the cowshed. To know her, to grow bolder, to steal into her courtyard at night, to ease open the door of the cowshed in the small hours. There is nothing he regrets, nothing he wouldn't lie about ten times over. To Devyani, who never dreams; to Amalendu, whom he despises. He lives in a frenzy of arousal every hour of the day. Ah, Mondira! His tongue traces the salt taste of her again against his teeth. The bounce of her breasts redolent with some intense fleshly juice, and their tightly pliant persistence against his palms. He remembers the delicate dimple at the side of her buttock, the petals of her dainty vulva. This was obsession—to remember a woman and find his tongue irresistibly exploring her remembered hollows, to find his nerves preserving the texture of her physical impress, his skin miming her touch, his nostrils full of the musk of her armpits. To find his mind returning in secret relish to the theme of her, appeasing itself with thoughts of her. To turn over in his mind some whispered quip of hers, and, smiling to himself, imagine what he might have answered but didn't. To put away his own thoughts because her voice keeps breaking in . . .

Sravan stopped writing. Rose from his desk and lit a cigarette before the open window overlooking the park. He found himself quietened with a vast, achieved blessedness. Buoyed up in a soft elation. As though he'd vented an unrealized lust of his own upon the page. As though he'd actually *written* that letter to Malini (and to all the others before her). So much that he wanted to tell others was in his books—oblique, no more his own. Surrendered to the pages that dumbly received the letters he never wrote, the confessions he was too proud to make, the apologies he was ashamed to utter. He shook them off his life, renouncing his claim, consigning them to literature's common reserve for anyone who cared to pick them up.

He returned to his chair and sat, thinking. The mellow contralto of Malini's voice declaring—My liberation is tempered with deliberation, Sravan. Or—When I buy shoes, they've got to be car-specific, brake-sensitive, clutch-friendly and stride-effective. Or—While my husband's drawing up the balance sheets in his office, I'm drawing up the balance sheets of my life. Or—at my age I've crow's feet, laugh lines, a philosopher's frown and five strands of grey eminence. And I'm enjoying it all. Why?—he'd asked. It's the receipt life's given me—for all the years I've invested—this positive feeling about myself. Her voice, starting in a slow drip and gathering force until the words fall in a rich downpour. Her laughter, built of gleaming soap bubbles . . .

He'd never courted her with words. He'd sent her, soon after they first met, a card he'd personally designed and photographed. An open book of erotic verse, with the print faintly legible. A rose against the edge and a feathered stylus. It'd caught her fancy. In those days they hadn't quarrelled over trifles.

He looked at his watch. Almost one a.m. He heard low voices in the sickroom next door. Movements. The light was switched on. In the stillness of the night the words carried easily. His father's apologetic mutter—I'm very sorry about this, beta, I can't hold it back. The tinny knock of the bedpan in the bathroom and a tap running. Buddhoo's voice—No problem. His father's—That's the fourth time tonight. I'm keeping you from your sleep. And Buddhoo—Arré, Babuji, not to worry. I sleep and dream serially. You're like the ad in the middle of the episode. *No problem*. He mimicked the Japanese voice, laughed. The bedpan clanged against the bathroom floor again. The tap stopped running. The lights went out. A long silence tucked itself about the house.

13

Pragya, like Sravan's mother, wrote poetry. For her own satisfaction, as she laughingly claimed. Your writing's part of your public existence, she'd quip, but mine is strictly private. In Buddhoo she seemed to have found a sympathetic audience and, wonder of wonders, was now reading aloud. Some of the words wafted over to the study. This one appeared to be written in ghazal form. Urdu-Hindi, which Sravan contemptuously dismissed as a mongrel mode.

Pragya's perennial subject—love:

Of the black-haired one with the silken eyes
Give me the truth, beloved.
I would not be gulled, give me no lies,
The truth want I.
I could not bear a lie.

She paused for appreciation, which Buddhoo noisily provided.

Of the white-cheeked one with the eyes of fire,
Tell me no truth, its lies I desire.
No, give me but lies, beguiling and fair,
Give me no truth,
Just lies that may soothe,
Lies need I, the truth I cannot bear.

'Great!' cried Buddhoo. 'But is this a single poem? Two opposite ideas?'

'I don't know,' said Pragya. 'They're two sides of one feeling, I guess.'

Pragya no longer showed Sravan what she wrote. Sometimes, tucked into a bunch of laundry or shopping lists, he came upon a strange paragraph. A sketchy diagram of her mood in a clutch of garbled lines. Something like:

> 1 double bedcover
> 3 towels
> 6 pillowcases
> 2 nighties

And then:

> 1 Vim
> 1 kitchen scrubber
> 1 Surf Excel
> 1 Nescafe – 100 gms
> Pears Face Wash
> 1 carton Nutrinuggets
> 4 packets chow
> 1 Carefree
> Chericof cough syrup
> 2 kgs, Rajma

And quite suddenly, out of the blue:

> Oh, give me such love for a day, beloved,
> That years to come my days be filled.
> No, give me no love if it's but for a day
> If the rest of my days bereft I shall stay.

A typical Pragya verse, that. Ambiguity, contradiction, neither this nor that, both or none, and everything cancelled out to its present nullity. Maybe we've cancelled one another out by now, he thought, and we stay together because it's too much of an effort to actually break away and rebuild elsewhere. Especially without knowing whether the other options won't be just as barren, or worse than the present one. Ha, the enduring Indian marriage, that much-touted institution. This boredom with Pragya may well be boredom with myself.

Once, when he was away on a research trip to Shimla she sent him by post a long thread of silver hair.

My first grey hair, she wrote. *May I dedicate it to you?*

She played a lot of psychological games, this Pragya. Poetic and desperate gestures, reminding him continually of her claim on him. Just after their wedding, when she had come home to his parents' house and relatives sat them down to play the ceremonial game of 'hunt the silver rupee' in the large brass platter of water, Pragya refused to win. She let him grab the silver rupee each time, and told him later—See, I've chosen to lose each game to you. It left him a little bit ashamed of having grabbed the coin without noticing her gesture. Oh, she knew how to weigh down a man with shame. Now they played complicated, hurtful games all the time, Pragya often winning hands down.

Her poignant, stinging letters. Copious communications in a steady barrage. *I congratulate you, Sravan. You've found love many times in life. But I lost it the only time I found it.* He found this sort of thing immensely irritating, particularly that favourite word—love! Overworked to death in her head. Some years back he'd written serious replies, poetry for poetry, tragedy for tragedy. Two could play that game. Things like: *You're the lucky one, Pragya. You were privileged to experience life and love. I only got to write about them.* But he had no time for that sort of correspondence now. He only felt like shouting—Come off it. Climb down, and none of your heroics!

He shrugged Pragya and her poem off his mind and considered the scene at hand. The sequence in which Devyani kills herself wasn't the next one serially, but it was pressing so hard on his mind that it was better to have it off his chest. Clear a space for other scenes. Might even unlock his brain on the journalist and inspector sequences.

Devyani is slow, and large with child. She speaks even less than she did before. Eats little. While she knows the ravenous hunger pangs of the pregnant woman, she tells no one. In the afternoons she sleeps, listless, on a mat on the stone floor. As though God put her to sleep while He worked on her.

She is roused from her sleep by confused cries in the courtyard. The groan of cartwheels. Shouts. Battering on a door. A woman's piercing shriek. A platter clanging to the floor. And then a man's guttural oath. The sound of racing feet on the stone cobbles of the yard. Through the half-open door Devyani sees Mondira and Mihir clamber up the stairs in a frantic rush. Amalendu follows. In a matter of seconds, she sees her sister turn and deal Amalendu a swift, expert push, sees Amalendu lose his balance, stagger, take a backward sprawl. Sees her sister thrust her own husband into the room, then herself, and bar the door. Leaving Amalendu at the mercy of the killers.

By the time Devyani can haul herself to her feet and reach the window, Amalendu lies in a pool of blood and a horde of bearded men in checked lungis and singlets tower above him with hatchets and butcher knives clenched in their fists. Cowering against the wall, incoherent with panic, are Mondira and Mihir. Outside, kneeling in tearful supplication, are their old servants, Qadir and Hasina.

'Spare our masters, men of the faith, spare our masters. They have been good to us, they and their fathers. They mean no ill. Be merciful, O men of faith!'

The killers' eyes are narrowed slits of impersonal venom. Amalendu is bleeding to death on the ground. The blood snakes across the courtyard towards the cook-house drain. Mondira staggers, hugging the wall behind her with a stifled sob. The stream of blood courses, sinuous, across the yard.

'We shall be here again tomorrow,' threaten the bearded men.

Flight. Is there time to cremate Amalendu? Not likely. Mondira stands above her husband's corpse with an impenetrable face, then glances across at Mihir, who stands, face working in spasms.

It is their old Muslim servants who arrange the cart. Who load the scanty bundles, the few pots and pans, and lift Devyani across the rear.

'Come, Bau-ma. Lie down so.' Hasina gives her a bag of gram and a cone of fluffed rice, a lump of jaggery.

The cart has to be abandoned. I've got to arrange events that way, thought Sravan. Easily done. An axle broken. A dead horse. Or, better, a stampede. The downrush of a manic mob. A frenzied race for life, leaving cart and horse behind.

Devyani stumbles off the cart, into an orchard and down a ditch, then sinks in a tired heap among the rotting leaves. The child kicks in her belly. She is alone. She crouches in the ditch till darkness falls, then creeps out and makes her way to a well. She remembers her sister's words: 'If we're forced to flee, if we're all separated, go to the nearest village well at night. We'll return to it. We'll come looking for you.'

The hours pass. A sinister, congested monsoon night, the air swollen with damp and dread. Far away, on the highway, vultures gather in small groups, fluttering wide, funereal wings. On every gust of wind is the stench of what they devour. The hours of the night pass. Then the entire day. The village abandoned. Weak with hunger, Devyani crouches on the ground against the brick wall of the well. No one comes for her. She wonders if they're alive. She wonders if they've managed to get away. Then she asks herself whether they got away singly or together.

Before she plunges into the well, she glimpses a fragment of her face telescoped in the sleek lens of the water. Featureless, too far away. Sparks of light slither across the surface. She takes a deep breath, plummets headlong in, slams into her own palpitating image. A crash, and the black mirror smashes around her, the shards fly, the spitfire brew bounds mountain-high around her, seizes her, sucks her down. She gasps for air. A faded cry. She fights it, clutches at it, spews it out, but it slips out of her grasp, it drains into her lungs, floods her brain. She rises once to the surface, coughing, to claw at the slimy wall. Thrashing in panic, the deafening hoofs of water drumming in her ears, she is dragged into its cold, black, snaky maw.

Sravan collapsed into himself, drained. That scene had lain dense and heavy on his heart for weeks, like a threat commanding a reckoning. He had given it all he was capable of, and now an unearthly fatigue gripped him. A dehydration of soul. Devyani's death was enough to squeeze his throat to aching. And he was hungry. Ravenous. The frantic hunger of a man who's just past his ordeal.

He walked into the dining room to raid the fridge. Found Pragya whipping batter in a bowl. She looked up, enquiring.

'Famished,' he explained.

She rose, opened a cupboard, produced a tin of something and put it on the table. 'There're some *dhoklas* left over, too.'

'Why don't I take you out for dinner tonight?' he asked.

'Why not?' She caught his eye and laughed aloud.

At its best, Sravan's marriage was a careful matter of small charities and big diplomacies.

'But I'm sorry to disappoint you,' she went on. 'I've got to do some shopping and visit Chand Mian, my tailor. Some new designs I've sent him for the next exhibition. I want to see how they've turned out.'

'So? Do your shopping and the rest, and dine with me later. I've got to see Farooqui about something, but I should be free at eight.'

'Tell you what,' she suggested. 'I'll drive down and finish my work and come down straight to the Piazza. You can come down separately.' Then she added, flushing, 'Thanks, Sravan. I didn't think you'd remember it.'

Hell, it must be one of her endless symbolic anniversaries. She had so many of those—first date, first award, first present, first tiff. He wondered what this one was, and kept his face suitably enthused.

He was at the Piazza at a quarter to eight. No sign of her. He consulted his watch, felt curiously uneasy. For some incomprehensible reason he was morbidly worried about Pragya. The market was closing, so what the fuck was she up to? Pragya was a lousy driver. A traffic hazard, he called her. A lurch here, a lunge there, a reckless swerving overtake. Anything was possible with her at the wheel. And when she went lane-surfing, the bitch, and when she braked as though she was giving a mobike a kick, and when he tried telling her, it was—Now who's doing the back-seat driving, dear Sravan? Shall I quote you to yourself, dear Sravan? He cursed her, more anxious and incensed than he understood. If she turned up now, the evening would probably start with a quarrel. There must be something seriously wrong with me, with us both, he thought bitterly. Things inevitably go wrong, even when I try to make them right on the page.

Impulsively, he decided to buy her a gift. Just a small something for her wretched commemoration of some miserable memory. He walked along a row of shops, looking in at the windows.

When he returned to the Piazza, his gift in his pocket, she was standing in a huff. 'Another ten minutes and I'd have gone home,' she said drily. 'I've been standing here like an idiot for half an hour. The doorman kept wondering what my story was.'

'Oh, come on, you could've waited for me indoors. And anyway, you look too old to be a tart.' Sravan recognized his own habitually hurtful voice. He had to be on his guard; at the slightest sign of softening in his tone, she usually overpowered the situation.

By the time they had made their way into the restaurant and found a table, a nasty strain had lodged itself in the air. Troubling and potentially explosive. That rash, black humour throwing up tiny acid gibes in his head, each a finely crafted insult. 'Sometimes I think you practise offensive dialogue with me,' Pragya had once said.

This was hardly a suitable time to produce his gift. The thing would seem off-key. Thaw the dignity of his constraint and inflate her self-righteousness.

Look at her, the little dart fluttered in his head. Someone ought to put a label on her—Combustible. Handle with care. Store away from heat and light.

He sometimes felt that some powerful negative expectancy of hers had urged his life away from her. Now he caught the glitter of furious tears in her eyes and groaned inwardly. Pragya often worked herself up to a pitch of exhibitionistic emotion in public places.

'What's up now?' he hissed. 'What're you turning on the water works for?'

'I'm not!' she spat out in a savage whisper. 'No, don't look at me—*please*.'

'Everyone here soon will,' he said wryly.

'No, it's only you who notices these things—you're that critical of me!'

'What've I done now?' he sighed in exaggerated injury.

'If you don't know, you don't know. Just don't scrutinize me that way. Give me a minute. I'm just . . . throwing this misery off. It's got to spend itself . . . like vomit . . .'

What a lovely word to kill your appetite, he reflected wearily.

She bowed her head. Her voice was misshapen, but her words were always precise. Pragya had perfected this bitter poise, and she used it in the most stagily awkward moments.

He hazarded a remark to restore peace, but at the first false note she drew herself up in her chair and mocked him.

'Is it possible that you're taking a romantic interest in me tonight?' she asked.

'Am I wasting my time?'

'Absolutely.' She waved her hand upon a non-existent swirl of smoke. Really, he thought, we're the most abnormal couple in this place tonight. He decided to try again.

'But aren't we celebrating something? A romantic memory, right? So for old times' sake . . .' Now, what the hell *was* the memory?

At that she suddenly relaxed, essayed a watery smile. Took out a book from her bag. One of his earliest novels. She opened to the title page and turned it round for him to see. Suddenly he remembered what it was. That first drive.

An overcast August evening. The sky had sparked, blown a fuse. The windscreen of the old Ambassador had prickled with sudden rain. In a moment the street had been crêped in silver foil. Gathering and dissolving under the swathes of the wiper. Rain had lanced down on the bonnet, made an uproar on the hood. When she'd offered him his book, it had seemed a simple thing to scribble those words on the title page. He now reconsidered his spare handwriting, the faded ink, with some surprise. Wondered if the coldness lodged in him was just the complication of some of those initial simplicities.

To Pragya, my ultimate reader. He'd meant it, too. She was then that just-right being, the ideal receptivity. *To Pragya, my ultimate reader, for whom I put in my finest shades, sure that they'll be noticed and treasured, the way I want them to be. In whom my words might grow to touch their richest bounty of meaning.*

I didn't know you but I identified you—instantly, he'd told her that day in the car, in the rain. I'm grateful and relieved that you *are*. Believe me, you do me a favour by just existing in the same world and time as me. It might so easily have been my bad luck to miss you by a century or a city.

They'd met at a music conference two months before. He and Pragya had both dabbled in Indian classical music in those days.

It's the first time I've actually met a writer, she'd said. Oh, I'm quite normal, really, he'd laughed. He was young, already famous. Sure of himself. Shall I tell you what I do to young women who pay me fake compliments?—he'd flirted. No, what? She was simply and expensively dressed in pearly silk. I pick up my pen—like this—and I autograph their beautiful silk saris. Like this. I'd love that she'd said, cool and exotic. Graciously she'd turned round on her high-heeled sandals and presented him, with a dancer's flourish, a shapely, silk-draped shoulder. He'd taken his autograph Mont Blanc and signed his name on the splendid silk. She had then rearranged the drape of the palloo, carefully varying its fluid fall so that the signature sloped across her left forearm, or clung to her neck, or rested like a luscious stroke across her breast. She didn't care what people thought. She'd flaunted it all evening and he had caught each one of its several signals. Subtle and sensuous. It was that quality of indecipherability about her—he had found her psychologically challenging. Once they were married, he had, on her insistence, autographed her naked body scores of times in one of their early bedroom games. Best signing spree of my life, he'd told her. Nothing like signing your name on a woman's body. As though I have authored you. That's why you're just so—exactly the way I want. But he had also vaguely resented the fact that it was probably for his signature that she treasured him.

What annoyed him now was Pragya's insistence on his total regard. Like an imposition of will it had irked him into permanent rebellion. She had no right to claim this exacting lifelong devotion. There were days when he found it hard even to be polite to her. He found her loud-voiced, didactic, cocksure, mawkish, unpleasantly insinuating. And every word or gesture was an implicit appeal or command for his admiration, which he honestly did not feel. He felt no connection with the man who, years back, had found her overpoweringly attractive.

During the first few weeks of their marriage she used to sit sentinel over his sleep. After hectic sex he'd plunge into mindless slumber, only to wake up with a start in the middle of the night and find her propped up on an elbow, gazing fixedly at him. It was uncanny. When they slept and he, always self-enclosed, appeared to take leave of her and turn away to the wall, she protested, insisted that even in sleep he should lie facing her. Nothing should take him away from her, not even sleep. But his side ached. She kept watch over his sleep, and the softness that filled him turned slowly to unease. She wouldn't let him get away; she cherished him too much. Over the years, he was to realize the horror of this exacting love and the stress of being an overvalued person.

He'd tried telling her. That there was a last lap of self that jealously guarded its privacy. That after every spell of intense contact, he wanted her to move away discreetly, allowing him his space. But she felt threatened by a mysterious peril. She wanted to speak, share, question, confide, explain until she choked him under the weight of a constant and unremitting invasion. And the closer she drew, the more uncertain and resentful she turned, the more frantic her gropings—as though she sensed his determined refusal to cede himself exclusively to her. Honestly, he reflected, she'd always been a borderline case but now she acted plain crazy. There seemed no way out except to keep her at bay. By not answering her questions. By not acknowledging her presence. By curt, monosyllabic replies. And when necessary, by rebuffs. It had become second nature to him. Between the two of them, his father and Pragya, they'd managed to foist on him a whole new personality.

Now she shrank from the glint in his eye, the unrelaxing immobility of his jaw. His unpleasantness had gone up as his desire for her had declined, until it was replaced by another desire—to lash, to make her cringe. He deplored her emotional grovelling and gushing, her cloying pride in him, her reeling chatter. He'd learnt the useful skill of slamming shut his mind and going reckless with his speech, but Pragya, with the door slammed in her face, wouldn't accept this. She insisted on knocking, scraping, hammering, seeking admittance, and it drove him up the wall.

And here she was at it again.

'Okay,' she was saying. 'Granted, this isn't your idea of a relationship. Point taken. We're that much older. Every decade of life's got its own definitions. But let me tell you mine. Sometimes I try to guess why I'm feeling seedy. Is it my BP? Indigestion? A pain in my joints? Low blood sugar? Nervous irritability? Menopause? Then you return—and I snap back to normal. Then I know it's just your absence.'

She looked at him hopefully. Sravan listened, his face impassive. She went on: 'When I'm alone, watching TV, and there's a good film, I want to share it with you. Instantly. A good sentence in a book. Or a snatch of music. I . . . I feel defrauded of the completeness of my own pleasure . . . when you're not around.'

He still chose not to react.

'But you haven't been around for years, Sravan. D'you know? There's a man I'm missing deeply—for fifteen years now.' She paused dramatically. 'He doesn't exist anywhere . . . you're the nearest approximation, and yet so different from him.'

Her eyes grew compulsive. Got to say something, he thought. Anything except the real thing. Anything but that old question between them. *Why did you do it?* He considered her in silence. He knew the thought was in her mind as well. They'd gone through that matter so often, there was nothing left to charge or to defend. The destroyed book blocked the space between them for good.

'Bit involved, that,' he observed cautiously. Listening to her, his instinctive reaction was—Bullshit! Why's she always trying to compose this relationship, as she's so fond of calling it? Like she's writing an interior novel about us. I feel as though I'm being made to act out an unnatural part, dressed in a ridiculous costume? Why does she want to organize us round ideal lines of her own fantasy? But was she reading his mind? They did seem to read one another's thoughts sometimes.

'I wonder,' Pragya mused, 'if all my fantasies are someone else's reality.'

'You've not shared your fantasies with me. Not lately.'

'Oh, they aren't much. Nothing original or special. Rather gross, actually.'

'I'm always interested in the gross,' he assured her, smiling crookedly.

'But I'm not too ambitious, Sravan. There's this silly romantic dream—a tryst—wine—confidences to share—moods, terrors, childhoods. So commonplace, no?'

'How boring. Is that all your grossness consists of?' he pulled her leg.

She flushed. 'No. Much more, actually. But let me get the atmosphere right. Okay, where should all this be?'

'A shikara on Dal Lake? Or the Udaipur palace?' he laughed.

'No, an ordinary room'd suit me fine.'

'Indoor location? I begin to see.'

'Exactly.' She produced her old, sudden smile. It took him by surprise, stirred him with an unforeseen pain.

'Actually, it's all hopeless, Sravan, so far as I'm concerned. I'm so disappointed—as you must be.'

'Hold it. What's this?'

'Let me spell it out. Things aren't right with me. No, really. I hurt inside. My mind wanders. My muscles strain towards a peak I can't climb any more. It must be bad for you, too.' She looked at him intensely.

'I don't know about that,' he said. 'You're pretty reliably orgasmic—assuming you're not acting.'

'But I've got to work hard—with my mind—see? I've got to concentrate on a bunch of powerful turn-on images. Words.'

He was genuinely intrigued.

'What I'm trying to tell you, Sravan, is that it isn't a nervous or muscular matter. I've been waiting for a master fantasy that'll set me off—launch me, sort of—but there isn't one. I've been waiting for a real person and there isn't one. And there's this tiredness that won't go.'

She'd put it well in her fumbling way.

'You could write a poem on this sort of thing,' he teased her. 'Call it "Mid-life Blues".'

She was incensed. 'Write? Why should I?'

'But you do write poems. This'd be better than the whatzit one with the silken eyes . . .'

She eyed him, suspicious. 'Are you making fun of me?'

'No, but don't you often scribble things?'

'Yes,' she conceded grudgingly. 'All that's part of my emotional management. When I'm miserable I make something out of it—so it's not wasted. Like using yesterday's mashed potatoes for today's cutlets. Never liked throwing used feelings away.' She was laughing now. So was he.

'Always a good housewife. So you could use today's confessions for tomorrow's custard.'

'Oh, you! Everything needn't be usable and marketable that way. I'm not like you,' she retorted. 'You look at everything so bloody . . . managerially.' He was glad the evening was going to be a success after all.

'But coming back to my ideal fantasy, I happen to know yours.' She smiled. He shrugged. 'I know you need to think of her. You-know-who. Even when we're at it. Especially when we're at it. I know that's all there is to it. Nothing more. You only think of her. But I don't even have that. Well, there is something. A tiny leftover bit. Sravan . . .' She looked solemnly at him. He was still reeling with the shock that Pragya really did not know! 'I must tell you—I've been unfaithful to you rather often.'

Shock upon shock. He almost spluttered over his food. He put down his spoon and stared. She was smiling blandly. Enjoying herself. Could all this be one of her subtle acts?

'Why don't you believe me?' she giggled. 'I'm insulted, Sravan. Do I look so chronically moral that I might as well be dead? It's true. There's something I've never told you, and I might as well now.'

'I'm pining to hear,' he said in affected amusement but his voice had a false note he couldn't conceal.

She took her time spooning up her biryani, daintily sopping her gravy as though her plate were a canvas she was thoughtfully painting. He was surer now that she was playing one of her games again.

'When I was in college, Sravan,' she began speaking meditatively, 'a stranger wrote hundreds of letters to me. In Bengali, alas, which I couldn't read. He wrote reams. I still don't know which guy it was. Someone in the boys' hostel opposite ours. I kept all the letters, and one day I got one of my friends to translate some. Oh God, Sravan, those letters! They were bombshells! He'd poured out his poetry, his misery, his erotic longings for me—they were just too much!'

'And you never actually saw the person who wrote them?'

'No, honest. He was under the mistaken belief that I knew him by sight and that I knew Bengali. I don't know what gave him the idea. He probably felt more comfortable writing in his own language. We passed out of college and I burnt up those letters. Sometimes now, Sravan, when I'm getting on in years, I think of those words and they're a real turn-on. I let those words loose in my head when you and I . . .'

'Pornography, in other words.'

'No, charged with quality feelings. Literature,' she insisted. 'That's what old, faded words can do.'

'Now I know why you're partial to writers,' he said. 'So what would you like me to do? Recite my steamiest passages for you?'

She laughed heartily. 'You could try. Words have greater variety than the stupid body, you know.'

When Pragya discovered the little felt purse with the Hyderabad pearls in the pocket of his trousers, crumpled away in the laundry bag, there was a big scene. Pragya jumped to her own conclusions. Classically comic. Iago's handkerchief! Why didn't you give it to me first thing last evening, then? And I really opened out with you! After so long! Oh, Sravan. He gritted his teeth. *Oh, Sravan*!

If you'd really got them for me, you'd have given them to me then . . . when I opened my heart to you! Opened her heart, fuck-all! Just open that window first, he said. She did. Striding up to it, he hurled the pearls out. They landed in a slushy flowerbed in the park. And Pragya let out a shriek. She rushed out of the study and Sravan heard her race down the stairs. In a couple of minutes she was back, her face blotched with tears and mud. Like the pearls she carried in her hand. Every bead caked in wet earth. She came up to him, sniffling, and handed them to him. Put them on me, she sobbed. They're filthy. Wash them, he said. No, just as they are. Now. He shrugged. She turned and he unfastened the clasp, mucking up his fingertips, and gingerly put the string round her neck. She turned round to look at him and she looked a fright. Her face and neck were streaked with dirt, and the muddy pearls looked weird—like nicotined teeth closed round her neck, he thought with a shudder. And that pearl necklace was called a choker! Oh, God! She came closer and whispered—Thank you, Sravan. And he started with sorrow and aversion at the sight of those filthied pearls. They looked as though they'd lain for months in the depths of a well.

She was picking up his thoughts again in that sinister way she had. All's well now, Sravan, isn't it?—she whispered, moist-eyed. It's all ended well, hasn't it? Say it's all ended well, please. Until he gritted his teeth and hissed, 'Yes.'

14

The chapter sped across the page with Sravan panting after.

Mondira calls out, hammers on the door with both her fists, but no sound comes from within. She goes round the back, tries the windows and the rear door to the courtyard but finds them barred from within. She comes back, strikes at the door with all her strength. The heavy black door groans at its iron chain but will not give. A queer look comes on to her face. Fear and fascination at an unuttered possibility. A forbidden hope, unseemly in her face. If he were lying dead within . . .

Then come the farmhands with ladders and logs. Battering at the door is no good. A boy hoists himself up the notched courtyard wall and edges across the narrow ledge to the upper terrace. Disappears into the chamber and appears, the next moment, on the trellised balcony.

'In here, Bau-ma!' he calls.

The question shapes itself on her ashen face. 'Alive?'

'Sleeping the poppy slumber,' calls the boy timidly. A riot of farmhands' throaty laughter.

Mondira's face is aflame. With a deep oath, she turns on her heel and strides away, squelching across paddy field and palm clump and banana thicket and bamboo forest. Striding across the rotting bridge between the twin ponds and into Mihir's estate . . . She returns home after a month. She is with child. The pangs of hunger knife at her, but she does not touch the handful of rice and lump of jaggery that her skinflint husband leaves for her on the mat. He keeps the keys now and lives on rice and jaggery, too. They feed their hate, grow thin and starve their bellies, spitting and hissing at one another across the stone floor.

The farmhands' wives bring her food in secret. Rice paste in milk and sugar, chillied gram and pieces of fish in mustard. She accepts it with the humility of hunger. The child is fed and is born. The old maidservant hears the baby wail, rushes to the prayer room and blows three nasal blasts on the conch in the small hours of the night. Amalendu staggers out of his opium stupor in a storming rage. He knocks the conch out of the old crone's hand and it rolls away on the stone paved floor.

A child despised by all save his mother. A toyless child of rags and frights. His mother is good with her hands; she makes him toys with garden clay and flour. Elephants and horses and camels. She bakes them in the hearth and paints them. His rhymes are the names of river fish and country flowers. His playmates are the farmhands, sorry at his plight. Once Amalendu charges across the plantation, whiplash in hand, to find his wife. Now, when she returns from her daily visits to her sister, she finds him sitting on the stone flags of the courtyard. He lifts his tousled head and hate-sodden eyes to gaze at her. The little one drools in the inner room, thumb in mouth, beside his farm-maid nurse.

Mondira visits her sister's house across the twin ponds every afternoon. It isn't simple desire any more. When her head hurts with the misery of it all and her breath comes short, when her cramped limbs ache and a listlessness comes over her, she knows it is his absence. A snatch of a folk song or a line of verse in a travelling play and she feels defrauded of the completeness of her pleasure if he is not there. One day he will stop caring and prefer his wife again. So she wishes she could give him something

> in memory of this time. When the sky had gone dark as night and a chill had stolen over the earth, when birds had made a nervous clamour in the air, and he had shuddered and achieved the summit and lain spent, she had looked up through the arch of the cowshed roof and seen the magic ring in the sky. So marvellous, so perfect, that to look on it long would have been to wreck the sight. She had known then that she'd been gifted that moment, a priceless inauspicious gift. A solar eclipse doesn't happen every day.

He stopped writing and considered the page for a while. All the scraps had been thrown his way, almost by clever predesign. As though the pieces were part of a bigger, anterior composition. His novel had pillaged all it had found and gorged itself on loose details. True, he'd drawn upon the accounts of others, but it seemed to him that the disjointed fragments, scattered over a dozen separate narratives, belonged together, gravitating irresistibly towards unexpected unities like far-flung parts of a dismantled continent. I'm only a speller of maps, he thought, a geographer of life texts. Observer and commentator. This was the sort of writing he loved, each sentence finding the next without effort.

But what of the things he left out? The situations that resisted representation? Someday, he thought, I'll write a book made up entirely of my deletions. All the things crossed out, the bits found unsuitable. The bits that couldn't be forced into moulds. The people edited away. Who knows? What's left out might be more important than what's retained. What's not the point may be the real point. I know how to sift and patch and cobble and pare and varnish. I know what I want. Like a diligent rag-picker rummaging in a potentially rich jumble heap.

Yet perhaps not so rich. The same few hundred patterns of life have been written about many times over. What gives each book life is the breath of the particular. The perishable immediate. And after it's been pulped and forgotten, a few dozen or score or even hundred years hence, someone will come along and write another book exactly like this one. What disturbed him was this exasperating tendency to lapse into distracting reverie when he sat down to write. Idle questions popped up and his mind went chasing after them. Like—Had nature realized all the variations possible in situation and character and event? No, because none of these were historically fixed and static things. Why am I writing at all? Being a writer is an item in my narrative about myself. He sank deeper into the quicksands of idle reflection. A small paragraph in nature's narrative, he thought, that's me. To be eventually edited as one who does not matter. But might there not be a super-narrative, encoded in the blueprint of the world, in which nothing is deleted?

A flurry outside. Buddhoo burst in.

'The secret of my friend Vinod's virility? Mutlub, how come the man was such a super-screwer? What happened now? One day he happened to go piss against an abandoned factory wall. A live wire had broken and fallen in the undergrowth. His dick got electrocuted. Energized, if you get what I mean. That's how he . . .'

'D'you mind allowing me an hour's work? I'm busy finishing a chapter,' said Sravan irritably.

Buddhoo backed out of the study. 'Oh, sorry, yaar. Okay, I'm off to the market for a bidi—back futafut.'

Sravan had problems refocusing. Every step of the way he faced the same question—whether life was one long contemplation into which events broke, or a long sequence of events into which thoughts broke. When he wrote he tried to yoke events with rhythms of thought. Unless thought and event were the same and the writer could find some way of fusing the two integrally . . . He forced his mind back to the page. Lit a fag.

> So when the little toddler sidles up to Amalendu, whimpering 'Baba!' Amalendu deals him a push and the tiny creature falls. But as he lies on his belly, squealing on the stone flags, his small face contorted with grief, Amalendu feels something clench up in his innards. He looks around, sees no one. He stoops in haste, gathers

> the child to his breast, crows, 'Eh, eh, my brat, eh, my mynah bird, eh, my child, my golden child!'
>
> But Mihir has sworn vengeance. His rancour festers within him. He is more self-righteous, more punishing than the most sanctimonious husband. When he breaks the news to Mondira that his wife, Devyani, is at last with child, he does it in cold revenge. It pierces Mondira to the hilt. She goes mindless with rage. She'd destroy child and mother both if she could—only the wife happens to be her trusting younger sister. Hurtful images swell in her head. Excruciating pictures of contact and furtive exploration. Each breath and whisper and rustle and creak, until she could tear her throat with hoarse screaming. Instead she sits, turned to stone.

Suddenly he stopped writing. A dead clump in the next room. An avalanche of thuds, wood clattering against floor. Tumbling human stuff—bone, flesh, cotton cloth, iron walker, steel spectacle frame. Then a blank silence. Not a murmur or a call. He knew even before he sprang to his feet. This time his father hadn't had time to call out.

The old man lay bunched in a sinister huddle on the ground, stunned, the walker turned on its side. His eyes were misty with stupor. An elbow had twisted beneath him in frightening asymmetry. Sravan flew to the collapsed heap of body and garment, crouched beside it, lifted and cradled the bruised, eyeless head, felt the pulse, cried out, frantic—Beta! Beta! What happened, my child? Then he bit his lip, startled by the clamour of buried echoes loosed in the air. He put his head against his father's chest. A deathly stillness. He held his breath as the terror mounted. Then something happened in there. The ghost of a movement. A thread of air slid down a micro tunnel of lung-stuff and stole back again. A dim drumbeat sounded, tentative, in the innermost reaches of body-space. An assent floated up and a catch quivered in the old man's throat. His Adam's apple shook and he coughed softly. The glazed eyes opened, rested on Sravan. They seemed to consider him for a remote and final testimony.

15

Even after being pronounced temporarily out of danger, with his hypoglycaemia under control and his blood pressure stabilized, the old man lay still, withdrawn into a drowse. Then he appeared to regress into delirium. He looked shrunken, and he gave off an unidentifiable smell. Keeping vigil beside him, Sravan thought of praying. Always a difficult thing for him—he wasn't the praying type, and the words came out all wrong. A broken, internal monologue addressed to his father. He seemed to be trying to transmit urgent thoughts to his father's brain, into that part of him that was unsmall and unsleeping. He seemed driven by an unspelt haste, lest the chance of the transmission be lost forever. Of what use then would be all those reams of words he'd written? The clock ticked noisily on the wall. A row of ants on the floor made Sravan superstitious. Sometimes a branch of the gulmohur knocked on the glass pane with swift, significant taps. When Pragya held the medicine to the old man's mouth, his slack old jaw stayed open on the spoon, like an infant bird's, and a fermenting smell foamed up from beneath the coated gums. 'Close your mouth, Babuji.' He did not hear. 'Close your mouth, Babuji.' The mouth lapsed slowly shut. He'd lost track of time. 'Is it evening?' he mumbled in the morning. And Sravan realized, in a moment of swift insight, that he was living a page from one of his early novels. Long ago, by directing thoughts upon a page, he had accidentally issued instructions to his own fate. The engines had started moving, and the instructions were now being followed.

Mid-snore, fragments of chopped words slipped out of the old man's lips like runaway morsels. Sravan strained his ears to catch them, but they were mostly disconnected. Agitated exclamations that wound down to a troubled grunt. There were times when the old man opened his eyes but didn't seem to be looking at anything. Yet off and on, between the grinding snores, there came two words, buzzed over with slippery tongue. Buddhoo noticed them too, and when they came slurring several times in a day, the two of them discussed it, puzzled. Late one evening Buddhoo came to Sravan's study.

'Got it. It's *neela jhola*—blue bag!'

Sravan started.

Several hours later they managed to identify the ancient travelling box. When the lock was prised open and the lid wrenched off, Buddhoo drew out a folded navy-blue cloth bag. Tucked away in it was a nondescript key with a number, and a tag with the name of a bank.

'Bank of Madura. Khusrubagh Branch,' Sravan read. 'Funny; I didn't know he had a locker there. It's at the other end of town.'

'Maybe he has a secret fortune stashed away,' Buddhoo joked. 'Bit like finding a bottle washed ashore by the tide, isn't it?'

But Sravan was past joking. 'He must be preserving something private. Something he didn't want anyone to know about. Something important and secret enough to make a longer trip for. I'll have to go to the bank and find out.'

'You'll need a letter of authority,' pointed out Pragya-the-practical. 'He's not in a position to sign. But maybe, if he's this bothered about whatever he's got hidden there, he'll be able to muster up the energy in a day or two . . . How exciting. Maybe its your mother's misplaced jewellery—the pieces she said she'd pawned and lost.'

Getting the old man's signature to the letter of authority was less of a problem than they had thought. Pragya had only to put her lips close to his ear and say, 'Babuji, we're going to open your bank locker in Khusrubagh. Will you sign this letter authorizing us?' and the old man lifted his creased eyelids and trained his foggy eyes on them. He had trouble holding the pen, but Pragya guided his hand.

It took Sravan more than a day to get over the shock of the discovery. As the bulky wads appeared from the locker and lay in close-fastened, dog-eared batches upon the branch manager's table, Sravan's jaw dropped. Buddhoo gasped. Comprehension dawned in their eyes.

'There it is, yaar.' Buddhoo recovered his wits first. 'Your father's secret fortune. How long d'you think that pile took to amass?'

Sravan was in no condition to make light conversation. The private wealth of a secret life lay stacked in four polythene packets. He had never had the slightest idea.

There seemed to be more than a dozen manuscripts and the records of a meagre savings account, fed pathetically tiny sums at irregular intervals and abandoned about four years ago—roughly the time the old man became housebound.

Now the discoloured sheafs lay on Sravan's desk. Through the open door he could see the feeble form on the sickbed, motionless but for the faint rise and fall of the frail ribcage.

'And to think he abused me all my life for being a writer,' said Sravan.

'From the look of it, he's been at it hammer and tongs, yaar. Years and years. If my hunch is right, that savings account was kept to publish this stuff at his own expense. And remember the story he told me? The book rejected twenty-one times? He didn't give up hope, poor man. All that disgust he aired—eyewash!'

Novels, plays, collections of essays, poetry. The titles sprang into view, neatly printed in faded blue-black ink on yellowing paper. *Kshamta. Astitva Ka Ek Adhyay. Satya Ke Chhutte Sikke. Yeh Nalanda Nivasi.* There were twin collections of poems called *Nirarthak Naad* and *Antardhvani*.

This was the man who'd poured scorn on all literary exercise. ('Self-expression? Give me one kambakht reason why the self must be expressed. All this self-expression is only psychological defecation. A purely laxative function, hah!')

There wasn't time to go through all the writings. Sravan felt the same reluctance before turning each page that he felt before stepping into the old man's room—as though he had to ask permission and wasn't sure it would be granted. There was a strong sense of trespassing, with the powerful possibility of discovery and chastisement.

Astitva Ka Ek Adhyay took him by surprise. It seemed an astonishing replay of his own current novel. An alternate view of the same situation. Why had his father's novel arrived at the same stalemate as his own? *Yeh Nalanda Nivasi* was a historical play set in the Middle Ages, at the time of the burning down of Nalanda University. About a man who manages to salvage sacred scrolls from the mammoth library—so similar to one of his own plays. The discovery filled Sravan with puzzled sadness—that the two of them should have experimented with the same thoughts but that he should have been the one to achieve results and not his irate, overbearing father. It also perplexed him that most of the manuscripts he skimmed through had a character whose name was Vanshi Dhar. His father seemed obsessed with the name. He'd given his fictional Vanshi Dhar a life multiplied by the number of times he'd plotted out a tale. Would he say why, if asked? Would he choose to tell? Better not to ask, to let some secrets be. Sravan regarded the sheafs of yellowed paper strewn upon his desk. He thought of the meagre savings account. Years back his father had divided his capital between his three sons, leaving a fourth for himself, and this account was his pathetic little clandestine wealth on the side, something he was not obliged to explain. He remembered his father's vicious jibes. An idea began to take shape in his brain, extravagant but well worth developing. He put down the script and crossed the corridor to the sickroom. As he entered, the branch of the gulmohur delivered two abrupt knocks upon the pane, and Sravan knew that things had to happen fast.

'Amazing!' was Farooqui's reaction. 'All my life I've had this zalim fantasy tormenting my head like a djinn from the Aliph Laila.

Imagine the scene, Sravan bhai-jaan: There I am, lying in my deathbed, the wick of my earthly existence burning low. Ah, the ache of it! I am a genius forsaken by the world of men. Then Allah-meherbaan takes pity on me. The impossible happens. I'm discovered at last! Visited by a farishta—an important publisher! He makes me sign a deal. He hails me as a lost icon. Is it a man or the angel Jabreel? The miracle is that it's a man and he takes on all my work, he pays me for every instant of labour in my long, despairing writing life. And what then? I am reconciled to God and man, all set to die content, praising Allah in whose world justice may be delayed but not denied, wondering if I'm already dead and the day of Kayamat is come and gone. That, Sravan bhai-jaan, has been my dream. And now here you come, asking me to act it out. That is what you want, no?'

'That's it. All you do is pose as a publisher. Tell him you came across a story by him in a journal. Tell him you were bowled over. That you see him as a major artist who was somehow passed over and ignored. That now it has become your mission to reveal him to the world of letters . . .'

'Has he published any stories?'

'I've just rushed one to press in the current number of *Swadeshi*. I'll let you have a copy. You must do your homework, Farooqui Sahib. Discuss it closely with him. Question the details. Mention how excited, how overwhelmed you were when you read it. How you showed it around. Tell him how you got in touch with the magazine and how you managed to trace him. Then, when he's primed with praise, spring it on him. Gently. The big offer. Say that for the time being you can't pay more than twenty-five thousand. You know it's too low for such a major talent, but for an Indian publisher and a first book, it's a proper signing amount. Show him the contract. I've got it ready here—you can familiarize yourself with the terms and conditions I've fabricated to his advantage.'

'Twenty-five thousand! Where does that come from?' asked Farooqui, suspicious.

'You sign a cheque from your own account. I'll return the amount to you in cheque or cash, whichever you prefer.'

'My begum will start getting ideas. She'll imagine I'm still supporting Rasoolan-bai . . .' murmured Farooqui, squeamish.

'Oh, come on, Farooqui Sahib. It's just for a day or two. You pass him one cheque, I pass you another—immediately afterwards, if you like. Or will your begum imagine you're being supported by Rasoolan-bai?

A soft gleam of a smile appeared on Farooqui's face. 'And now that I think of it, what harm will it do? Give the begum cause to think better of me. Which, I sorrow to confess, Sravan bhai-jaan, she has failed to do in recent years. Rasoolan's ghost shall exalt my worth, and no names need be spoken, no?'

It went off flawlessly. Sravan complimented Farooqui on his performance, thanked him profusely. Farooqui brushed it aside.

'It's easy to act out one's own vahiyaat dreams, Sravan bhai-jaan,' he said as he left.

His father could now sit up, propped on pillows. He had met Farooqui with majestic aplomb. Taken the news with dignity. He made a courteous, halting speech. He signed the contract with the same smart flourish that he used on his own dud cheques. Dud cheque for dud cheque, marvelled Sravan in the next room.

When it was all over, the sickroom was ominously silent. Despite his suave performance in Farooqui's presence, the old man seemed dazed by the developments. When Sravan ventured into his father's room that afternoon, a volley of crisp oaths greeted him.

'Who asked you to pry into my affairs, laat sahib?' Sravan caught the clink of battle in his father's voice. The sunken old eyes seemed to spit heat at him.

He found himself speaking in a high, persistent, defensive tone.

'Why, you did. You kept saying, "Neela jhola". So we had to ferret it out. I went down to Khusrubagh and discovered your manuscripts. Pretty good, some of them. I sent down a story to *Swadeshi* . . .'

'Keep your patronage to yourself!' slashed the old man. 'And even if I did mutter something in my sleep, what business had you to misappropriate my work? Publish my story in that useless rag? Without my knowledge? Without my consent?'

All of a sudden, and at the same moment, they both realized that the old man's voice had recovered its former strength. Sravan looked into the flushed face and noticed that his father was sitting bolt upright, unsupported by the pillows on which he had been slumping. Erect for the first time since his fall, his eyes burning with a furious jubilant flare. A shine of malicious rejoicing transformed the collapsed flesh of his face. An expression of demoniacal satisfaction. He decided to play his own role at least half as well as those two old men had done.

'I'm sorry you feel that way. I sent that story to the press because I liked it. I didn't realize it was private. And in case you resent the cheap exposure, as you used to call it, I can always ring up your new publisher and say you've changed your mind and regret signing the deal. I'm sure he'll appreciate your modesty and tear up the deal if you return the cheque . . .'

'That will not be necessary, Sahib Bahadur.' Snap and crackle. 'You keep out of my affairs—enough mischief's been done, thanks to your interference. What's done is done; there's no help for it.'

Sravan grinned to himself. Status quo. For all intents and purposes, his father looked completely restored. Smugly exultant. Checkmated at last in this game, and that gave Sravan the deepest pleasure. One last job: retrieve that dud cheque. The old man had hung on to it. That night Sravan stole into his father's room and cautiously switched on his torch. Buddhoo lay on the mattress, spread-eagled in sleep. The old man slept heavily thanks to his sedatives. He must have put the cheque beneath his pillow. If Sravan could just ease his hand in ever so lightly, he might be able to draw it out. He slipped his hand in and found what he sought—only to feel his father's knotty talon clap upon it. As though it was a lifeline.

No good. The old man wasn't going to let go, not even in sleep. He'd have to try some other time.

16

The parcel turned out to be a book. Good cover design, glossy paper, fancy font and on the back cover a known face, dimpling at the camera. It took time to register. *Reflections in a Lake*, by Malini Mishra. The title page autographed in green ink. And a slip of handmade notepaper with the words: *With best compliments to Sravan*. Unsigned.

He looked quickly at the name of the publisher. Eagle Books. Never heard of them. Probably a pay-and-publish concern. Vanity publisher. What hit him was that other handwriting, its letters so different from Malini's curlicued hand. *With best compliments to Sravan*. A known hand. The same spidery hand that had penned that biannual hate mail for years!

His first reaction was disbelief. His second, contempt. But the feeling that eventually prevailed was agitation. That handwriting had the sinister power to unsettle him completely. In the old days, he would keep going back to feast his eyes on it, masochistically teasing his flinching heart with the mere sight of it. Now, after a span of months, its effect was scarcely less potent. He marvelled at the neurotic dread that mere handwriting could evoke. He shoved the book away in the right-hand drawer, meaning to ignore it, but four times that morning he found himself taking it out and staring at those five innocuous words. *With best compliments to Sravan*.

He tried to dial Malini's mobile but it was switched off. He tried her flat. A servant received the call: Memsahib had been out since morning. He chafed, restless. A good, heated reckoning with her might have released his pent-up fretfulness, but she denied him even that.

Maybe he could write a damning review. His name alone would see it through—any journal, any tabloid. There was no need to *read* the wretched thing; he'd endured the torment of so many protracted readings by the authoress herself. He relieved his smarting heart by writing the review immediately, loading each phrase with venom. *Eminently forgettable. Altogether avoidable. Pretentious and clumsy pun in the title itself. Pseudo-reflection parading as profundity. Four hundred pages of tedious posturing. When writing turned as casual as a random fling, when the writing of a book was just a piquant novelty to a bored and jaded palate, one could only regret the irresponsibility of quality-waiving publishers who churned out any bilgewater as long as they were paid.* And as he disgorged his resentfulness, his complex infatuation for Malini suddenly resolved itself in simple loathing. One of those swift shifts in feeling that readjust one's troubled ambiguities in an endurable compromise. He sent the piece off to *The Letter and the Spirit*, the journal she set great store by, and, somewhat uplifted by this exercise of therapeutic malice, began to pack for his trip to Delhi the next day.

'You might like to tune to the national network at 9.30 tomorrow night—they'll be covering the Lotus Award festival,' he told Pragya before leaving for the station. She expressed no enthusiasm.

There was to be a glittering ceremony followed by a book launch afterwards. He didn't know this young writer whose first novel he was to launch; he'd have to snatch a copy at the reception and read bits to form an idea. It pleased these self-important little pen-pushers enormously when a well-known writer showed familiarity with their work. It was a woman writer. He hoped she was presentable. Lunch with her, so what a bore if she turned out to be a dowd! Then the afternoon at a book fair, signing books. Smiling blandly into faces. Mouthing pithy one-liners. At five, a recording for a talk show. He hoped they'd got his return ticket ready.

The receptionist at the Samudragupt Intercontinental gave him the message as soon as he stepped up to the counter.

'Mr Sravan Kumar?' (How he abhorred that *Mister* bit. Made him feel like the hero of a ridiculous sixties film.) The girl looked searchingly into his face.

'Yes.'

'Room 259, Lotus Foundation delegate?'

'That's right.'

'Urgent message for you, sir. It came from the foundation office this morning.'

'E-mail?'

'Telephone.' She passed the note across the counter.

He read it over twice before it made any sense to him. Then, in scattered segments of meaning, single words detached themselves from the brief paragraph. It took him a few seconds to speak.

'I'd like to use your phone, please. No time to go up to the room.'

'Of course.'

He got through to the foundation and spoke to Samarendra Dutta.

'Sorry about this, Dutta. I've just arrived and have to rush back right away. You'll have to do without me. My father had a massive stroke last night. If you could manage a flight ticket for me up to Lucknow, I could hire a taxi from there . . .'

'The flight doesn't leave till evening, Sravan-da. We could deliver your cheque to you at the airport.'

He was suddenly angry. Goddamn your garlands and your cheque and your silk shawl and your copper plate and your fucking citation! But he simply said, 'That'll be fine. But please arrange for the ticket first and get back to me. I'll be in my room.'

'No problem.'

In the lift, on his way to his room, a vicious thought swam into his numb head—He managed to cheat me *again*.

The five-hour taxi ride was an agony. His head drummed up a

squeezing ache. By the time he'd dumped his suitcase at the flat and rushed to the hospital, his father had slipped into coma.

For days afterwards it all kept coming back to him. The frozen sky, the grey river, the burning ghat stretched along the sand to a hump of hillock on the fag end of a dusty road.

The pyre had been built at the extreme edge. Nine mounds of wood carefully axed to slender faggots. The body—it was hard thinking of his father as a body—laid alongside. The garlands ceremonially removed. The cording snapped, the flowers cast into the grey stream, the shroud, the *Gita* on the chest.

Massaging ghee on the shrivelled body was like applying a lifetime's appeasing unction. Large dollops on the chest—the chest burns longest, he was told—and he had obeyed, smoothing the ghee in like a guilty caress, like an emollient to grease a rusty love.

Seven times round the pyre, then he thrust the bundle of joss sticks into the straw-filled hollow beneath the body and spoke the words of final offering—To you I offer the fruit of my good karma, I, lighter of your pyre. Your evil karma take I on myself. That you may go onward in peace.

The straw caught, a scarf of flame blew out of the body, and Sravan stepped back, recognizing the moment for what it was.

The body lit up slowly from within, a blood-red glimmer beneath a charcoal crust, its lines suddenly highlighted. And then those unmentionable sounds of incineration—the splutter of nameless organs, the snap of a muttering flame, the blast of the skull bursting, which no mantra could quieten as his father turned into a bulk of organic waste, a biodegradable thing.

Later Sravan took his dip in the river and came away, not looking back, carrying pot and knife as ritual prescribed. The lamp was lit in the sickroom. As igniter of the pyre he was to spend his days and nights in that room. Babuji wasn't much of a believer, he'd told the priests, insisting on a simplified ceremony and a shortened period of mourning. He knew the future would be one long ceremony of decoding his father and measuring himself against his father's lengthening shadow.

Sleeping in his father's room was difficult, even with Buddhoo on the floor. The queerest dreams narrowed into one another as his brain paraphrased the event in various allegories. In one dream he dithered about in an unsteady game of musical chairs; it wasn't a chair that disappeared with each round but a player. There were more chairs left than players. On the bolt of a window frame hung a small boy's coat. Sravan awoke with an inchoate trouble heavy upon him. The oil lamp filled the room with a rusty light. Could he be dreaming the dreams of a dead man?

He drifted into torpor. Couldn't move or turn with the weight of a massive book on his ribs. His lungs would not lift. He shook the book off his chest with a powerful heave. It crashed, pages crumpled, upon its belly on the floor. He awoke once again to hear Buddhoo's thin snore and see the ritual flame extinguished in its bowl.

They still looked at the empty bed when they spoke of the old man.

'I found that dud cheque for twenty-five thousand under his pillow. Pretty crumpled it was. And a long grey hair,' said Buddhoo.

'Remember that grand spluttering speech he made when he signed that fake contract? His bombastic air—*I had a script to show the world what I thought of it. Twenty years it's lain in a bank locker, biding its time. I knew its time would come. Its time has come now. I knew it.* What a sinister speech, Buddhoo. To think that he didn't know that his own time had come . . .'

'Don't think about it.'

'Can't help thinking. There's a sort of backwash. D'you think the satisfaction hastened his end? I mean, such things do happen. He might have dragged on. And how d'you know he was waiting for me?'

'He kept turning his head to look at the door, that night he came out of coma just before the end.'

'I wish I could be sure. But he didn't actually ask for me?' His voice was beginning to sound shrewish.

'He couldn't speak, Ravan,' said Buddhoo patiently.

'All the same, I wish I could be absolutely sure it was me he was waiting for.'

'You've said that a dozen times.'

'Something was unresolved between us,' Sravan tried to explain. His eyes were smarting. 'I tried to win him over—my way. He didn't want to be obliged to me. D'you think right at the end he was? Obliged to me? And when he was ill, the way he went feeble. Lost his fire. Hung his head and heard me scold. Went limp. To tell you the truth, Buddhoo, I couldn't bear that. I had to put the roar back in him. And I did.' He savoured the memory. Another thought struck him. 'He went away carrying this feeling, too. This unfinished business between us.' Buddhoo heard him out in silence. The final question surprised him even as he uttered it. 'Did I disarm him? Or merely defeat him? What d'you think, Buddhoo?'

'What would you like to think now? It was you he waited for.'

'Like that old woman in my book?' Sravan said ruefully. 'Why the hell did I write that scene months back?'

He was left with the manuscript for his father's novel. A strange sort of inheritance. Much of it dovetailed peacefully with his own. It inspired a mixture of infatuation and violent exasperation. He dreaded the handwriting that fleshed out his father's voice in an eerie posthumous persistence. He'd never be able to complete it, he feared. His own writing would be a superimposition, an afterthought, an insurgent editing. But in an invulnerable way that script would stay the same. It would drag his small rancorous dissents into its authoritative current and sweep on, neutralizing his voice. Like a father's genes active in his own, or a father's karma in his fate. That's all a man amounted to: some cells in his children's bodies. Some residual attitudes in his grandchildren's minds. But Sravan couldn't shake off a sense of guilty intrusion.

17

That voice on the phone again. Sober this time, with a smug note of self-righteousness.

'Just rang up to say that it doesn't become a writer of your eminence and seniority to belittle a starter. Even if she does happen to be an ex-girlfriend.'

'Did you pimp it through? How did you get acquainted with her?' Sravan said. He heard the other laugh in quiet triumph. 'You've been keeping tabs on me. Watching every move like a hawk. Hot on my trail for years. Haven't you found anything better to do? Silent phone calls to her flat—I might have known it was you all the time. Then at that party . . . what a good actor you've become!'

'All this is besides the point. I called to say that your review was highly unseemly. Haven't you learnt new ways of professional victimization? Your style is getting too repetitive. Some of it was in obnoxious taste. Hitting below the belt . . .'

'I'm not bothered with below her belt or above. I leave her to you!'

'I've known you to be a perfect bastard, Sravan, but I didn't know you could get this crude.'

Sravan uttered an obscenity. Gave him a semblance of composure.

'I warn you, Sravan, one of these days you'll learn this isn't a safe world for you . . .'

'Are you threatening me?'

'I'm only saying you're not out of the press's firing range. Nobody's so important that he's invulnerable . . .'

'Fuck-all to you and fuck-all to the press!' Sravan banged down the receiver and found, to his dismay, that he was hot all over, perspiring a little.

When Buddhoo proposed moving on, now that his job as nurse-entertainer was over, Sravan insisted he stay just a few days more. By now he had busied himself with outlandish handiworks. He settled down on the floor, surrounded by his gear. Strips of cane from a broken rattan chair. A discarded handloom sari, scissors, cellotape, fevicol, pencil, tape measure, needle, reels of multicoloured thread. Even a borrowed sewing machine. Pragya, just back from a shopping spree, flopped down beside him and watched. Buddhoo measured out the cloth.

'Kite?' asked Pragya.

'Wall kite.' Buddhoo gobbled on his words, his mouth full of pins. He took a pencil from behind his ear and marked the cloth, then pinned a hem round its length. 'I have an interesting relationship with kites,' he told her. 'Once while striding across the countryside I fell into a ditch and broke an ankle. My eyes had been following a kite in the sky. We'll need an empty wall to put this up when it's done. Mind if I remove those ghastly paintings?'

'They're lost on you, but don't call them names. Yes, we can move them elsewhere.'

'One hot summer, kites proved my downfall. Class seven or eight. Exams round the corner . . . Achha, three feet square, couple of inches for the tuck.' He began cutting, frowning, mouth pursed.

'Then?'

'I wasn't bothered. I'd made enough bandobast to get through the exam, see. Foolproof. I'd hired a dozen volunteers—a greengrocer, a sweeper, the maharaj in our cook-house, the cowherd who took our cow out to graze, two farmhands, the kasba barber . . .'

'To cram on your behalf?' Pragya giggled.

'Wrong.'

'To smuggle in scraps for you to copy from?'

'What bloody bukwas! This was all strictly lawful! No unfair means about it!' He put the scissors down. 'I hired them to pray for me. Their fee was high, but my faith in God was unshakeable. I said I'd pay them ten bucks apiece when the results were declared—and I flew kites all summer.' He began measuring out the cane strips.

'How long did your faith last?'

'I didn't blame divine grace; I blamed my useless volunteers. The results came out: failed with glorious distinction in all subjects! Hopping mad I was. Took the stick to some of my chumchas and chased them down the highway. Goes without saying that my father subsequently took the stick to me and chased me out of the house. I spent two months sulking at an uncle's house in a nearby village.'

The strips of cane were now being tied into a neat square frame. Pragya watched, interested.

'Funny,' she said after an interval. 'I've had a strange relationship with kites, too. Not half as innocent as yours.'

'Uh-huh?'

'When we went to stay at my grandpa's every autumn, I was the odd one out. Twelve years old and a stupid girl in a frilled skirt that had been lengthened twice and had discoloured hems. I wasn't ever invited to fly kites on the terrace, so I spent hours watching my cousins through a peephole in the second terrace wall. One day this cousin of mine—he must've been twenty-five or so—he noticed me spying and said—Come on, no need to lurk around, I'll teach you to fly a kite. I was thrilled. And you know what the chap did? He swung me up by the arms, clean off my feet, lifted me up just like that and swung me over the stone parapet—you know those carved stone railings in old houses? Dangled me over the edge . . .'

'Arré baap ré!'

'That's it. I was shrieking with fright. Trying to get a foothold against the wall, clawing at the cornices. He just kept laughing. He said—Now you can feel you've turned into a kite. Shall I let go, Pupu?'

Buddhoo had stopped tying the cane frame together and was gaping at Pragya, appalled.

'And d'you know, I go through that panic each time I look down from a high-rise building. Hanging in the air. Howling. My legs thrashing about. Screaming. And that beast cracking his sides . . . it all returns.'

'He was a monster.'

'Of course he was. He's in the police force posted somewhere in Bihar. Every extended family has its resident monster. Hypersexed.'

'Have I told you about my friend who got hypersexed from accidentally pissing on a live wire?' asked Buddhoo.

'Yes, you have.'

'So how'd he let go?'

She spoke softly. 'He made me promise I'd go into the bathroom with him every afternoon when everyone was sleeping.'

'My God!' said Buddhoo, just as low. 'Did you?'

'I had to. I was only twelve, and he was big. I had to keep going. That bathroom on the terrace was a secluded place. All through the autumn vacation.'

'No one you could tell?'

'No. I was ashamed. And the terror! He said—If you dare tell a soul, I'll chuck you down next time. And the thought of being dangled over that railing again . . . So much for the caring, supporting extended family.'

She shivered.

'Saala!' swore Buddhoo softly. He picked up the cloth and began folding the edges round the cane frame.

That afternoon Sravan got a brief note from Malini, delivered by hand to the Centre. *How low can you get? Have resolved to confess all to Pragya.*

Curse her, the bitch! He might have expected this. Here was another problem in the offing. He was reasonably sure this wasn't her idea; it was the brainchild of that bastard, none other. He'd now have to watch Pragya closely, gear up for an explosive scene, face recriminations, spitefulness, tears.

But the day passed without event. Pragya seemed undisturbed.

The next thing Buddhoo invented for Pragya was a punkah made of one of her old handloom saris. He climbed on a stool and suspended it from a couple of hooks in the ceiling, originally put there to support a fancy swing. The punkah had a long, tasselled cord that sloped across the wall like a streamer and disappeared onto the balcony through the ventilator. Outside, craftily concealed behind a row of crotons, Buddhoo had fitted up a most original contraption: an engine run by sand. On a tin wheel fashioned out of tin cans and two buckets, fastened back to back, a steady downpour of sand emptied slowly through a couple of improvised nozzles, first on one flat spoke of the wheel, then on its opposite. The weight of the sand made the wheel swing in a vertical semicircle, first to the left, then to the right. Inside the room the punkah waved in wide swaths, generating a soft breeze.

Pragya stared at it, open-mouthed.

'Genius!' she exclaimed. 'How long will it run?'

'As long as it takes fifteen kilos of sand to seep down. Then all you have to do is pour the sand back through this funnel here—back into the buckets. Look, no mess. You can even regulate the speed by shifting the diameter of this nozzle a bit wider. See?'

Pragya gazed again at the punkah.

'Needs an autograph of the designer,' she remarked thoughtfully. 'Since it's one of a kind.'

'Oh, bukwas!' scoffed Buddhoo, slapping sand off his hands.

'No, really. Get up on that stool there and sign your name.'

'Nonsense. A real artist isn't bothered with all that bundul.'

'How d'you know what real artists are bothered about?' she asked cynically.

'Is the Taj Mahal signed? Ajanta? Ellora? Are the Puranas signed?' Buddhoo discoursed, striking a pose. 'The greatest works in the history of the world are often unsigned, sisterji.' He began rolling down his sleeves, glowing with the satisfaction of a functioning invention.

At his desk next door, Sravan had a disconcerting vision—Buddhoo signing Pragya's naked body. One of those impish, clandestine fancies that came to his imagination when his brain locked up. The fantasy gathered detail. A perverse little thought that he gently uncensored in his head to allow free play. It was one of his many little islands of escape when the book preyed on him. It was hard detaching himself from the accursed book—it fed on him all hours of the day and appeared, thinly disguised in inverse fantastications, at night. Yet he couldn't set down a decent page! My God, he groaned, it's like a boa constrictor, drawing me up in its entrails. Squeezing the life out of me. He felt like a run-down engine on a cold morning, revving and revving but not starting. He made compulsive attempts at the problem scenes and gave up.

Something had snapped. Overnight he'd lost the ability to see a face in words, hear a speaking voice in his head. Dialogue came out wooden, actions flat. It had something to do with his father, he suspected. Dynamo, menace, crisis, threat—that's what he'd been, that impossible presence in the next room. Was this lassitude, creative withdrawal or genuine mental fatigue? It might not be a bad idea to say—To hell with it all, there's more to living than writing, and as Buddhoo put it, it hasn't been a life for me, only an account of a life. I haven't known the wood for the trees; so much time lost. But when the writing goes—if it goes—what will take its place? An uncertain thought, yet not comfortable. Maybe we're both burnt out, my father and I, each in our way. He on that pyre (that horrid highlighted, charred silhouette, that choking smoke) and me here, at this arid desk.

He had often said—When a writer begins jabbering about the theory and process of writing, beware. Yet here he was doing just that. Pragya had only to point out the handloom kite to him and he'd start off—Writing's like flying a kite, did you know? The thought tugs at you, takes off, becomes airborne. The words pour through your fingers like kite string unrolling from its spool. Until the kite is racing across the sky and you're panting headlong after it. Down the steep gradients of experience . . . He stopped, uneasy. What was he nattering about now? Pragya had only to put a plate of mangoes before him at lunchtime and he'd be off—Fell off in last night's storm? That's just how a mature book should be written. None of the effort of plucking it from the branch: let it hang upon the bough, scenting the air. Grow from flower to fruit, realizing its inherent possibilities. Swell. Round itself and ripen. Then gently drop at the peak of its fulness.

He intercepted the look that passed between them. Pragya didn't exactly say—are you all right?—but he read the question in her anxious face. Surely she hadn't failed to notice that he wasn't writing anything? He could see their faces signalling the problem that their words refused to frame. *What's wrong with him? Shell-shocked*. He wished their conferring faces would shut up. He wanted to quarrel violently with someone. Anyone. To set his disconnected life in motion again, like slapping a defective torch to set it alight. He sometimes felt like Amalendu in his impotence—again that dismal novel of his! And Pragya still did not mention Malini's name. The suspense was sinister.

Days before the outburst, he could sense the storm clouds gather. The big row, when it came, driving back from the Riverside Resort, released a drenching tide of relief in his head. But it wasn't over Malini at all. It wasn't what she said—he hardly remembered what it was—but the snide way she'd said it. Her soft lollipop-sucking way of whispering a jibe. He braked abruptly, his throat rigid. Just get out of the car, will you? She turned to look at him. Very slowly. With idle contempt. Her smile scorched his face with its challenge. His hands clenched the steering wheel. Then, with one of her sensational shrugs, she flung open the door and stepped out. Stood with a provoking swagger on the pavement. A faint spasm twitched in his face. He stepped on the accelerator, and as the car picked up speed Buddhoo hissed from the back seat—Are you mad? Sravan ignored him. The car sped down the long cantonment avenue. Buddhoo thumped his heavy hand down on Sravan's shoulder and snarled—Stop, saala, stop, will you? Sravan braked with a teeth-grinding screech. Tell you what: why don't you get out, too?—jeered Sravan. Give her company. Exactly what I had in mind! Their voices had risen. Buddhoo blustered out, slamming the door hard. Sravan drove on. His head seemed to have gone toxic with sour words. He'd always had this tendency to go into silent convulsions of black humour. Made him enjoy these situations, the nastier the better. His father gone, he was looking for someone to ignite his old angers again, someone to stub those angers on, some flint to strike sparks against.

He reached home, checked the time. Nine in the night. He wished them a happy six-kilometre walk—no public transport on that route. He locked up; Pragya had a key. The kids were subdued. He stretched out in his room, relishing visions of the two on their late-night hike. Imagining the two of them. Imagining . . . One day you'll reawaken to your original book, he thought, as you rediscover your wife after an inconsequential fling. He felt like the director of a secret blue film, imagining the two of them. Sets, camera angles, special effects—a fascinating composition. Potent enough to overpower his malaise. Like a dose of creative Viagra. And those two going about in original innocence, not guessing a thing!

18

Looking back in later years, he never forgot the innocuous way the events began. He saw himself on the front steps. He saw, in his memory, the front door locked. He remembered thinking that Pragya had probably left the keys with the neighbours. He rang the Pawars' doorbell. Subhash Pawar saw him and expressed a strange condolence.

'Really sorry about this, Sravan. I just don't know what to say. Terrible thing to happen.'

'What's happened?'

'But don't you know?'

'No.'

Pawar's jaw dropped. Then Sarita Pawar appeared, fat and concerned. 'Now you come right in, Sravan, and drink a glass of water first.' She steered him in, pulled a chair. They sat down in front of him, gazing at him in dumb sympathy. He felt like hitting them.

When they broke the news a shiver passed along his nerves and jammed against his brain in a grinding screech.

In the silence that followed Sravan looked from Pawar's face to that of his wife. His mind rejected the information.

'A lively kid, and so intelligent,' Sarita said. 'It's usually these extra-bright ones that go off the rails.'

'But wild, mind, wild,' added Pawar. 'Always had the wits of a whiz-kid. A little devil sometimes. I told Sarita here—that kid's going to make his mark or end in jail.'

'I read of a case in which five teenagers raped and murdered a lady doctor . . .' put in Sarita Pawar.

'The things he could think of! Such brains! Once he smashed the headlights of all the scooters parked in the scooter park. Said he needed something for a scientific discovery he'd thought of. Ingenious!'

'And when I pulled him up for it, know what he did? He stole up to the terrace where my washing was drying and ripped all the clothes to shreds! With a blade!'

'And the raffle-ticket business, Sarita. Tell Sravanji about the raffle-ticket business.'

'Oh, yes. He came up with a handful of colony kids and sold me a ticket—five bucks—for a school raffle. He sold tickets to the entire building. It was later that Mrs Bajaj and the third number-wali suspected something was wrong, and they compared tickets and came over to my place. Know what? They were all photocopies from the same original! Very nicely photocopied, too. Now tell me if that isn't the work of a genius!'

'I cornered him on the stairs and got him to confess. He said the idea was his own—he'd made a nice little profit and given the other kids a cut. But of course the other parents in the colony didn't like it one bit.'

There was a nerve shrilling in his temple, so painful that each thought hurt.

'And don't forget that business with the salt.'

'Yes, Sravanji. That time when there was this wild rumour that after the onions, salt had gone out of the market. Ashu said—Auntie, I'll go get you a pack from Gupta's store. I gave him thirty bucks and he brought me a pack. Later Gupta swore he'd sold the pack for just six bucks. Gupta also said he'd caught the kid shoplifting, but since it was just stickers and things and you're such old customers of his he was too embarrassed to complain.'

'Look,' gasped Sravan, managing to get a word in. 'Why are you telling me all this now? Why didn't you tell me earlier?'

'We told Pragya. She was very upset. She begged us not to mention it to you. Said it might disturb your work to get mixed up in these day-to-day jhams. She said she and Prabuddha would talk to the kid.'

'Talk. Take him for counselling, eh? When all the time what the brat needs is a good old-fashioned hiding. Sorry, Sravanji. Didn't mean to alarm you but I'm a blunt man.'

Sravan had the feeling he could still escape the situation. Tear the whole miserable chapter out, crumple it up and cast it into the wastebasket. Then the awful sensation of captivity overcame him. Trapped in this draft, assigned a character he didn't feel comfortable in, an action he couldn't relate to.

'Where's Pragya? Where's the kid?' He found to his loathing that his voice was unsteady.

'Prabuddha and Pragya rushed to the school. I believe the school's closed for the day after the incident. The headmaster is detaining your son. Obviously a police case, Sravanji, and we can't tell you how sorry . . .'

All the way to the school the nausea followed him. He felt physically ill, stumbling through a situation he couldn't grasp. A funny dizziness in his head and a shortness of breath in his cramped chest. By the time he reached he was calmer, with a desperate determination to work out the crisis to a satisfactory end. Once again, and quite absurdly at this inappropriate moment, he had that feeling of blankness that came over him when he was stuck on a particularly ticklish point in a book and couldn't see how it would work out. The thing to do then was to trust the script. Scripts acquired an initiative of their own and carried you along—you had to follow their volition, not your own. Which was what he was doing now.

19

'It isn't I who shall decide, Mr Kumar, but God. He and the Indian Penal Code.'

The Reverend Isidore D'Souza had sunken eyes. Pugnacious for a small man. He had bony, bat-like hands at the ends of wide cassock sleeves that conducted his rhythmic speech. A six-o'clock shade coated his face like mildew on a discoloured stone wall.

What confused Sravan was the range of judgements in the Reverend Isidore's discourse. Almighty God's, the Bishop's, and the Indian Penal Code's. The Reverend Isidore was given to citing the Bible and the IPC with equal readiness. He'd spent the last couple of hours in troubled perusal of both. Now he let Sravan have the full force of it, mixing chapter and verse and section of the IPC in a disconcerting mash.

Pragya was in the anteroom, with Buddhoo waiting outside. She had been crying. Her face was blotched. The strain had told on Buddhoo's face as well.

When the kid was brought in by a peon, Sravan's heart hurt. A small, hunted animal. Panic scurried about his eyes and he looked tinier than he was, his curling lashes fluttering in terror. Sravan looked mutely at his son and felt a physical contortion of pain in his chest. The beastliness of it! The kid looked stupefied. Sravan had a rash impulse to snatch up his son, to hide him, hit out. But all he said was, 'Don't be hard on him—he's only a child, Father.'

The Reverend Isidore farted with his nose. 'The boy he tried to murder was also only a child. Now you see him wroth and his countenance fallen.'

"Murder! He isn't dead, so how can you use that word?' cried Pragya.

Isidore looked at her in grim satisfaction. 'He's close to it.' He induced his spongy lips into a flat horizontal stretch. 'I'm in touch with the Medical College Hospital. He's in their emergency unit. His chances are slender.'

Oh, hell! Sravan gripped the arm of his chair. Tried another voice. 'You realize, of course, how we as parents are feeling? What we're going through.' It was a wrong voice.

'The injured child has parents, too,' was Isidore's stinging rejoinder.

He tried another voice. 'You must be so used to injuries in the school campus. When one is handling a thousand boisterous kids . . . it's an occupational hazard, I should imagine . . .' He wasn't too sure what he was saying. 'When one kid accidentally inflicts a serious injury on another, isn't it what the law calls a non-cognizable offence?'

Any reference to the law set Isidore alight. 'You aren't quite understanding the seriousness of this, Mr Kumar. Here there was an intention to kill. Ask your son—he confessed before two witnesses. And anyway, the IPC may not cognize this offence. I as headmaster have to.'

His son couldn't be completely beyond his protection. The wires in his head cut deep. Strident words tingled on his tongue, but despair made him lower his voice suggestively. 'The school needs a new gym or generator, perhaps?'

Isidore's eyes shone in grisly malice. 'I suggest you hold on to your money. Mr Kumar. You're going to need it to bail out your son.'

'Bail! But he isn't under arrest.'

'Not yet. When the warrant comes, he will be. Maybe he will be remanded in custody first. The matter will be sub judice. Meanwhile, as headmaster I am detaining him here. I have unofficial instructions.'

'From whom?'

Isidore wouldn't say.

'You've actually . . . you've actually phoned the police! Over an accident? Over two eleven-year-olds having a scuffle?' Pragya's voice had risen in near hysteria.

'Not I but the hospital, Mrs Kumar. It's normal procedure. When any suspicious case is admitted, the hospital notifies the police. As for your son being a minor, that's immaterial. The IPC has the same law for children and adults. Murder or intention to murder meet with the same . . .'

'How d'you know there was an intention to murder?'

'That's the boy's statement.'

'Statement? A little kid's adventure fantasy.'

'Parents are blinded by affection, Mrs Kumar. But the law is very definite about this. I sent for a copy and have read all the sections very carefully.'

Sravan turned to the kid. 'What happened, beta?' he asked in an altered voice.

The kid looked up slowly at him. His eyes shivered with tears.

'You pushed him?'

The kid had gone dumb. His lower lip did the shrieking for him.

'How did he fall?'

Silence. The kid's face puckered in a soundless bawl.

'Did he jump?'

No answer.

'He jumped, didn't he?' The kid slowly nodded, his face twisted.

Sravan advanced, feeling his ground cautiously. One false step and they'd be undone.

'He . . . he jumped,' whispered the kid. Sravan groped a few steps forward.

'Superman or Spiderman or Batman? Or was it Godzilla?'

The kid's eyes sparked. 'Spiderman,' he whispered.

'I can't allow this,' interrupted Isidore. 'Mr Kumar, you're prompting the child. This will not do.'

'Can't I at least have a word with him in private?'

'Impossible. You go on and say what you have to say here in my office.'

Sravan shrugged and turned to the kid. 'Which one of you was Spiderman?'

There was an answering gleam in the kid's eye. 'Him.'

'I will not have this. Mr Kumar, you have just helped your son fabricate a complete statement to repeat. Here before my very eyes.' In a disgusted aside he added, 'I always say children learn lying at home.'

Oh yeah, scoffed Sravan in derision. Here you teach them truth and moral science. He masked his irritation and kept his voice as composed as possible.

'Nevertheless, you heard what he just said. This is his account.'

'His previous statement was very different.'

'D'you have it on record?'

Isidore smiled. Thin slivers of teeth showing between loathsome purple lips. 'Yes, Mr Kumar, I have it on record. And two witnesses' remarks, too. And to my records I shall add how I have just watched you dictate a false statement to your son. Very quick and inventive, I must say. No wonder you are a writer and your son comes to be such an arrant liar. I've had complaints about him before. But a false witness shall not be unpunished, and he that speaketh lies shall perish. And if you continue to prompt the child I am sorry to say I shall give instructions to the security guards not to let you all enter the premises.'

Sravan planted his elbows on the table. 'Till when, say?'

'Till this matter is decided. Or twenty-four hours.'

'All without a warrant?'

'A person can be arrested even without a warrant.' Isidore swivelled round to the side cabinet and picked up a book. Ah, the Indian Anal Code! Sravan jeered inwardly.

Isidore read in tones of a Sunday sermon: ' "Section Forty-one. Any police officer may without an order from a magistrate and without a warrant, arrest any person . . . ah, um . . . against whom a reasonable complaint has been made, or credible information has been received or a reasonable suspicion exists, etc. etc. The boy will have to remain here, and depending on the course of events he shall have to appear before a juvenile magistrate." '

A sob burst from Pragya. 'You don't mean this! And the warrant hasn't even come!'

'That will not be necessary,' said Isidore. He opened the IPC again. 'It says here—Section Forty-three—"Any private person may arrest or cause to be arrested any person who in his presence commits a non-bailable and cognizable offence." '

'Just a minute. In his presence, did you say? But this thing occurred . . .'

Isidore faltered, then regained his balance. 'You overlook that phrase about credible information. It's no use, Mr Kumar. The boy has given us enough trouble. He is not a normal child. He needs treatment and rehabilitation and the law must take its course.'

'Tell me, please,' begged Sravan, reduced to emotional appeal now, 'what possible satisfaction you as an educationist will get from seeing a child's spirit broken because of an unfortunate accident. The child's going through hell as it is. Let him go home. Rest and get over the shock. The law can take its course. Or some agreement out of court with the affected party.'

The Reverend Isidore was unbending. 'My position as headmaster is crucial. It is a question of responsibility. Moral accountability. Setting an example. Up to twenty-four hours I can keep the child here. Till news from the hospital arrives. Or a warrant of arrest.'

'Why should that be necessary?'

A wry smile from Isidore. 'Mr Kumar, nothing that I have seen of you so far has encouraged me to trust your word. If I let the child go with you . . .'

At this point Pragya began to cry. 'How can you be so inhuman?' she sobbed. 'He's just a small kid. An ordinary kid, not a criminal. We're ordinary parents. You don't know how hard it is to bring up a disturbed child.'

Weeping women were outside Isidore's script. He looked at this Magdalen with an impenetrable face and demanded austerely, 'Then why do you beget them? A foolish son is grief to his father and bitterness to her that bore him. Thank God that I am a gentle and humane headmaster and I have not laid a finger on your son.' He turned to Pragya. 'Please don't worry. The boy will be comfortable here. Tomorrow we shall see which way the wind is blowing.'

'Can't I at least bring meals for him?' begged Pragya.

'That will not be necessary. He shall have what he needs. We'll give him rice and dal and vegetables and whatever you people eat.'

Sravan smarted. Bloody cur! He felt like asking, And what do you people eat? Fucking black English pariah? Steak-and-kidney pie?

He tried one last time. 'I find this absolutely amazing, Father . . .'

'What I find amazing, Mr Kumar, is that you haven't even once asked about the other child—the injured child dying in hospital.'

Sravan fell silent, overcome by confusion.

'And now, please, I have work to do.' Isidore dismissed them summarily with a wave of his bat-like hand, lolling out of his wide cassock sleeve. 'You, boy, sit where you are.' He rang for the attendant. 'Send Brother Eugenius.'

The kid began to whimper.

'Quiet,' snapped Isidore. 'Not a sound, mind.' The kid collapsed in a spasm of sniffles.

Pragya could not hold herself in check any longer. She flew to Ashu, knelt before him, flung her arms about him. 'I'm not leaving you here, baby,' she sobbed. 'I'll sit on the pavement outside the school, baby. You shan't be alone.'

But Isidore thundered so imperially over her bowed head that she subsided. 'Control yourself, Mrs Kumar. In case you're thinking of sitting outside and making a spectacle of yourself, let me advise you not to. No good will be served. You'll only attract attention to this incident. The press and then the other guardians. Believe me, no one will be on your side. Public sympathy will be with the hurt child and his parents. In the interest of your child I advise you to go quietly and leave him in my charge.'

The terrible reality struck home. Pragya, growing pale, staggered to her feet and clutched at Buddhoo's hand for support.

'It's okay, Father,' said Buddhoo smoothly. 'I'm not a parent or even a relative. And I'll be outside the gates. Just for the kid's consolation and his mother's confidence. I assure you I won't attract anyone's attention.'

20

He was surprised it was not a private ward. That there was no glass door to stop him, no uniformed guard or sentry or board listing visiting hours. A government hospital. Only government hospitals register police cases.

The ward was shared by three other patients. A burnt woman beneath a metal mesh, two road accidents and, in the corner, the case he'd come to check up on. He still preferred to think of it as a 'case'. He prowled around the passage, nervousness locking his jaws. He sat on a bench, lit a cigarette. A young doctor passed, told him to smoke outside. Relieved at the chance to get away, he nodded and fled to the green patch outside the emergency block. In a few minutes he slunk down the corridor again, stood outside the ward in question and peeped in at his 'case'. He could see the top of the drip stand and the inverted bottle of glucose. Tubes. Blood-transfusion kit. He could make out the little black cart that held the oxygen cylinder. And three persons.

Through the gap in the screen, his eyes settled on a small hand, held stiff along a splint with the glucose tube attached. He could feel his breath turn laboured at the sight.

The young doctor passed again, carrying a file. Saw Sravan lurking at the door and raised his eyebrows quizzically. Sravan grew instantly self-conscious, began walking slowly down the corridor, exaggeratedly concentrating on the numbers of the wards. When the young doctor vanished into an adjoining ward, Sravan made sure no one else was about and made his way back to the door of the ward. He studied the three around the bed. A scruffy woman with hair a dusty henna and puffy eyes, her face streaked. She wore a faded green salwar-kameez that she'd had no time to change out of. A short, mousy man with scanty hair, wearing a creased safari suit pulled on in haste. Or maybe he had just been informed at his workplace. A girl in a skirt and rubber slippers. The woman sat on a stool, holding the hand flat upon its splint. Sravan had come with a chequebook and a mouthful of words. At the far end of the corridor the young doctor appeared.

Buddhoo let him in when he rang the doorbell. 'Back for a bite of dinner,' he said briefly.

He crept into the dining room like a thief. Pragya was sitting stock-still at the table. Her eyes drilled into the depths of his guilt and fixed him, impaled him to his shame. He stood there, helpless. 'I couldn't,' he said.

She scorched him. 'Why?'

He shook his head. 'Don't ask me why.'

Her eyes clutched at his face. 'You didn't speak to them at all?'

'No.' He tried detaching his face from her grip. He wasn't up to this; it was a situation beyond his capacity. Sometime in the future, in secret, he'd try writing it all out—the faces, the cross-fire of suggestion and threat, the appeal, the terror. He feared that even on the page he wouldn't be able to manage it. 'I spoke to a doctor instead.'

She looked ready to fly into a passion. 'A doctor! What good will that do?'

'He explained the exact situation to me. Medically, I mean.'

'Oh, God!' she gasped in exasperation. 'Medically!' She mimicked his voice. 'Listen to him!'

'I had no words,' he said lamely. He envied her gift of release in simple anger.

'Funny, isn't it? You weren't required to deliver a soul-shaking speech. You just had to go and stand beside them. Say you were Ashu's father. Say you were grieved. That you wanted to share the work and the expense . . .'

The sharp blade of her voice sawed at his raw heart. Her eyes narrowed. 'Or were you scared? Or are you incapable of direct words now?'

He couldn't risk using real words now—no matter how he used them, they sounded professional. Like something in a shop window.

'What did the doctor tell you?'

He told her. Repeated the medical terms, not daring to look at her. She had screened her face with both hands.

Presently she removed her hands and asked, her voice queer: 'What does it mean—this four-quadrant aspiration? And this . . . this diagnostic peritonial lavage?'

'I think they're tests. To check rupture of abdominal organs. Putting in fluid and then taking it out and checking it . . . That's what the junior doctor said . . .' he finished weakly.

'Coma?'

'Yes.'

She was always one for lightning decisions. She picked up the car keys. 'Pass me that chequebook,' she said briskly. 'I may be late. Don't wait up.'

'Where're you going? The hospital?'

'Yes.' She turned to Buddhoo. 'You coming?'

'Sure,' answered Buddhoo, and he followed her out.

Sravan bolted the door after them, sank into his chair and waited for the enormity of the thing to come and capsize him. All of a sudden his head unlocked and the horror came lurching up. He had to set his teeth and gulp it down. The medical terms became ghastly visions. Hemiplegia. Intra-cranial haemorrhage and contusion. There was also the rupture of a lung, resulting in blood and gas collection in the pleural cavity. Fracture in the lower back and paraplegia of the lower limbs. The kid might be paralysed for life. The poor mite. Here Sravan was, trapped in a runaway script, resisting it with all his might and unable to suspend or change it. He wished he could unknot and weep, simply and exhaustively as a child does. He tried. A horrible cramp travelled up his throat.

He sobbed to disgorge the gob of pain—for that kid, that other one with whom he felt this awful connection, linked by this umbilical cord of guilt.

Much later he found himself thinking straight again. It was a quarter to ten when the doorbell rang.

A youngish man with a camera, a notebook and a cocky face. Reporter from a local paper. A card. S. Moolchandani from the *Clarion*, sent to cover this incident.

'Incident?' queried Sravan.

'This St Benedict Public School case. A kid's been hurled down from a fourth-floor balcony.'

'Criminal Violence in Local School'. This young jerk probably had the headline all ready in his head. Sravan cursed him with all his venom. But kept his face mildly enquiring.

'Who tipped you off?'

'Kids, parents. Rumours afloat . . .'

Despite his manful effort to wear a mask, Sravan couldn't bite back the grim retort. 'Pity this is all they picked for you. Your paper, I mean. Playground politics.'

The young smughead stiffened and Sravan instantly realized his error. Wrong thing to say. This guy took his job seriously. A new hand, painfully conscientious in his obligations to truth and to his paper, pathetic bastard! Going against the grain, Sravan managed to expel the glint of mockery from his voice and produce the proper tone of complimenting appeasement.

'What I meant was—how's it they send the dynamic young guys to cover these trivial Page Six items and keep the useless old fogeys to cover the real issues?'

He'd touched a raw spot. The young man's face turned sulky. 'I can't choose, can I?' he shrugged.

'Oh, I'm sure you can't,' said Sravan. Then he added lightly, 'I've been a bit of a newspaper man too.' No, wrong again. He somehow always managed to use the wrong voice. This one now sounded kind of condescending. He switched to a more casual, offhand tone. 'Used to be. They'd send me out on the most boring assignments. So I'd inflame them into red-hot controversies. Pure spite, you get me?'

The young man did. And didn't think much of it. 'Good for you,' he remarked. A hardened cynic, this constipated turd!

'Now, about this incident . . .'

'Accident,' corrected Sravan.

'There's a kid seriously injured. Reports say he was shoved.' He held his ballpoint pen like a stiletto. 'Getting down to the intention part of it . . .'

Sravan pulled a chair.

'Why don't you sit?' he urged in a voice of suave persuasion. 'Shall I make you a drink?'

'No, thanks.' The young man looked irritated at the interruption. He sat. Sravan sat on the divan opposite the rug.

'What d'you mean? That the kid who fell off the balcony did it intentionally? Juvenile suicide?' he asked innocently.

The young man jerked his head in annoyance. 'Juvenile homicide's more like it,' he said. 'The *Clarion* picked up this story from a parent who wishes to remain anonymous. The headmaster of the concerned institution cannot be contacted for an interview at the moment, but we have reports that the guilty party is being held at the hostel of the institution. For tomorrow morning's edition we'll make do with your version. Now, your son is alleged to have declared his attention to kill minutes before the victim crashed down from the fourth-floor balcony. What is your account of the incident?'

In what he congratulated himself was a superbly bemused tone Sravan answered: 'If I were to lose my temper at your question and shout, "Blast you!" and if, an hour from now, you were to get yourself bumped off in a bomb blast, would you say—no, of course you wouldn't be in a position to say anything—let's put it this way—would it be logical to say that I slung the bomb at you? Or if—forgive my language—if you made a "Fuck you" sign at a girl on a bus and she happened to be raped an hour later in a park, would you be construed the rapist?'

His brain was lucid, performing splendidly. The young reporter looked disoriented and Sravan seized his chance. 'As for my son's threat to kill, practically every eleven-year-old threatens his peer group with mutilation or murder every day of his life, thanks to the sort of psychological climate we live in. The fact that the kid actually fell off a balcony doesn't necessarily mean that he was physically pushed.'

'Your son was with the victim when the incident . . .'

'Threatening to kill is not in effect culpable. A shout at a strategic moment can disbalance a tightrope walker. Would that be culpable?'

The young fellow was by now at a loss.

'No one actually saw my son administer the push and the kid himself remembers nothing. The only person who would have the true facts would be the victim, but I'm afraid he will not be in a condition to speak or recall much for a long time, if at all.' He was trusting the average man's reluctance to serve as a witness in a criminal case.

But the young man's confusion was momentary. In a voice of dismissive command he broke in: 'You can suggest all those possibilities to your lawyer. All I want is the details. Name?'

'Whose?'

'The victim's.'

'Sorry. I don't know.'

'Your son's?'

'Ashvin Kumar Nishit.'

'Father's name?'

'Sravan Kumar Nishit.' Would this turn the item into a major scoop? Enlarge the font? He expected the fellow to be surprised but was disappointed.

'Profession?'

'Editor, teacher, writer.'

'Teacher of what?'

'Creative writing at the Nehru Centre. Editor of *Swadeshi*.'

The young man considered, pen poised. 'I once published an article in *Swadeshi*. That was before I joined *Clarion*. The only one.'

'Why only one?' asked Sravan. This very cautious.

He seemed unwilling to confess but he did, despite himself. 'I sent in four or five articles. Travel pieces. Rejected.'

Sravan could see that it still rankled. 'Did you send them elsewhere?'

The young man nodded. 'Came back with a bang.' He grimaced.

Sravan chose his words. 'Why don't you send them to us again?' The benign editor, keen on encouraging young enterprise. 'We'll look at them.'

The signal went across with clarity. There was a longish silence. Sravan continued, 'We pay rather well. In fact I was considering introducing a regular travel column, and we needed a columnist with a flair for . . .' His words trailed off as he tested the vibes in the air. 'We also award an annual prize. Ten thousand bucks for the best travel feature, provided it's a place in India and relatively little known. A link-up with the tourism department, you know. *Swadeshi* can just break even—what with our management's rigid stance regarding selective ads . . .' this last thrown in to cover that small inconsistency about paying well. 'You can send in a special entry—I'm on the jury.'

He did not look at the young man as he spoke. But he was aware that the ballpoint pen had stopped. A minor alteration of inflection, that's all it took. The young man assessed his proposal without comment.

Then he ventured, 'Would the magazine also fund the travel expenses?'

Bastard, thought Sravan. Aloud he said, 'The plan would have to be submitted and passed by our finance cell, but it could of course be considered.'

The young man turned back to business. 'Now this incident . . .'

'Accident,' prompted Sravan.

'I'm sorry—we can't regard it that way. It comes under a specific criminal charge.'

The little runt! That was the way it was going to be, was it? Sravan seethed. 'I don't understand.'

'The injured child is a Dalit Christian. The school management has released a damaging report.'

'To your paper?'

The fellow nodded. Sravan had his doubts.

'The AICO has entered the fray.'

Sravan did not speak. 'I'm beginning to see it all,' he said cryptically. An array of possibilities flashed through his mind. 'Okay,' he said. 'You've come for my report. The facts of the case are—and I don't care what the school management has reported—it was a game between these two kids. They were on this balcony. One of them, that one in hospital, climbed the railing. Spiderman or something. My son was too incoherent—shock—but this is what I gathered. What my son actually did is produce a blood-curdling yell, something to the effect that he'd kill. That's the "intention to kill" the school management's harping on. But it was just an innocent yell.'

'What makes it innocent?' asked the fellow shrewdly.

'What makes it innocent is that the so-called accused had not *foreseen* the consequences of his yell. That shout made the other child lose his balance, but to foist culpability on a child because of an accidental sequence is deliberate and mischievous politicizing. Which paper did you say? *Clarion*?'

'That's right.'

'Katrak Group?'

'Yes.'

'Oh, all right.'

When he had shut the door behind the fellow he stood a while, resting his back against it, thinking fast. In a couple of minutes the phone rang. Pawar's voice. The fucker must've been posted at his window, looking out for the departure of the journalist.

'Who was that, Sravanji?'

'I'm sure you don't need to ask.' Try as he might, he couldn't be polite. 'Did you send him?'

Pawar sounded injured. 'I don't know what's given you the idea. Sarita and I just wanted to tell you that we're all keeping mum—not saying anything. That fellow's been around, asking questions about the kid.'

'Oh, yes?'

'We didn't say a word.'

'Thanks,' said Sravan drily. 'Good of you.' He put the phone down. What a ball the neighbours were having. Paying him back for years of snobbish aloofness. He felt reasonably sure the journalist had every detail about the kid's advanced delinquencies. And there was no knowing if his offer to that jerk would be taken up. For all he knew, it might be put down as conclusive evidence of his general corruption. He found himself pacing the floor and realized that he hated this house, had hated it for years without being aware of it. Parts of it felt close, dense with noxious stress fumes. He decided to pour himself a drink.

He'd just settled down on the settee when a shattering rap descended on the front door, an imperious rain of thuds. He put down his drink, unbolted the door and took in the swinish insolence of the uniformed figure that strode in with an air of unchallengeable gumption.

'Sub-inspector Satish Dubey. Nazirabad Police Circle.'

The offensiveness of the voice dared him to resist. Prompted him to realize what resistance might cost him.

He regarded Satish Dubey's flabby, sweat-slick face. His loose-packed belly flesh spilling over his leather belt. His huge hams tight in khaki. The paan reddening his clammy lips.

'There is a doorbell, Mr Dubey,' he said quietly.

His visitor apparently found the civilian address provoking.

'Sravan Kumar Nishit? Father of Ashvin Kumar Nishit?' he read out.

'Yes.'

'I'm here in connection with the case in St Benedict Public School. The attempt-to-murder case, Section 307. The accused is your son?'

Sravan kept a disdainful silence.

'You are to produce him. He is to be taken into police custody.'

Even more pressing than the need to preserve his dignity was the urgent need to still his face.

'My son isn't here,' he answered.

Dubey reverted to bluster. 'Did I say right now? You are to produce him tomorrow at the Nazirabad Police Station at 10 a.m. sharp."

'My son is a minor. Eleven years old. He can't be placed in the common sort of lockup. What arrangement have you for minors?'

He'd taken in the situation somewhat, decided to play cool.

Dubey threw him a searching look. Assessing his response. There passed into his bragging voice a micro-inflection that Sravan instantly caught—a faint dip of tone he himself had used with the journalist a short while ago.

'Once the arrest is made—even before the warrant comes—we can put him elsewhere under police surveillance,' Dubey said.

'A hotel?'

'Why not? If you pay the tariff. Understand?'

Too well, thought Sravan. 'How much is the expected . . . tariff?'

Dubey turned evasive. 'That depends on the nature of the crime—and your paying capacity. This being a murder charge . . .' And now it was in a pungent aside that he went on. 'We might decide to lodge the accused in a private house—before he appears before the Juvenile Magistrate.'

Sravan spoke in a finely calibrated murmur. 'I wonder—could I suggest—under the circumstances—my own apartment? Could he be brought back from the police station to his custodial cell in this very house? Under your surveillance, of course. Seeing that he's a minor. If I pay your . . . tariff?'

Dubey leered acceptance, even a crude semblance of approval at the finesse in Sravan's mode of suggestion. One artist saluting another.

'We'll see about that tomorrow,' he said, friendlier now that the deal had been struck.

'This is an arrest without a warrant, right? Section 56?'

Dubey's friendliness vanished. 'That's my business, not yours. Ten a.m. sharp. Produce the accused before we come down for him.' This delivered with due rhetoric effect. A policeman's last word.

Sravan could hear his heavy boots clumping down the stairs,

then the revving of the Honda mobike outside. He didn't go to the window lest he catch Pawar spying on him.

The strain was getting unbearable, a huge threatening nimbus engulfing him. A journalist and a police inspector! Those two scenes he'd laboured to write during his long spell of sterility. How had those scenes been tossed into his life with such sureness of aim? He had the nightmarish sensation of sinking powerlessly into the quicksands of his own book in a horrid, paranormal subsidence. The house felt too still. Refrigerated silence massed up on all sides of him, impossible to defrost. His nerves felt the numbing chill of it. In one gulp he downed his drink and hurried to the phone to dial Mridul's number.

21

Mridul drove home at four in the morning. At nine he called up.

'Relax, Sravan. I rang up Shukla. He's SSP for Nazirabad Circle. It's okay. No FIR lodged so far. The cop who called last night was hoaxing. Shukla's made enquiries. Fellow named Dubey—sub-inspector, Nazirabad Thana—he's working on a burn case. Attempted dowry death. He went investigating at the emergency unit of the Medical College Hospital. Must've picked this up there. Sravan—are you there?

'Yes.'

'That Dubey bastard must have been a freelancing shark come to extract a cut . . .'

He heard Mridul's earnest voice and remembered the night they'd spent in their chairs in the flat. He thought of thanking him. For his decency, his uncomplicated concern. Then the thought of Mridul phoning from that familiar bedroom filled him with acute discomfort. Not to mention Mridul's obvious ignorance of the review he had done. His tangled vocal cords struggled for control.

'Isn't it too early? There's still time for an FIR.'

'There's nothing on at the police end—so far. Maybe there won't be. Hope for the best and see if you can stall it. You'd better handle that journalist and the paper he works for. I'll be round in the evening. Straight after office. Six-thirty.'

Six-thirty! As if he, Sravan, didn't know it. He'd always taken care to leave Malini's apartment well before that.

There wasn't time to spare. He consulted the directory and dialled.

'This is Sravan Kumar Nishit. I'd like a word with J.B. Katrak, please.'

The morning edition of the paper carried a tepid account of a fall in a local school in which a child 'sustained injuries' and was 'hospitalized by the school authorities'. A casual 200-word affair tucked away on the third page. There was nothing in the account to suggest any other way of reading the event. The word 'accident' appeared.

It was past eleven when Pragya and Buddhoo turned up, sleepless and dishevelled. He gave them the newspaper without a word.

'That's the official hospital record, too,' said Buddhoo after he'd run his eyes quickly over the report. 'By some merciful stroke the hospital's recorded it as an accidental fall.'

'But the other party? The parents?'

'They're only human. Sravan. They're furious. Emotional. Actually they're not sure exactly how it happened, and there hasn't been time to pursue the point. They're short of hands. The poor kid needs every minute. And we—Buddhoo-bhai and I—we've managed to persuade them.' Her voice was deathly tired, her face white with strain. 'In fact they even said this morning as we were leaving that even if they had lodged an FIR they would've submitted an affidavit denying their charges. That's big of them, isn't it? But then, often the police aren't willing to drop the case. Mercifully it hasn't reached that point. Though some AICO activists did call on them for a statement and tried provoking them. Turning it into a class issue.'

'But if that kid should recover both speech and memory?' He uttered the question bothering him.

'Oh, Sravan, shut up! Don't make it difficult for me. As it is I'm sick of these strategies and subterfuges.'

'But just in case the kid does remember?'

'Then you've got your unfailing yarns to fall back on.' He was taken aback by the bitterness in her voice. 'As for me, I'll take the situation as it comes.'

He looked from Pragya to Buddhoo. 'How'd you talk them out of it?'

Pragya clicked in weary irritation. 'You've got it all wrong. Sravan. We didn't "talk them out" of anything. This wasn't lawyer or writer stuff, for God's sake!'

He saw his overstep, wondered if it was some sort of moral limitation of his.

'Oh, okay. How'd you do—whatever you did?'

'I didn't go rehearsed and prepared. It wasn't an act. Sravan, that poor kid's in a terrible state. They saw my horror was real. They saw that anything the law could extract out of me, I was only too willing to double. Treble. It wasn't compensation—that's a dirty word, after you've taken one look at that poor mite. It was buying peace for myself—if that's at all possible.' Her voice trailed off.

'So now we're on hospital duty as long as we're needed. Pragya pays for things; I do the running around. They attend to the kid. Fair enough,' added Buddhoo.

One last point of curiosity. 'You didn't convince them it was an accident?' he asked cautiously.

'It wasn't an accident,' said Pragya in a low voice. 'You know that. Nothing but the truth can work in these situations, Sravan, though you may not take me seriously.'

He didn't want to argue with her. He told them about the visit of the reporter, the sub-inspector, his talk with Katrak.

'And now I think I'll phone Isidore. Another hour or so and he'll be guilty of illegal detention of a minor.'

Isidore's voice was emotionless. 'Yes, you may come and collect him,' he granted. 'There has been no FIR. It is God's mercy to you.'

There was a moment's silence. Then Isidore added, 'I have to tell you that I am expelling your son. That is something I have to do. For my conscience. I have the whole parent body to consider. There are many rumours. There will be no peace until and unless some action is taken. So I must ask you to take your son away. Put him in another school—in boarding school, if you like. I will give him a transfer certificate.'

That evening they sat alone watching TV, the kid and he. Pragya and Buddhoo were away at the hospital. They sat in what Sravan imagined was a companionable silence, experiencing, in their separate ways, the backwash of a hideous experience.

The animated film on TV showed the final episodes of a sailor story. A ship on the horizon, a faint mast, a puff of white sail, a dark hull looming. Then a flash of telescope lens in the sun—an outcry of shouting and waving. Ship ahoy! A boat cleaving through the choppy waters. The English sailor lands on the shingly strand. Advances, hand extended. Bos'n Martin Shrewsbury of Her Majesty's Patrol of the Spanish Main . . .

Sravan rose and switched off the TV.

'Did you do it?' he asked the kid.

He'd wondered if this kid was merely dazed, or whether he had some kind of crisis-proof armour. All evening the kid's utter normality had baffled him. As though the horror had dripped off him like water off a duckback raincoat.

The kid looked at him, straight and unflinching. 'No,' he said calmly.

Pragya had not asked the kid any questions. She'd left all that for later. Poor kid—there'd be weeks of conscience-raking, psychological drilling, parental counselling, confessional therapy. He knew Pragya. It was going to be a moral third degree. As for him, he recognized the protective capacity of denial.

'I know you didn't,' he said to the kid. A gentle lifelong fiction they would foster and share. Absolutely reciprocal.

But always under threat from so many things. Like the phone call from the hospital saying the kid—the other one—had emerged from his coma. It would take time, Pragya said, probably months, but his spine would mend. The surgeons were hopeful. What was troubling was the brain. The MRI reports showed partial cerebral anoxia, which in lay terms was a lack of oxygen in the brain, and also cerebral atrophy of the temporal lobes. The speech centre.

Now this sort of thing rattled him. Horribly. There was no easing off the nausea of that knowledge. No payment could be enough. This soreness in his soul. Unless he tried rinsing out his heart with words again. The old doubtful potion. Alternative healing. He looked at his son sitting there in the armchair. He didn't know the guilt he'd inherited, but he would. Soon enough. All his life that brain-damaged kid would lurk in the hidden recesses. Sravan saw his son twenty years later, a young man with a dark responsibility. Visits to a mysterious 'friend' in hospital or asylum or suburban home.

The idea began expanding in his brain, claiming all his concentration. He turned to it in relief, grateful for its distraction. The pain turned into a bait: an exciting theme and a demanding plot. It obsessed him. The protagonist's sinister secret life, suspected by his family. Disappearances, bank drafts, telegrams, phone calls, railway tickets. Great. It was there, ready-made, just spinning forward the way the best themes did. He'd have to jot it down before it evaporated—as so many excellent ideas did now. It needed a climactic discovery, naturally. All the clues were already there, but capable of gross misinterpretation. The brain-damaged classmate of thirty years back.

Sravan's first reflex was to head for his study. He didn't know what it was that intervened. An unpleasant subversive voice in his head, an idea he'd been offered on a silver platter, a hospital bed? Not this time—he stopped himself with an explosion of intuition. By God, this time I'm not writing it out. I'm going to act it out—watch me now.

22

'Don't mince words,' he told Pragya. 'I understand what you're getting at. You're leaving me. Not a judicial separation—a situational one.'

'I wish you wouldn't use that tone,' she bristled. 'It isn't anything so dramatic.'

She looked him squarely in the eye, across the old battleground of the writing desk.

'We can't send Ashu to a local school. The story's going to follow him round the town. You can't quell these stories, Sravan. They cling to people like nasty smells.'

He had to concede that.

She went on in a reasonable voice that he'd come to regard as specially suspect. 'We can't even keep him in this colony. You know how the neighbours are. This thing needs careful handling. He's got to start afresh. In a new sort of home environment, a new equation with . . .'

'You could advertise for a new father,' he interrupted bitterly.

'Don't be difficult. All I plan to do is put him in a good school in the hills. Not a boarding school; a regular day school. I'll rent a house. Shift my design biz upcountry, that's all. Mussoorie'd suit me fine. The right sort of market in the holiday season. In time I might even go in for a showroom. And Chand Mian, my tailor, is quite keen to shift and try his luck in a new city. And there's another thing. Chetan's going to be moved to Delhi for treatment and I'd like to be close at hand, helping out.'

'Mussoorie's not close enough.'

'Closer than this.' She was using her heiress voice now. Gone were the giddy-girlie tone and the sulky-sneering keeper-of-your-conscience voice.

'Ah, the principal financier,' he couldn't help remarking unpleasantly.

'That's exactly how I want it to be,' she answered. 'I want to see both the kids through. Properly. It's very important to me. Otherwise it's going to be an awful feeling, Sravan—not having done one's best.'

It's an equally awful feeling, not having loved enough, was the thought that crossed Sravan's mind.

'So how're you going about it?'

'Well, I've sent for application forms for the entrance tests at a number of schools. As soon as they arrive, I'll be off with the kids. Coach them up a bit. I'll look around for a nice place to rent and furnish . . .'

'And all this you propose to handle alone?'

'No. Once I've found a place, I'll send for Buddhoo-bhai. He's promised to come help me set up and get started . . .'

'Good,' he said, derisive. 'Excellent planning.'

She took no notice of the jibe. 'Yes. Seems a practical sort of plan.'

'Except for one niggling little detail,' he mocked. 'What's to happen to this pile of lumber in the backyard, honey? This morally defective, old-model, non-functional husband?'

She smiled. 'Don't be self-deprecating,' she said. 'It doesn't suit you. You aren't an old model and you're extremely functional, I happen to know. You're just a husband with the warranty period expired. And you weren't ever a high-fidelity product.'

His silence was active with protest. Then he asked. 'Just what is the problem?'

Her voice hesitated, hovered round a word but came to settle on another.

'Okay, put it this way. I'll tell you what my Shakuntala Bua once said to me. She said, "I could've left my husband four times in my life—the provocation was enough—but I didn't. Now it's too late—the chance is lost. But that's what's written here in the lines on my forehead." I don't want to be ruled any more by things like that. Lines on the forehead or genes or disposition or personal script, as you call it. To break out of them—that's what I want.' There was an undertow of emotion in her voice.

'And you don't want to let this chance go? The kid's done you a favour.'

'Try to understand me, Sravan. A marriage is like two gamblers counting their losses, you know. It's what survives destruction when most of it is gone.' She spoke in a strange, shredded voice. 'What I regret most is that we—you and I—have lost our better selves. All these years—they've brought out the worst in us. I don't regret losing anything else—my youth or you—but I regret losing my better nature. Like that time when I burnt up your novel . . . I know you hold it against me. You'll never forget that thing. You'll always go on punishing me. And why shouldn't you? It was a terrible thing to do. I'll carry that shame till I die. For years I haven't been easy in my mind about that book. It was like . . . like killing a child. Your child.' She uttered a wry laugh. 'Medical Termination of Creative Pregnancy. Like a woman jealous because her lover has fathered another woman's child. Now d'you get what I mean by better self? I just want to see whether going away might restore that to me.' Her eyes grew troubled, braked on a word. As for him, his mind was in such an uproar, he was deafened by the clap of thought against thought. He saw that there was now no persuading her. She was perfectly calm, and now she turned flippant.

'You can join me whenever you can get away. And we'll come down when the schools close for the winter. You'll be able to write much better with us gone. We were always disturbing your work. And when you come up every summer, think how well you're going to write up in the hills in a mountain retreat. Maybe you'll be able to write that burnt book again—from your notes and memories. Please. Nothing will please me better. I'll do up your study for you—a room with a view, what say?'

He lost his head. 'Write! Write!' he fretted. 'Is there ever to be anything else for me?'

She put on her innocent face. 'I wonder. It's what I've always been curious about.'

He decided to try one more thing.

'Look, Pragya,' he began. 'There's something odd I'm going to tell you.'

'Uh-huh?'

'Something funny's happening to me. I hardly know how to put it. There's been this problem with the kid. You're taking him away. We're going to live separately—on what terms, I don't know. There's guilt in the background. Someone's died—no, not in real life. But in my book . . .'

She looked stricken. 'Your book? That one?'

'The one I'm on now. Don't butt in. Let me speak. Someone died. In my book it was a young woman. She fell—jumped—or was pushed by her circumstances—into a well. Her death hangs like a threat to the peace of a family. There's been infidelity, betrayal . . . And a man's been pushed to his death as well, denied shelter . . .'

'How exciting,' said Pragya softly, thinking aloud.

'The truth comes out and the family breaks up. The breakup's brought about by the kid . . .'

Pragya uttered a stagey gasp. 'D'you mind going a bit slow?'

'Pragya, what I'm trying to tell you is this—everything that's happened to us lately—all this trouble—it's all a rehash of my book. Yes, I wrote it all in a different order. But it's happened to us. Organized differently. That family broke up through a kid. Ours is about to. This thing you just said, about murdering a child—or a book—because it's been conceived—or fathered—by another—this too! This jumped-or-was-pushed question. This too is a situation in my book. I've begun feeling that I've got to pay for every word I ever wrote. I have to account for it somehow. Every story I ever wrote is going to rise against me and demand its due—in reality. There's something funny going on. It's closing round me like a curse.'

She didn't let him finish. She rose to her feet. 'Hyper, that's what you are. And who said we're breaking up? I'm just going to live somewhere else for the sake of the kid.'

'But that's exactly what she did—Mondira.'

'Who's Mondira? Another of your women?' She said that in a spasm of vengeance she couldn't help. He gulped down his agitation, let it pass. She still hadn't uttered Malini's name, depriving him of the opportunity of lying his way out.

'A character in my book.'

'There you are. Hyper,' she exclaimed, patience wearing thin. 'Now you know what I mean. Writing's driving you crazy. That's what's closing round you. Simple as that. What was that word Buddhoo-bhai used the other day? Ah, monomania. That's it.'

Long after she'd left the city, Sravan kept brooding on her words.

When Pragya was packing up to leave, she carried out a thorough spring-cleaning of her room, leaving a heap of half-torn paper on the ground. Old recipe books, do-it-yourself manuals, design pamphlets, old magazines. The morning after he put her on the train he found, carelessly abandoned in the discarded mess, one of his early novels. A more fluent rejection wasn't possible. Hurt, he picked it up and carried it into his study. His father had deliberately never read his books, probably didn't even remember the titles.

So there it is, he thought. Unbelievable but true. My life's cracked apart, accurately along the line I plotted for my book! Like the earth's crust, silently crumbling along a zigzagging fault. He went back to his work, disoriented at the strangeness of it. My mind made it happen on the page. Now it's happening in my life. There I was in control. Here I'm not. He thought distractedly of Atreya's words. A paragraph in a weekly assignment. With amateurish gravity she'd penned: 'Every few years, the map of our life changes; the country of our consciousness comes to have different frontiers; its territories are redefined; and all our psychological self-administration given a new slant of strategy.' His remarks on grading the piece B+ had been: Ponderous. Avoid semi-colons. Shorten length of line. Reduce thoughts into simpler units.

The thoughts in his own head now wouldn't reduce to simpler units. He sat questioning his book for traces of prophecy. What's going to happen to Mondira's small son? His mind prompted the answer—Mondira and Mihir will part ways. The child will never return. The territories of their lives will have to be redefined, and all their whatwasit 'self-administration' given a new whatzitcalled 'strategy'. He sat searching his book to read his own future. Trying to decant fiction for truth. Believing that the truth might be still there, settled at the bottom, and that the fiction might float up and be drained off. Then he rapped himself hard and thought—bullshit! My head's caught in an idea warp, that's all.

The last two chapters. He felt such relief, striking each character off his soul. Detached psychically at last. Thank God I don't have to go on feeding each character my own vital energy. But the damn idea kept returning, and he had to share it with Buddhoo.

'You must take this seriously. By intuiting an outline for the book, I willed it to happen in my life.'

'Then it's simple,' said Buddhoo. 'Go ahead and rewrite it. Change the script, since it isn't working too well for you.'

'I haven't any alternative drafts. And my novel's as fixed upon the page as my life is fixed in time. Rewriting won't be easy—my brain's going to fight every word. By the way, there's something on my mind. What's going on—Pragya and you?'

Buddhoo looked astounded. 'Have you taken leave of your senses?'

Sravan kept silent.

'You've written so much about infidelity and betrayal in that wretched book of yours that you're obsessing about betrayal, you're enacting betrayal, imagining betrayal all around you.'

'Sorry,' said Sravan, contrite.

'Sure,' said Buddhoo. 'Come out of that book, for God's sake. You'll wander round and round your own pages without ever finding a way out.'

'Until another book comes along.'

'Like they say, it takes a spell to break another spell. But Sravan yaar, how do you get to free yourself? There's nothing on between Pragya and me. What the hell! Don't be a bloody fool. You're imagining things. Actually,' said Buddhoo, 'we're in the same boat. I'm either making things up in my mind or making things with my hands. I can't live without an audience for my buk-buk. You can't live without doing your buk-buk on the page and then spinning it all around yourself. We're both trapped, we two buk-bukaneers. Or, in your case book-bookaneers.'

'That's just what's bothering me. That out of all that suffering shall come not an action but a book. For me books may well be surrogate deeds. After so many of them, year after year, what I want to achieve is a real, consequential deed, not a mass of words.'

'Don't go and shoot yourself like those jackasses in your boring existentialist novels,' laughed Buddhoo.

'Well, my novel's done and finished. I'm left with a blank quarter page at the end and my signature. At the end of one's life there must be some sort of a karmic signature, you know.'

'Your essential ISBN code?'

'Yes. Okay, suppose I take your advice? Can't rewrite my life so I might as well go back and rewrite my book. But not just yet.'

'Why?'

'I like this blankness. This post-signature emptiness. No obligation to spin another tale.'

'Moksha?'

'Absolutely right. That's exactly what it feels like. But there's another thing disturbing me. Ever been nagged by silence, yaar? As I wrote these last chapters I felt such a *stillness* close around me. I'm not used to it. This absence of people. And I wonder if I'm guilty—of rejecting them all.'

'Let them go now.'

'Will I get them back?'

'I don't think so . . . no, I really don't know.' Buddhoo forced a laugh. 'Maybe if you write a reunion sequel. It'll be one way to test your theory.'

Sravan brooded. 'It's this writing of mine that's always been in the way. I've always known it. Everything would be restored to me if this writing was abandoned. But that's just what I can't do. I let go the rest—so long as I preserved this. But I'm angry—that this choice had to be there at all.'

Buddhoo kept silent.

'Go on, say something. Haven't you any of your stupid stories for me? Your *Mithyopanisad* or anything. You've been playing Krishna to my Arjuna long enough. I can just feel my pen fall from my hand . . . like Arjuna's Gandiva fell from his. Only he was in a battlefield full of family and kin and I'm in an empty thought-field in which everyone's gone and I've got to start fighting the page alone and I don't see why I must.'

'Yaar, you make too much of everything. That's your fault. Too much of your family going away, too much of your books, yourself. I'll tell you a fable I like. Suitable for a jittery writer at the end of his marriage and the end of a book. Narada once asked Krishna the meaning of maya. He was always doing that, you know. So Krishna took him walking across a desert waste.'

'The page, was it?'

'If you like to read it that way. The sun was hot, the sand burned. Krishna stopped suddenly and said, I'm thirsty, Narada. Fetch me some water.'

'I've heard this one. But tell on—I'm waiting to see what twist you're going to give it.'

'So when Krishna asked for water, Narada set off, pot in hand, looking for water. Before I go on, I'm hellishly thirsty, Ravan. How about some beer? It's a longish story and the throat needs moistening.'

'Right. Get it.'

When he'd poured the beer into mugs and settled down. Buddhoo went on. 'At the verge of the desert, Narada spotted a village and a well. Beside it was a beautiful woman.'

'But of course.'

'Well, Narada, laying eyes upon her, fell headlong in love. (Confirmed bachelor though he was, he was always doing that.) Forgot what he'd come for. Went pleading for her hand. Her father insisted that Narada stay on as groom-in-residence in their village and help to till the fields.'

'Another heiress.'

'So Narada married the maiden and settled down as a householder. Years passed and they had many lively children. Then, one Shravan night, the river rose. Higher and higher. The flood waters came lashing and swirling into Narada's village. Narada couldn't protect his house, couldn't save a pot or a cauldron or a casket of gold. All he could manage was a boat. He bundled his wife and his kids into the boat and tried to row them across the flooded river. Failed. The wind was wild, the waters choppy. Suddenly a child tumbled off. Then another. And another. Narada beat his breast and tore his hair in grief and despair. Then he lost his oars. Before his agonized eyes his wife was swept off, and he couldn't do a damn thing. Then the boat capsized. Blinded by his tears, wailing loudly, Narada found himself sinking, too. Thrashing about, gasping for air, floundering, spluttering. Cursing the water he swallowed in gulps. It poured into his lungs and choked him. It closed over his head. He lost consciousness. And as he faded out, he heard a voice in his head—I'm thirsty, Narada. Bring me water. Narada was furious. Water! he shouted. Who is this that dares mention water to me when it is water that has wrought my ruin? From the deep river bed came a voice—It is I, Krishna. I'm thirsty, Narada. Where is the water you promised me? And suddenly Narada awoke from the spell—to behold Krishna smiling before him. He was bewildered. Where's the woman, my wife? he wondered. Where is my home, my village, my family? The fields tilled, the hearth I tended? The river? The flood? To which Krishna replied, Now do you understand the meaning of maya? So that's it, Sravan, mere bhai. Virtual reality, you could call it. You thought you held the oars. You thought you were rowing confidently across your book and your life. But your book's overpowered you. You're capsized and cast ashore. It happens. Here we are now. No family, no fucking book, no relationships, no characters. It'll start feeling real by and by.'

Sravan drained his beer. 'I don't even know if I found what I set out for.'

'Oh, you did, of course. An overdose of it. That's the lesson: you get what you want. More than you ask. More than you bargain for. Until it becomes the element that drowns you. If you imagine you're out to gratify yourself . . .'

'Please, please.'

'No, seriously . . .'

'Cut out the preachifying, pundit.'

'Oh yeah. I know. You're like that guy in the limerick—the one who had a quarrel with every moral. But this is a law of reality we're on.'

'Oh, I forgot you're playing Krishna to my Arjuna and it's got to boil down to something like this. But don't forget it was Krishna who sent Narada to fetch water in the first place, so what was Narada's fault?'

'That's just the point I'm trying to make. Narada's only fault was that he forgot who that water was for. Tell you what, yaar. We aren't like Krishna and Arjuna on Kurukshetra. The roles don't suit us. We're more like Don Quixote and Sancho Panza—ha! Can you imagine what would happen if Don Quixote found himself at Kurukshetra? Great! This is going to be my next project. A multicultural comic myth. On screen if possible. In an Indian idiom. Only you'd have to be called Don Kya-hota and I'd have to be Succha Punj. And we'd have to have a lady love called Dulhania-dil-Tabassum and a nag called Rosie Nanda. I can just see you attacking clouds of dust with your pen. And tilting at dish antennae . . .'

Sravan began to laugh. 'You know what? That's just what I suspect I've been doing all along.'

'So there's nothing better to do at the moment than repeat the old cliché that something new shall come of this mess. Or something old and troublesome might renew,' wisecracked Buddhoo.

The phone rang and Sravan picked it up. 'Oh, okay,' he said to it. 'I'll come.' He switched it off and grinned at Buddhoo. 'You're right, yaar. Something old and troublesome has just renewed.'

'The little lady with the assets disproportionate to her intelligence?'

'Don't be daft. That was Ranjana Devi. She's seventy-five if she's a day.'

'Outside your sixteen-to-sixty-five range, you mean.'

'She's asked me to drop in tomorrow, God knows why. She's such a droning old crone, I think I'll pick up Avasthi on the way just to divide the focus of her chatter.'

23

Ranjana Devi dragged out her sing-song welcomes, modelling the words with her mouth. She surprised Sravan with a birthday gift. But it isn't my birthday, he protested. It's mine, she announced. And I celebrate my birthdays differently.

'Each birthday I give a gift to one of my friends. It's your turn this year. And my gift always suits the person who gets it, though a minute before I fish it out of that old aluminium trunk, I haven't the faintest idea what it's going to be. Watch.'

A large trunk stood alongside a wall in her room. Sravan had not noticed it before. 'I keep it covered up to look like a divan,' she explained. 'That trunk is a metaphor, my dear. It's ugly, I know, but I can't wish it away. It's like the management of grief. Since it won't go away, you've got to make a place for it in your mind. Cover it up with a beautiful cloth, or compose your room around it or say, I defy this thing and shall build myself up positively in relation to it. Something like that.' She knelt before the trunk and undid the clasp, then paused before lifting the lid.

'Don't gape like that.' She smiled. 'It isn't a coffin. It's a treasure trove.'

It seemed to be packed with bric-a-brac.

'I've got a lot of beautiful things here,' she said. 'Things I've been giving away. That's the way it is. First you collect things, then you go about clearing them away. It's a bit like a lucky dip. Put in your hand, Sravan, and pick up anything. It's bound to be just the thing for you.'

Sravan obeyed and lifted the small package wrapped in tissue paper. Ranjana Devi exclaimed in amazement. 'Ah, didn't I tell you? Just the thing for you. This is my husband's mascot. His ivory Saraswati. Take it, Sravan, with my blessings. And wish me a happy birthday. I'm seventy-seven today.'

He was out of his depth. He wished her, and gazed mutely at the exquisite figurine in his hand. Avasthi embraced the old lady, touched her feet. Ranjana Devi pronounced benediction, glowing with pleasure.

'An old woman's idiosyncrasy, no?' She smiled sweetly. 'But it gives me such joy. And there's something more coming, Sravanji. Instead of serving you a slice of cake, I shall treat you to a slice of my life. It goes with the gift—a package deal. Do you understand? I'm distributing my things and my secrets equally among my friends. When I am dead and gone you can get together and pool the slices and get the whole cake before you. I promise you it'll be different from anything you ever imagined.'

'You chose the Saraswati so you get the Saraswati story. Why do you think he kept this image on his writing table? Because she's the muse, you imagine? You're wrong. This Saraswati stayed on his table as a gesture to Saraswati Shandilya. Yes, a flesh-and-blood woman. Did you know her? She was a brash, brown-eyed, big-hipped woman, a social siren who paraded as a poet and a party singer. But my husband was besotted with her. You didn't know this small detail, did you? Nobody did. Except me, of course. Oh, he played me false, he did. And he paid for it. Dearly. From the time that woman came into his life, his writing went downhill. Until he couldn't write a page. It tortured him, made him rave, but there was nothing to be done. That is the way it happened—I'm not making it up. No biographer knows this. My husband did not write anything after he met that woman and after a while he grew desperate. So he invented that hoax called *Antim Aadesh*.'

'That was the mega-novel he was working on for six years—his incomplete novel, wasn't it?' asked Avasthi in surprise.

'There was no novel,' she said. '*Antim Aadesh* is a rumour, no more. To save his reputation. To stop the press saying—he's finished, the great Maheshwar Dayal. For years now scholars have been writing to me, asking for his papers and the remains of that so-called incomplete masterpiece, and what do I tell them? I say it was misplaced, lost when we changed houses. Then, when that woman left him, he had a heart attack and it took him off.'

Sravan looked at her composed face. This one-poem, memory-counting, legend-immortalizing woman. He wondered why she was telling him all this. He asked.

'Because,' she answered, 'you picked up the Saraswati and this secret was reserved for the person who picked up the Saraswati. No other reason.'

'You don't want to protect this . . . secret?'

'Not any more,' she said. 'For me there's nothing left, nothing more to do. I want to go into the next century without any baggage. I'm joining the Gaudia Mutth on the first of January with a different name, in a different city. I'm leaving my things and my story behind with friends. You can do as you please with them—they don't concern me any more.'

To Avasthi she gave a framed poem by her husband beginning, '*Bhool gaye thé ki ek aur bageecha hai seenchne ko*.'

They were both a little subdued when they left her.

'Do you mind if we drop in at Farooqui's? Since you're here,' suggested Avasthi. 'He's in a peculiar mood. Sold his library.'

'He's clearing away, too?'

'Not the same way. You'll see. He's become very touchy. I've brought something for him here.' He tapped the cloth bag slung across his shoulder. Sravan didn't ask what it contained.

They seemed to be enclosed in a bleached cage. The empty shelves of Farooqui's whitewashed room looked like the picked ribs of a cadaver. Sravan was used to seeing it fleshed out with glossy books in several languages, but now it was a monk's cell, a catacomb.

He turned to Farooqui in silent query.

'You could call if bibliophobia,' was Farooqui's explanation.

'No, seriously . . .?'

'They'd begun oppressing me.'

'Books?'

'Yes. Every time I stepped into a library or a bookshop, I felt choked.'

'I don't understand this. You've spent your whole life reading and writing . . .'

'Have you felt this heavy weight . . . of human experience . . . pressing down on you in a library? This roar of human thought? Janab, I felt deafened. Crushed. Ah, I know what you're going to say, Avasthi, mere bhai. Once, long ago, how good books smelt. Like oxygen in a rain forest. It's all over for me. Khatam! I feel tired, just looking at the kambakht things.'

'Surfeit,' murmured Avasthi.

'No. My soul's sickened of this whole wretched *junoon*. Seeing the books heaped upon pavements. The ones unsold are pulped down later. Some poor bewaqoof's work, written with the blood of his heart. The book fairs! Frightening! The stalls look like cars on a highway. Too many, too bright, too loud.'

He gestured nervously.

'Yet you add to the pile by writing more,' smirked Sravan.

Farooqui was revved up in self-defence. 'Hasn't Avasthi told you? Ask him.' He turned to Avasthi. 'Go on. Tell him,' he said with obvious pride.

'Not long ago Javed Mian completed a novel. Took him all of eight years. He used to sound me out over it. Read out bits. I found it very good. Suddenly he was seized with this madness. Went and sold it, along with his newspapers and old books, to the *kabari*! That's how serious it is. Javed Mian needs to have his head examined.'

'How much did you sell it for?'

'The handsome sum of eight rupees! Waste paper by the kilo! A rupee a year, good bargain, no?' Farooqui gave vent to a crazy, sobbing laugh. 'Did any publisher ever buy a script for a sum as low as that? My kabari's a deal better. Ha! I've set a world record!' He brayed like a joyous lunatic.

'Why did you bother to write it at all?'

'Enlightenment came to me, my son, just after I completed it.'

'Eight years!'

'A little over that, actually. It was a kind of shelter, that book. Helped me across eight difficult years. A bad time. Kept me distracted from my troubles. I'm safely across that time and it's served its purpose.'

'That's just what some of my books have been. But I didn't get rid of them.'

'There's another reason. I couldn't bear to read a single page of that book. Not a page. I don't mind telling you this—many times during those eight years I touched rock bottom. There were times when life had battered all the literature out of me, and my so-called philosophy had drained away. Weeks when I wrote only a para a day, then only a line. But always a line, never less. I swore to myself that come what may, one line would be written. Defying my situation, you understand? Now when I read that book again, somehow I can't concentrate on what's there on the page. Instead, I'm reading a horrible undertext—all that happened to me the day I wrote that particular passage. Say I come across a fictional situation I've built, and my accursed memory gets active and I start saying to myself—That's the part I couldn't complete because my Ishrat vomited blood and it was a Sunday evening and I ran from pillar to post and couldn't fetch a doctor. I read the next para and say to myself—This bit's more poised—I wrote this a while later, when she was dead and buried and I could think in straight sentences again. I crossed out fifty-seven lines in between—they didn't seem right—until fifty-seven days later I found this line. Simple, rounded and true. I go over the next chapter and I remember—this was written on the day my son abused me, threw a shoe at me, attacked his brother with the kitchen knife and my wife grabbed at it desperately and cut her hand instead. After a few more passages I read a page and recall how that day I received a legal notice from my younger brother, Kamran. And the next chapter, written on the day my son smuggled important title deeds across to Kamran and I received a threat to vacate the house, else our things would be thrown on the footpath—and someone hurled bricks into the courtyard at night. Allah knows, it wasn't an easy time. I needed something to keep me sane. This book, all two-and-half kilos of it, was my asylum. But I can't bear this embalmed text of pain. It's like being forced to watch the happenings in the green room when you'd rather watch the stage. Each time I look at that book, it hurts my heart. I had to put it behind me. And yet I couldn't bear to burn it . . .'

Farooqui's voice had sunk to a reedy musing, his face fallen slack in a myriad intersecting lines. He cleared his throat loudly, rose and drank some water out of the surahi in the corner, turned and offered them some. He carried the surahi to the verandah, splashed water on his face, and mopped it with his sleeve. He came back beaming, replaced the vessel and produced his malevolent laugh again.

'So I'm doing humanity a great service, sparing it my talents as a hack writer. Sometimes I feel the whole of my life coming up in my throat like a ghastly vomit and I'd like to spew it all out, but that's no reason to write, is it? I've started a campaign to discourage misguided idiots from unnecessarily burdening our shelves. Starting with you, young man. Now consider—all your life you're like Pavlov's dog, conditioned to record and reflect. Rushing up with each new experience. Encashing it for words. Until one day the account's depleted and you're bankrupt. All your life you've shut yourself up. Told people to clear out, not disturb you. Then one day you find your house gone ghastly still. Everyone's gone. The old are dead, the young flown off. What do you have? Dead books, silent walls, rags.'

Sravan felt himself shiver. It was hitting too close. But Farooqui's acid voice wouldn't leave off. 'Know this,' he persisted. 'As you grow older and improve in your chosen work, a curious thing happens. That skill that was your greatest joy turns into your bitterest ache. It feeds on your lifeblood. Claims more and more of you. Thrills you. Punishes you. Drains you. Lashes you on from performance to greater performance. Loneliness to greater loneliness. It's like a boa constrictor. And all the time a fellow doesn't stop telling himself his own story. When the narrative stops, he dies. Even when he sleeps, oblique stories go on. A pseudo-order, janab, a completely fake thing! I tell you—all my life I've been possessed by this punishing demon that dragged words out of me in never-ending command. Books and more books. One day I awoke to find that a world had passed away under my nose. I'd known, I'd seen it going, but it hadn't registered. But when the knowledge came, it struck at me so violently there was no writing it down, no.'

He fixed his burning, broken eyes on Sravan. He looked much like a boa himself, tightening his mesmeric persuasion around Sravan, watching him like a predator. There was a moment of silence. Then Avasthi's sane voice broke in.

'Don't let this old fool get the better of you. That's not the whole truth, Sravan, just his side of it.'

'What's yours?'

'Mine? All right—it's not pretty but I'll let you have it. I've come to suspect that I'm surrounded by parasites. Yes, they're my family, but what of that? Time-servers, every one of them—wife, daughters, sons. None of them worthwhile in my sense of it.'

'Your standards of sincerity must be impossibly high,' remarked Farooqui with a gruff laugh.

'Think what you like. It is the harsh truth of years. There are only two things I can count on: my pension and my writing. The only two things tried and tested.'

There was no trace of complaint in Avasthi's mild voice. It seemed to rattle Farooqui's querulous soul. He produced a scornful snort. 'One day,' he predicted, 'one day they'll let you down, too. The pension when you find you're too old to go to the bank and collect it and have to live on the sufferance of insolent bank clerks; the writing when you find there's no excellence there, either.'

Avasthi abruptly lifted his dun-coloured cloth bag off the floor, laid it on the table and turned to face his friend sternly. 'That will do for now, Javed Mian,' he said summarily. 'I know excellence when I see it, just as well as you. I picked up something excellent yesterday afternoon. From Santosh, your kabari. I consider the three hours I spent on my gouty knees, rummaging in his bundles of waste paper, well spent.'

Farooqui's eyes recoiled. He looked from the bundle to his friend and his brow crumpled.

Avasthi continued lightly, 'Yes, all two-and-a-half kilos of it. And I must tell you, Javed Mian, your signing amount's gone up by two rupees. The kabari paid you eight rupees—I paid him ten. Congratulations.'

Back home that night, Sravan placed the Saraswati on his table beside his PC and thought by turns of the three old men. Writers all, they had depended on their work for sanity and sense and had come to fear and despise it. And none of them could ever break away.

He'd never thought of himself as superstitious or suggestible, but he studied the ivory Saraswati on his desk with foreboding. The carving was exquisite, the eyes slumberous with thought. She was curved in a danseuse's slender droop over her veena, one hand lapsed in mid-lilt upon its strings, the other flowering upwards in blessing. A delicate leg folded in feathery drapes upon her swan, the other melted into the snowy froth of its down. He marvelled at the craftsmanship that had created her creamy sheen. Looking at her long enough in silence was enough to stir a silver spray of strings in one's pulse and sprigs of verse in one's head. There was no doubt about it—Ranjana Devi had given him a valuable piece. But not even Saraswati could give Maheshwar Dayal that last book he hankered for. *Antim Aadesh*, the last command, ever to remain unfulfilled.

Sravan had never been religious but he needed a rite, however foggy. He lit a single mogra joss stick. He piled up on the table his files and his floppies, his handwritten notes, his diaries and jottings, his albums of cuttings and citations and all his published works. Saraswati's hand lay upon her veena, frozen in mid-strum.

He counted the things he had to be grateful for. The instant when a book found its truth. Or when neutral words acquired a miraculous personal sound and it felt as though living sap had risen in a dry shoot. Or when a spell of aridity broke and a reward came, a brand-new idea, complete and searching like a laser beam. There were things he'd miss. The scuff and scrabble of small sounds—pen on paper, the stutter of typewriter keys, and, lately, the milky moonlight of the computer screen, the still-life calm and coherence of this room. The west window, framing a large day like a dusty windscreen, the road in the park outside sparking hot light. And the articulate space beneath the lamp as he wrote. The shavings of light sprayed in through jacaranda branches, lying in thin glass slides upon his worktable. All the writing accessories that somehow went into what he wrote.

He watched the joss stick burn down. His eyes felt studded with shards. He put everything away, out of sight, locked it all up in his cupboard. Dusted away the ash from the joss stick and unlocked the door of the study. He stepped out, feeling unsteady.

He was tempted to share the experience with Buddhoo. But Buddhoo was wildly excited over a new project.

'A TV serial, no less!' he proclaimed. 'I must get someone to buy the idea. A spicy, slapstick side-splitter! Called—guess what?—*Income Tax*! Have you time to hear the story?'

'All the time in the world.'

'Sit. This idea came to me like a thunderbolt. Must be your new Saraswati in the house. It's crazy, yaar, but a delight. There's a couple—married—stinking rich. Rolling in the stuff. The first few episodes devoted to the stinking-rich syndrome—no moral attached except that it's moral to be rich and if you aren't, too bad for you. All descriptive, nothing prescriptive. Okay, they have just one misery in life, this couple: the income tax they have to pay. Get it so far?'

'Hmm.'

'One day their chartered accountant comes with a great proposal—that they go through the motions of a legal divorce. No hard feelings, everything perfectly hotsy-totsy between the two of them, but just as a legal necessity to cut down tax. They jump at the idea, and a few hilarious episodes revolve round the divorce case, etc., etc. At length they're pronounced ex-man and ex-wife, sorry, ex-husband . . .'

'Then?'

'The capital's nicely split up in two, get the idea?'

'Then?'

'Then, hey presto!—she ups and marries the chartered accountant! D'you like the storyline? Maybe with Satish Shah or Raghubir Yadav in the lead, it'll be a small hit. All I need to do is find a sponsor—and why not the income-tax department? I mean, the underlying moral is, pay tax like all law-abiding citizens and don't try monkey tricks else you'll come a cropper. Hullo? You look cheesed off, Ravan. Is it this income-tax reference? Touched a sore nerve, have I? The lady with the assets disproportionate to her intelligence?'

'It's off,' said Sravan curtly.

'How d'you mean, off?'

'I mean off, finished. I'm not going to see her any more.'

'End of an affair?' prodded Buddhoo. 'How? Suddenly?'

'Not in the mood.'

'Oho, Ravan. The biwi walks out and you're called to heel.'

Sravan refused to be provoked. Instead he asked: 'It's Delhi now?'

'Looks like it, yaar. I'm getting restless here without an audience to hear my buk-buk. And Pragya wants me to go up to Mussoorie and help her set up.'

'Oh.'

'After this serial, I've other great ideas for the small screen. A second serial is about the elderly chairman of an insurance company who secretly goes around scribbling dirty graffiti in bathrooms.'

'You'll have to reckon with the censor boards. And maybe an insurance company or two.'

'I'll burn my bridges when I come to them, ha ha! I have two other projects. There's an inspiration boom in my head. A variation of my cassette venture: "Quit Smoking" cassettes. Electronic nagging for the woman of today. Good, strident, nagging voices that put the shits into a smoker-husband. You play it last thing at night and first thing in the morning . . .'

'Except that most married smokers won't need electronic nagging. And you're being dangerously sexist, man. What happens to smoker wives?'

'This is a—whatd'youcallit?—a culture-specific product. We can later introduce variety. There's another idea on my mind. Two, to be exact. I've a hunch I've hit upon a new energy resource. I mean to exploit the anger reserves of a dozen people and make a bicycle run. I've even worked out the formula: energy=pulse rate by bionic milliwatts upon microsecond by square root of brain-wave frequency whole upon force of stimulus upon surface area of brain! I call it the Buddhasen Effect. The other idea is that fantastic thing that came up the other day—what would happen if Don Quixote and Sancho Panza found themselves on the plains of Kurukshetra? All in all, I'm facing a creative bonanza. Got my hands full and it's time to move, get some change of air . . .'

'How about me here, stranded? Krishna abandoning Arjuna, what?'

Buddhoo guffawed. 'Oh, come on, yaar! You've got enough to do. I've been Yudhishthira's dog to you long enough. You just go ahead and climb your mountain alone, as they say in books. I'll look in from time to time.'

The evening Buddhoo left, Sravan decided to experiment. For the next four days he spent all his waking hours sitting in a chair, the TV gibbering to fill the emptiness. Scribbling was a behavioural addiction, he told himself. If it can't be replaced, it can be defied. It was disorienting to arrest this runaway narrative, but he tried to avoid all thoughts of himself or his book. He assigned himself thoughts to think, timed them.

He wasn't sure what he was trying to do. Corner the obstructions? See what his first impulse would be once the grit of habit was washed away? When he was stuck while writing he stopped and waited and was never disappointed. Some miraculous form of help inevitably surfaced. Now, stuck in a psychological groove, he tried the same thing. Put his trust in the waiting. Sat still.

What I have to practise, he thought, is containment. Like holding a glass of booze against the light, teasing myself as long as I can. Lengthening the span. Like keeping an unread book beside my pillow, allowing its aura to spill into my dreams.

But he worried; an anxious reflex ticked in. He had ideas for future books—what would happen to those?

I'm also worried about this death thing, he thought. Who knows, I may be let loose in a hell of my own uncompleted thoughts. All the swarming bogeys that I never incarnated in words and am denying expression.

He quelled his fear. So what if they stay unexpressed? Someone else'll come along in the future and do justice to them. Maybe I wrote out someone's unfinished work.

He soon faced the withdrawal symptoms of creative compulsion. Just keep still, he told himself. No matter what happens, keep still. His unripened book tempted him from the study, but he pushed it out of his mind. He put himself in limbo, made his mind drop its schemes. Its recurring themes. He scrapped his plots, plans, continuities.

Sit still, do nothing. Hold remote control in one hand, glass of whiskey in the other, keep eyes fixed on TV screen. Until stoned. It takes one addiction to defeat another. Above all do not regard the calendar.

If he could just manage to keep sitting still, evening after evening . . .

After the first few weeks his mind ran round, flexing and unflexing. Exciting imps of thought. His head began buzzing insistently. Threw up stray phrases, fluttering like leaves before a breeze. Little twinges of ideas awoke, twitched in tiresome repetition. He worked hard to ignore them. An hour of this onslaught and he'd be ready to rush to his study to jot it all down.

He kept it up for a month. Did nothing, just sat the evenings out alone. Rose only to eat or go to the loo or answer the phone or sleep. And honour his stints at the Centre and the *Swadeshi*.

Then acute depression gripped him. Slump in mental metabolism, he told himself. His brain began to regurgitate, with a palpable retch, a mess of bilious emotion. Forgotten aches swam up, burning old angers, stubs of injury in an uncontrollable outpour. For minutes at a stretch there was a constant shudder in his head, as though his mind was loosening its stern hold, discharging itself in long, subliminal quakes. What's this now? Cerebral ejaculation? He felt he was waiting for a sign.

Then, one morning, he awoke in a completely silent head. It

was so still—he could hear his mind knocking about far away. He inhaled its spaciousness. Gave himself one more day of sitting still. He no longer needed that TV screen or the remote control to calm his jittery hand. He shut his eyes, sitting in his chair. The wet lap and wash of this coolness! His heart drank at it, felt it sluice down and pool up in the dry depths within him.

He dropped off to sleep again, a sleep so deep that he was absolutely awake to himself. For a long time he stayed that way. Asleep, awash. A soft shirr of water in his ears: he heard its chill, sheer, regular plash. Strings of water spilled along his nerves. His brain seemed a hollow through which a healing river ran. He wondered if this was the sound of sleep, whether sleep had a sound. Or whether it was the flow of his own blood in the silence of his body. He felt himself slicked, drenched, sogged into soft fleece. Dissolved and resolved under a pleasing, soothing solvent, every nerve in his head moisturized, a cool flow pouring down the middle of his skull. He felt himself moving, marvelled that sleep was a movement, felt himself carried across large areas of sleep, marvelled that coolness could have different shades and textures, that he could see and smell its transparencies. This was the flip side of involvement, the relief the mind experienced in letting go of its precious compulsions. He was cast gently on a bank with a thump he heard clearly. He awoke.

The venture had taken exactly seven weeks. He had no wish to speak. He dreaded breaking the spell. He was still not sure what he had been trying to do, what this abstinence was supposed to generate, why he'd felt it necessary or what he believed he had found. But the phone call had to be made.

He found the number easily enough, scrawled obliquely across the last page of the directory. It had bided its time, else why had he jotted it down?

He dialled. The phone rang, twenty-five rings before the engaged beep took over. The owner wasn't in. He tried throughout the evening with no luck, and all through the next day. He was nervous. Grateful each time nobody received the call. Finally, on the fifth morning, he had better luck.

'Hullo?' said Vyas, sleepy or drunk.

24

Vyas turned up the next morning. He displayed no surprise at Sravan's invitation.

Sravan studied him closely. Looked at Vyas as he had not been able to do in years. A tall man with a stoop, hair like a mop and a discoloured smile.

'Anything special?' asked Vyas. The muscles of his narrow face held in place an expression of frayed politeness.

'Yes and no,' answered Sravan. 'I've been trying to get in touch with you for some time.'

'It's too late for that interview.'

'This isn't about that. Your phone went on ringing.'

'I'd gone home—to Faizabad,' said Vyas. For an instant his face slackened, allowing itself to lapse into a fleeting expression of apology. 'So what's all this about?'

'I've been wondering what you're up to,' said Sravan cautiously. 'What're you working on now?' He unfolded his subtle, friendly smile and placed it, carefully poised, upon his face. It wasn't easy. It was ready to overshoot the mark any minute.

'Why?' Vyas's eyes engaged his in squeamish trial, testing his face in quick scrutiny before detaching themselves warily from the contact.

'Nothing much,' Sravan lied. 'I was at a loose end. Thinking of the old times at the Samiti. You know the sort of low you go into just after you're through with a demanding book. Post-compositional sadness.' He laughed. His laugh sounded phoney to his ears.

'I haven't composed anything for some time now, so I wouldn't know,' said Vyas non-committally. That too sounded wrong to Sravan's lie-detector ears. They were lying to one another. And why shouldn't they?

'Pity.' He tried guarding his face with a show of graceful concern. 'Strange, the way things turn out.' He mused to fill the uncomfortable pauses. 'Sometimes life's developments read like bad literature, no? One's surprised it could be so clumsily put together. I've been thinking of the way you just gave up. Stopped writing. You needn't have taken the remarks of a few vicious critics to heart. No good talent is ever killed off by bad press.'

'That's what you said to me then.' For once Vyas looked directly at him. A searching look that asserted its enquiry right past the civilized formality of his social face and into the unprotected preserves of his guilt.

'Did I? What else did I say?'

'Plenty.' The flicker of a smile. 'You were a great consoler of failed men, Sravanji.'

Sravan couldn't tell whether Vyas was being ironical, but picked up the conversational thread quickly. Perhaps too quickly to be convincing, he felt.

'Oh, I've always been much more interested in the complexities of failure than the predictable machinery of success. The guys who don't make it are more intriguing than the guys who do. Haven't you noticed that I always write about anti-heroes? But about that time. What else did I say to you then?'

Vyas usually spoke in a rush, with a little confused frown. As though he were constantly quelling hurdles of speech. The result was a vaguely troubling timbre.

'You were full of historic precedents. Parading them for my comfort. You said to me, Remember what Sibelius said? He said never pay attention to critics—don't forget that there hasn't ever been a statue in honour of a critic. You quoted Samuel Johnson about someone called Foote, someone who was kicked around by the critics and Dr Johnson said Good for him, he's rising in the world, or some such thing, because earlier no one thought it worthwhile to kick him. High-brow, that's what you were. You spoke of Boyer, Donatello . . .' Vyas's voice slowed. 'And when you were editing my book for the Mayur Vriksha people, hacking and slashing the parts I considered my best work, then you lectured me on Rodin.' His eyes stopped on Sravan.

There was a catch in Sravan's throat. He uttered an uneasy laugh and said, 'You remember.'

'Can I forget?' Vyas whispered. 'You said Rodin hacked off the hands he'd carved on the statue of Balzac because everyone who saw it exclaimed over the hands. They seemed alive. So Rodin destroyed them. No part is more important than the whole, he said. Nothing should attract too much attention to itself. That's why you slashed the best portions of my book and wrote, 'Recast' in the margins. Only I couldn't ever rephrase those things. That's the way the book came to me—no other.'

Someone had told Sravan that Vyas had sat over his script for days, phrasing and rephrasing until he'd almost had a nervous breakdown, but that was literati gossip, no doubt. Finally the editor's opinion had prevailed, and a much truncated version of the original script had appeared. Even Sravan had had to admit that it did not read well. The gaps had showed. The press had trashed it up brutally.

'I told you then,' said Sravan in an unnaturally thin voice, 'and I tell you now, it's a mistake to be so unstrung by a dozen vicious reviews. Let me tell you of my own experience. When I was a new author, I had an upstartish critic named Ranjit Rawat. Fellow whose only source of publicity was his annual shit-spewing reviews of my novels. Sheets of invective—you should've seen them. He'd pound on each book and grind it to dust. It happened four times. The same words—my characters not properly realized, my plots incoherent, an underlying sentimentality. A review tells you more about the critic than the book under review, you know. There had to be a strong personal reason. It showed in that carping style of his. So I decided to play a trick on him. I selected an obscure story by Chekhov, and changed the proper nouns to Indian names for places and people. I gave it an Indian tone and sent it to *Pen and Parchment*. Prompt came the damaging review in the pages of another journal! Rawat was at his vicious worst, tearing the story limb for limb. Lambasting the author who hadn't the foggiest idea how a story should be written. Whose raw callowness showed in every line. I laughed my guts out. I wrote to my editor friend and he was appalled when he learnt of the trick. I wanted him to print a detailed letter from me, confessing the borrowing and stating my reasons, taking a few pretty digs at Rawat in the bargain. But my editor friend was upset. He said—Are you mad? What about the prestige of my paper? Is the "Readers Write" column a boxing ring? Reserved for personal scuffles? Just keep shut, will you? So I did. But I couldn't resist having the last laugh: I sent the tearsheets of that story to Rawat with a copy of the original, and congratulated him on his acuity as a Chekhov critic.'

'Did you hear from him?'

'No. Embarrassment shut him up forever.'

'I wish I had your resilience.'

Sravan stretched, yawned. 'It's got to be built up, Vyas. Doesn't come in a day. When my first books appeared they said I was like Murdoch, Maugham, Huxley—but, of course, less than them all. In short, I was a poor copy of every passé British or American author on the shelf. Not mature enough, sneered my seniors. Too intellectual, said my friends. Not original, said the academics. Nothing new, said others. Forgodssake, didn't André Gide write somewhere that nothing real can be new or original? The earth's too old for that. Every good work is a plagiarism from God, as a friend used to tell me. Does that mean it has no flavour? The old experiences have to be known again with a shock of personal truth. We pluck the fruit from the tree of knowledge and say—This is mine. I plucked it. I know the sharpness of its taste, its sourness or sweetness or bitterness on my tongue . . .'

'You were always rhetorical with me, Sravanji,' observed Vyas cynically.

'Sorry.' Sravan checked himself. 'You're one of the people I feel comfortable talking to.'

'I'm flattered.'

'By now I've worked out a technique for handling adverse criticism: I make myself a drink. Tell myself—By the time I finish sipping this, it'll stop rankling.'

'Does it work?'

'Unfailingly.'

'Good for you, then. I'd use it—if I were still writing, but I'm not.'

Sravan unfolded his arms, put his elbows on the table. 'That's why I called you today.'

Vyas looked at him steadily. Sullen. 'I feel no need to write any more, thank you.'

'Ofo! Hear me out, please. You might not need writing, but writing might need you . . .'

Vyas smiled crookedly. 'Rhetorical again. Why do your words always sound as though they have makeup on, Sravanji?'

Why did he so much want things to go right for this man? It was not that he specially liked him. But he desperately needed proof that things went right as often as not, even for the defeated and lapsed. That unexpected solutions arrived. He wanted to engineer and bear personal witness to this romantic improbability. To plot out a satisfactory end for a story gone wrong.

'I wouldn't want you to end as an extinct author.'

Vyas tried the ice before he stepped on it. One step at a time. 'Very kind of you, but it's possibly escaped your attention, Sravanji, that you were the writer to end all writers. You ended me.'

Sravan betrayed no confusion. He was expecting this. 'Nonsense.' He swept Vyas's bitter reproach aside. 'You know I did my best to improve your book. As I believed a book should be written, especially a first book. Then. I was twenty years younger in my beliefs, remember.'

'And I twenty years younger in my trust,' muttered Vyas.

'Don't go on like that. Let me tell you—I once reviewed a book by a second-rate author and came down very heavily upon it. I specially attacked a passage describing an old man's death. I called it trite, stale, pulp, mediocre, boring and plain bad. Much later, when my father died, I realized the accuracy of that passage I'd dismissed. It reminded me of you, Vyas, and your book.'

Vyas said nothing.

'I wish you'd realize that, after all these years. I did the best I knew—at that point in time.' This had become a disquieting internal question. 'And anyway, your second book was applauded,' he added, defiant under imaginary threat.

'Yes, a polite patter of applause.'

'Did you know that it was put on the shortlist for the Asian Vanguard Book of the Year?'

Did Vyas know that he had been first on the shortlist and Sravan second? That the delay in informing Vyas and getting his consent for the reading tour wasn't only a postal one? That Sravan went on the reading tour when Vyas's consent missed the deadline?

'Yes. I got a letter from the Academy of Letters,' said Vyas in a colourless voice.

This was the toughest moment of all. Meeting Vyas's eye. Resisting the immediate temptation to find a glib explanation. Sravan sat still. How much more did Vyas know? Did he know that he, Sravan, had been on the Adhunik Upanyas Puraskar jury? That he'd turned the vote deliberately against Vyas? He'd never told anyone these things. Editing the truth—he was good at that.

But the editing that disturbed him most was the book he'd hacked and mauled. Mayur Vriksha often sent him scripts to edit. His reasons for accepting the job were unconfessed: he took it on because often there was a lot to learn from these freshmen writers, no matter how unpolished they were at first. Vyas's novel had agitated him beyond measure. His own book was due to be released at about the same time. He recalled his shock, displeasure, panic—those breathtakingly brilliant passages. Balzac's hands.

The silence had extended itself to an unnatural length.

'I asked you to bring me your original script—the one before I edited it. I'd like to read it again.'

'Whatever for?'

'I don't know—I've been thinking about it. Maybe we could bring out a fresh edition. I'd suggest it to the Vriksha editorial office—a reprint. Put all those passages back. Give Balzac's statue its living arms again . . .' It wasn't coming out too well.

'A reprint—twenty years later?'

'Nothing unusual about that.'

Vyas was faintly mocking. 'Please yourself. I brought it anyway. Do as you see fit. To be honest I've lost interest in that book.' As he handed the script across, Vyas's hands actually appeared to wince, wary of the exposure. He drew them quickly back into the shelter of his waistcoat pockets.

'There's one more thing,' Sravan added. 'A favour I'm asking.'

'Of me?'

'Yes.'

'I have to tell you what's happened to me lately. It has a direct bearing on what I'm asking of you.'

Vyas nodded. Sravan told him the story.

'That's when this idea for a new book hit me,' he finished. 'See it this way—a man, middle-aged, has a secret. He makes trips to a distant city. Keeps sending sums of money. For years. His wife and sons keep trying to find out what's going on. They suspect a woman, a second family somewhere. He is tight-lipped. Finally, he's trapped by his elder son. It comes out that his "other" family isn't a woman but a brain-damaged childhood friend, a kid he'd pushed off a high balcony in school. The idea's obsessed me. Not for what it is at face value but because it spells out a partial answer to a question that's bothered me for years: whether humanity can ever rise beyond its inherent instinct for violence. It seems to me that one can do little about the chronic impulse to injure. The best one can do is step up the empathy levels of the human psyche. Even a microscopically tiny advance is a betterment of spiritual stock. Strange—a stray situation crosses your path, arrests your imagination, becomes the touchstone of your whole life . . .'

'What do you want?' asked Vyas flatly.

'How do I explain this to a cynic like you?'

Vyas looked through the dusty window. The road sparking hot light. The shavings of light slipping in through the jacaranda leaves. His eyes travelled to Sravan's bookshelves, fixed reflectively on the small ivory Saraswati, then back to Sravan's waiting face. The seconds beat in Vyas's stare like a pulse.

'You're a strange guy, Sravan,' he said at last. 'How self-important you've always been. Doling out your precious ideas for the poor dolts to scramble for. The kindness of your heart, no doubt.' His voice took on a biting note. 'And what if I say it's not up to my standard? I don't pick up the leavings of others. I'm quite used to having others scramble for my leavings, Sravanji. For a big price.' His manner had changed abruptly. Turned sneering. Arrogant. 'I suppose you can't help it. In your own vainglorious way, you might even be meaning well, I suppose it's years of smugness—this insufferable patronizing voice. But let me put you right on one point, Sravanji. When I said I haven't written for years, I was lying, of course. And you knew it. But I'm not into art stuff now. I'm in big business—doing very well for myself, thank you. Want to know more?'

He surveyed Sravan thoughtfully. Assessing the wisdom of impetuous self-disclosure. Then he began to speak, still in that biting voice.

'It's like being in computer software, or molasses or teak plantations or property development. No, more like running an exclusive boutique . . .'

Sravan gaped, not getting the drift. Vyas smiled balefully. 'Designer writing—my line. Made to order. My own spring, summer, autumn, winter collections. For a discreet, exclusive clientele that knows a good thing when it sees one, and doesn't mind paying for it. Only the label isn't mine once the payment's made and the product changes hands. The label becomes the customer's. That's why my products are highly priced. Steep, some feel.'

'Vyas—do I get you right? You're *selling* your work?' gasped Sravan.

'Aren't we all? Aren't you? Selling to a publisher or selling to their so-called writers—one and the same thing, no?' It was Vyas's turn to relax, play games with his host's disturbance.

'You're joking. Or lying.'

'Why should I want to do that?'

'But . . . for how long?'

'About six years now.'

'And who're your . . . your select customers?'

'Sorry, Sravanji, no names. Professional discretion, breach of trust, etc.'

Sravan couldn't digest this. Caught entirely off guard, he struggled to get a grip on Vyas's astounding confession.

'But you can tell me your tariff, at least?'

Vyas uttered a laconic laugh. 'That depends on the piece. It's a hard line. Plenty of discernment needed. I have to spot the likely customer first, get his drift—his choice of subject, his vocabulary, timbre, right? The same piece can't be shown to other customers. It's got to be altered according to the next man's writerly measurements. My rates take account of all the labour involved, and the risks. Say, two thousand to five thousand for roughly every ten pages. Poetry is priced by the word—I have a price list . . .'

Sravan had no words.

'Vyas, this is totally bizarre.'

'Is it your faith in my unspoilt virtue that's causing you problems, Sravanji?' asked Vyas sardonically.

'How many works've you sold?'

Vyas thought. 'More than a hundred.' He laughed in Sravan's face. Malignant. 'The name of the game's money, Sravanji. Don't we know it? You with your big sales and awards and promos, and me with my little writing emporium. Next time I'm expanding my business, I'll take up your offer of that charming idea you just outlined for my succour. Maybe that'll be your next book.'

Sravan decided to ignore the slight. It was the least he could do.

'Bit late for new books, Vyas. I'm tarting it my own way. Mortgaged myself to the Katrak Group. Doing a biography for J.B. What's that saying? In trouble, even the donkey must be adopted as one's dad . . . I'm doing it in return for doctored reports of that incident concerning my son—you get the idea? So much for my artistic freedom. But you: I'm impressed. A hundred works! At two to five thousand for ten pages. Neat.'

Vyas's face was dark with savage mirth. 'That's just the customer's initial outlay.'

'I don't understand you.'

'There are subsequent small instalments he or she has to cough up from time to time. Maintenance costs for personal reputation . . . in the face of possible exposure. I retain copies of all works. I also have some taped conversations . . .'

This was so explosive a revelation, uttered in a low, halting voice, that Sravan's own voice broke into a stammer.

'You're . . . you're into blackmail, too?'

Vyas leaned across. 'Mind if I bum a cigarette, Sravan?' He extracted one with finicky care, picked up Sravan's lighter, flicked.

'*Blackmail* doesn't have an aesthetically pleasing sound. Unbecoming. I have a sensitive choice of words. Let's give it another name—penitentiary account? Caution money? Precaution money, rather. Please yourself, so long as it sounds right.'

But Sravan was sick with the outrage of this decay. The enormity. He stared dumbly at the man across the desk.

'Vyas, what've you let it do to you? So much going for you. You could've been . . . one of the biggest names. A literary star. Solid, real stuff. I'd even risk the word "genius". You could've done so much . . .'

His voice tailed off lamely.

'Except that you didn't let me.'

The words were spoken without rancour. Toneless.

'Oh, I'm not being dramatic, not blaming you, Sravan. I know I'm good—why else does my work sell? Mark my words—half the scribblers in your literary circuit have bought my work—and don't know that the others have bought it, too. It's damnably funny—like women who visit the same jeweller or tailor in secret! Or,' he laughed bitterly, 'the minister and the terrorist sharing the same slut!'

'It's not funny,' remarked Sravan weakly.

'Oh, I know it's all terribly sad,' Vyas mocked gently. 'A heartbreaking business. A bloody shame. The shipwreck of a major talent. A genius cut down in his flower. A great voice destroyed. And worse—the tragic compromise of an artist's conscience. I know the pained emotions troubling your heart.' His mouth twitched in a soundless laugh. 'All I can say, Sravanji, bare bhai sahib, is don't mind me. I'm perfectly pleased with myself.'

'But when your work appears under another signature? When it gets rave reviews?'

Vyas pulled a grimace. 'I've taught myself to enjoy the irony. What's the old gag?—The real artist isn't bothered with signatures.'

'I don't believe you. I just don't believe you.'

'That's your problem.'

'Can't you retrieve it all somehow? Recover it? Pay back the money and . . .'

'It runs into quite a bit.'

'I could help . . .'

Vyas eyed him keenly. 'I'm a mean guy, Sravanji.' He mimicked a Bollywood bad-guy voice. 'I'm in no mood to help you unwrite that sorry chapter between us. If you aren't easy about me, you can just live with the discomfort. But no noble gestures, please. I won't give you the chance.'

'I was only suggesting recovering your work. Lending, not donating you the cash . . .'

'Impossible. Published under too many names. Scandal. Copyright litigation.' He shuddered. 'Hardly worth my while. Now, if you don't mind . . .' He stood up. 'I see no point in discussing this.'

Neither did Sravan.

'I'll leave this manuscript here if you like, but I lost interest in it long ago.'

'I haven't,' was Sravan's limp protest.

'Do as you wish.'

Sravan walked him down the stairs and saw him start up his old TVS champ.

'Just one small question, Vyas. Why the fuck did you tell me those things? How d'you know I shan't talk?'

Vyas stood, considering, one foot on the pedal. 'I don't know why,' he said slowly. 'I guess there's a kind of . . . honour among thieves.'

He buzzed away on his moped. Sravan climbed the stairs, pondering those last words. He felt an unpleasant heaviness upon him.

It was hard getting started on the Katrak assignment. A pile of tedious contextual material to wade through and sift. Did I really think I could quit writing? The acid taste came up his throat again. No, sir, no such relief. It's use it or lose it, this writing business, and the terror of losing exceeds the agony of using. No creative

Viagra for writer's block. Fellows have shot themselves—or lost their minds—trying to cope with it. Even when you know you're burnt up—like your father. Even when you know you stopped being a real storyteller ages back. The real storytellers aren't sitting at PCs or typewriters; they're still in the tea stalls, kitchens, courtyards, coffee houses. The footpaths, dhabas, highways, barber shops. No writer's block for them, by the way—that sort of storytelling enjoys natural immunity, for it's seldom such a self-intensive trip. As for me, I'm a literary technician now, and what's wrong with being a paid hack to a newspaper company? I was a good liar, on-page, off-page, so it's custom-made lies from me now. A reader-friendly fictional autobiography it's got to be. Still, it's depressing to be doing nothing better.

He didn't know exactly when the images began to appear. In a mind floodlit with amazement, snatches of language blew in, slack and imprecise, mirroring the asymmetries of knowing. There was no word for it except the old one—inspiration! An alpha rhythm in the brain. A pollinating breeze. A frequency in the sensorium, a kinesis in the psycho-plasma of the mind. Awaiting the witchery of an uncanny hand. He waited a week to be sure. To test the idea, turn it over in his head. Confirm its substance against the litmus of each passing day. Seven days of gathering drama in his head while Katrak's bio waited.

He phoned Vyas again.

'Come and pick up your manuscript.'

'Done with it?' Vyas sounded faintly derisive.

'Yes. Come down and let's discuss it.'

'You were right, Vyas,' he opened when Vyas turned up the following evening. 'It's twenty years too late. What sounded strong stuff then seems excessive now. That's the law of styles, I guess. What's natural and just-right now will sound featureless and lacklustre in another twenty years. Style's an inconstant thing. Sorry to have bothered you.'

Vyas picked up the script without comment and dropped it into his saddlebag.

'But before you go,' Sravan went on, 'the more I reflect upon your upbeat business firm, the more interesting it seems to me.'

A glimmer of amusement came on to Vyas's expressionless face.

'Considering a rival company, Sravanji?'

'No.'

'A partnership?'

'No.'

'Surely you're not thinking of joining the select club of my customers?' Vyas loaded each word to offend.

That five-second pause came from Sravan's innate theatrical instinct. He underplayed perfectly the role he'd been rehearsing in his head for a week.

'There's an idea I'm keen to explore, but this Katrak biography I'm doing has a one-year deadline. I'm out of sorts—something's not going right on the page—and the new idea's too pressing to ignore. Ideally I'd like to be able to break my own record and do two books this year, but your discreet little writing firm [he smiled subtly] has offered me a better option. I'm sure you get the drift . . . I am, in short, accepting your tender . . . If I commission you to do this novella . . . it has to be a novella, a hundred and fifty pages or so. Do you have to check with your secretary?' He was openly smiling now. 'Is there a long waiting list?'

Vyas broke in. 'You're serious?'

'My sense of humour is generally inoperative by this late hour.'

'In that case, Sravanji, I deserve to be congratulated,' said Vyas, smiling crookedly, 'on netting such a large account, no?' He pronounced his words with the right corporate inflection. 'But I'm sorry,' he hesitated, 'I discuss business only in my official chambers in Darbhanga Lane. Mezzanine above motor garage—number 17. You're welcome tomorrow evening.' Sravan could see that Vyas was kidding.

'So you can tape my voice, Vyas?' he laughed. 'No, I insist on discussing the project here—and I insist on home delivery. Chapter by chapter and subsequently in full. I'm an interfering client, as you'll see soon enough. Come on, what's the going rate for a 150-page novella? A parable genre?'

He'd mastered the situation for a minute. Suspicion flashed in Vyas's eyes.

'Are *you* taping *my* voice, Sravanji? Gathering evidence against me? What's your game?'

'Haven't you learnt to believe me?'

'Frankly, no. You haven't given me cause.'

Sravan sighed. 'I'll only ask you to suspend your disbelief then for fifteen minutes. Let's go down to the colony park in case you imagine this room's got a concealed microphone or something. And in case you think my pockets could do with a search, go ahead. I also recommend the use of a lie detector . . .' Funny how much he was enjoying this game. Like two small boys enacting a favourite thriller.

Vyas looked uncertain. 'You're absolutely serious about this . . . order?'

'Pity I can't prove it in writing. You'll just have to make do with a gentleman's word. Sorry, all that's passé—no gentlemen now, only salesmen, so we'll have to content ourselves with cordial threats of mutual exposure, if that's any good.'

Vyas relaxed. 'Oh, okay. One's got to bank on customer goodwill, I suppose.'

'Quite an entrepreneur.'

'A born manager,' grinned Vyas. 'Triple charge. Production, marketing, personnel, all rolled into one! But just one permanent risk—a vindictive customers' union someday. Wonder if the Consumers' Forum covers a line like mine. The precaution-money bit makes HRD difficult . . .'

They laughed.

Out in the park, punctuated by sounds of traffic and phrases of breeze, Sravan verbalized his images.

'Four men visit a village. Or a small town, if you prefer. You've got to highlight their telling features. Their sternness. Softness. Humanity. They're different, but obviously related. Now this has to be done in a time-surpassing allegory vein. No magic realism, please. Something Bunyanesque. Epic. Get it? They've come looking for a man, a kinsman whose address they've lost. They ask their way down that village. There are many misleading reports—so-and-so answers to the description of the sought person—and they hasten to identify him. But they're always disappointed. Okay.

Right at the end they do manage to find the man. And this is going to be the toughest bit—the nature of the man they eventually find. He's unlike anyone else. Nothing to recommend him. Dirty and fierce. He left the settlement and he's a healer of beasts, a sort of male witch. An outcast by choice. Rough—yet plants grow under his touch and animals are cured. And humans. He's given to beating people, too, and is believed to be subject to fits. He greets the four with abuse, asks them who the fuck they are, says he doesn't know them and has no regard for ties of kin *or* unknown visitors. They say they are men of peace. He lifts the hempen curtain and says gruffly, I don't care who you are, but if you are men of peace we are brothers. Now, can you see why an epic tone is important?'

Vyas wasn't impressed. 'A hundred and fifty pages of this?'

'Not reader-friendly enough?' Sravan queried in gentle self-mockery. The four men have to unfold slowly—right from page one. One has a faded robe and carries a bowl. One has an unkempt beard and has lived in a cave. One has matted locks and wears ash on his forehead. One has long, flowing hair and the marks of nails on his body. And don't turn them all into women to give it a provocative twist . . .'

Vyas stood still, unblinking for an instant.

'Are they recognized?'

'Only by the reader.'

'I'll do it,' said Vyas, a little breathless.

'Good.'

'When d'you want it?'

'How long d'you need?'

'Can't say offhand. A year? That suit you?'

'Don't push yourself. Take your time. Give it your best.'

Vyas grinned. 'Guaranteed perfect after-sale service. Motor warranty a hundred years.'

'You're a vain bastard, Vyas. I wouldn't ever claim that for any of my books.'

'This,' said Vyas, '*is* officially your book. Wait and see.'

'I believe you,' said Sravan a little sadly. 'Now, your invoice?'

Vyas thought. 'Considering the appeal of the idea and

considering that the idea is yours, not mine, shall we say twenty-five thousand only?'

'You're giving me quite a discount.'

'For old times' sake, Sravanji,' said Vyas meaningfully.

'Done,' said Sravan. 'Payable in advance?'

'Ten as earnest money. Fifteen on delivery.'

'And afterwards?'

'What d'you mean afterwards?'

'Your royalty. No, that'll be me getting it, no? Your silence account, precaution money, whatever you call it?'

Vyas eyed Sravan with renewed mistrust. 'Somehow I can't believe you mean it.'

'Shall I give you a cheque to prove my seriousness? Or do you have problems with income tax?'

'I'm really excited about this subject,' enthused Vyas on the stairs. 'It's got the promise of . . . ignition!'

'Yes, I know,' said Sravan. 'Now, since you prefer cash, you'll have to wait till tomorrow. No monkey business, right?' Still mimicking the trigger-happy tone. 'If you try anything funny I have my answer ready. I'll say you're a practising gay—and that's the amount I paid to . . .'

Vyas roared with laughter. 'Not a bad story. Might be the best hype line to promote this book. Senior Author Confesses to Buggering Up Junior Author. And it's true, in a manner of speaking.' Though it still rankled, Sravan tried to make a joke of it, too.

As he re-entered the study, Sravan's eyes fell on Saraswati. Ranjana Devi's words stirred in his head, this time with exuberance. Nothing more to do except think of a title for the book, speak to Mayur Vriksha and arrange for it to appear under the name of Veerendra Vyas. He could anticipate their curiosity. Veerendra who? The same Vyas who was hailed as a writer of uncanny promise twenty years back but who, by some mysterious conjunction of circumstances, went out of circulation, dropped by the wayside? Nothing more to do except, perhaps, practise forging Vyas's signature for the contract and its counterfoil. And the fellow swallowed the bait, a savvy guy like that, Sravan chuckled. Ten thousand down and fifteen on delivery! Giving me a discount, too!

Then another thought struck him. Twenty-five thousand! The same figure used on Farooqui's dud cheque. Twenty-five thousand seemed to be the recurrent quantity in all his spiritual swindles. Life's script repeated its circuits with breathtaking symmetry, too precisely and too often to be entirely accidental.

He'd copied Vyas's signature from the old manuscript. It was strange now, practising and practising a signature not his own. He had it almost perfect now. Quite a penance. Gave him a paid-up feeling, the relief of a forgotten rightness. Fiction had been his lifeline, and forgery would be his salvation. Odd thought. Did justice to his sense of equivocation, his plight of inhabiting qualified realities. His tempered truths.

He wondered what luck Pragya was having with the injured kid's treatment. He thought of Buddhoo's theories of hurting and healing motives. He speculated on the book now taking shape in Vyas's head. His own plans had suddenly clarified: the Katrak biography but nothing more. He would wait until Vyas's book was through. Only then would he unlock his cupboard and, when he felt equal to the task, write a real book again. For real books, even when they happened on earth, were made in heaven.